THE CHINA ALAMO

HOCK HOCHHEIM

WOLFPACK PUBLISHING
— EST 2013 —

Published in the United States by Wolfpack Publishing, Las Vegas

Wolfpack Publishing
5130 S. Fort Apache Road, 215-380
Las Vegas, NV 89148

wolfpackpublishing.com

Paperback ISBN 978-1-64734-772-7
eBook ISBN 978-1-64734-771-0

THE CHINA ALAMO

A JOHANN GUNTHER WESTERN

Chapter 1
The China Shanghai

San Francisco Bay, California, 1900

"Doctor."

"Doctor."

"Doctor."

The three doctors touched their beer mugs over the center of the table in congratulations. Then they looked at the attractive Chinese waitress suddenly standing by them.

"Doctors?" she said.

"Yes, ma'am," Dr. William Bellmont said.

"You *tree* men doctors?" she asked again.

"Yes, we are," Dr. Henry Hedgecock said.

"Just yesterday," Dr. Jason Telemore said.

"Just...yesterday?" she said, balancing a tray with three more beers on her one hand.

"We graduated San Francisco, Cooper Medical College only yesterday," Telemore said.

"Ooooh, doctors. Real doctors," she said. "And you have

come down here to the docks to eat a dinner, and…"

"Celebrate," Bellmont said. "Yes. It's my fault, I wanted to eat Chinese food and I love the Bay here. And the docks."

She placed the three new beers on the table.

"Yeees, congratulations," she said with a big smile. The three ogled her shapely figure in her tight, yellow-gold silky dress with its low-cut neckline.

"What is your name?" Hedgecock asked.

"Oh, my name is Linda."

The men giggled.

"Ohhh," she said with a saucy expression, "you no *beleeb'* my name is Linda?"

"My dear, I would believe *anything* that you told me," Bellmont said.

"Then you will *beleeba'* me that your Peking ducks are coming to you *bery* soon. *Bery* tasty."

The three doctors made a case study of the men and women around them like voyeurs in the underworld. *Red Keleton's Peking Duck* restaurant was a rowdy, loud place of mostly men and some women. While some of the men looked like sailors and workers, many didn't, and might've been businessmen or even tourists like they were. Some of the women looked like prostitutes to them. Some not.

Outside. Across the wooden boardwalk, the bay just after sunset was still full of incoming and outgoing ships. Freighters, cruise ships, military ships, loading and unloading people and goods, all visible through Keleton's front windows. The dock's boardwalk and side streets were lined up with hotels and eateries, import and expert offices, and shops.

"This was such a good idea, Dr. Bellmont," Telemore said.

"I thank you, Dr. Telemore," Bellmont said.

The ducks came with many side dishes. More beers followed. As the night fell, a classic bay fog rolled across the water and onto the coastline turning the streetlamps into blurry, colored orbs. They ate, they laughed, they ogled.

"Good evening, gentlemen," said a stout man in a flannel shirt and blue jeans.

"Good evening," the three replied.

"My name is Red Keleton. I...own this place. Did you enjoy the ducks?"

"Ohhh yes," Telemore said.

"Linda apprised me of the fact that you three are newly graduated doctors?"

"Yes, we are," Hedgecock said.

"Where are you boys from?"

"Sacramento," Bellmont said.

"Utah. Salt Lake City, Utah," Hedgecock said.

"Los Angeles," Telemore said. "Where are you from, sir?"

"Victoria, Canada," Red Keleton said, "but I've lived in Liverpool, England for many a year."

"I think I can detect a bit of an accent," Bellmont said.

"Well, Doctors, how's about one last round of beers, free on the house, and good luck!"

Three thank yous followed.

"He's a mighty nice ol'chap," Telemore said in a bad English accent.

After that last round, the three men paid, stepped outside to the chilly fog, and walked over to a railing by the water's edge. They leaned on the top rail.

"Hello again!"

They turned to see Red Keleton with a big grin walking up.

"Listen, boys," he said. "Tomorrow is my birthday. There is my celebration anon. You see that paddle steamer over there? The Goliath?"

The three strained their eyes to see the white and red ship through the fog, midway down the dock.

"Yes," Bellmont said.

"I am having a little cruise tonight for a few hours. A birthday party. Free drinks. Free drinks *and*...there will be some ladies aboard too! Very friendly lasses. You three are welcome to join in."

"Well..." Telemore sighed.

"Of course," Hedgecock jumped in to interrupt any Telemore excuses.

"Excellent. We leave in 20 minutes."

******

Men and women from Peking Duck soon emerged from the double doors, laughing, and talking, some with drinks in their hands, led by Linda to the Goliath dock. Hedgecock noted there were more men than women, a disconcerting fact encouraging competition. Red Keleton burst out following them, laughing with a wooden box under each arm, followed by another Oriental man carting packages.

The three men joined in with the group. Dull, yellow, electric light bulbs in a long strand draped post to post, marked the way. They filed down the dock, walked a ramp onto the Goliath, which upon closer inspection was a rather large and modern boat. A man sat at a piano and started a ragtime song. Chinese

4

and American women already on the deck smiled and handed out shots of whiskey and beer mugs to everyone. Everyone mingled. Many were strangers to San Francisco.

The boat eventually coasted out into the bay, working in and out of waves of fog.

"He's mysterious," Bellmont said to his friends, his pinky raised from his beer mug to point at an older Chinese man, dressed in traditional Chinese clothes of robe and hat. He wore a mustache that hung in two strands from his chin. Sprouting from his long black hair was a thick braid with a dark red piece of cloth tied at the end. His hands were folded in front of him. He stood back off in a corner of the big party area, watching.

"Yeah, but," Telemore said, "he's just another Chinaman in San Francisco."

Another Oriental approached him in what might be coined an "American" outfit in comparison. They seemed to whisper to each other. Then Red Keleton joined the pair. And for two or three quick seconds, all three of them looked at the doctors with serious expressions.

Telemore waved and smiled back at them. They looked away.

"What was that all about?" Hedgecock asked.

"I don't know," Bellmont said, "but that younger Chinese guy? He's got a big, I mean a *big*, knife on his belt under that jacket. You see it?"

"He's probably a fisherman," Telemore said.

"Hello again, Doctors!" Linda said, with a huge tray of many whiskey shots.

"Hello, Linda," Telemore said, as the three each carefully extracted a shot glass from the tray, hoping not to unbalance it.

The Goliath left the bay and entered the Pacific. They saw

several large ships sitting still in the ocean.

Then Dr. William Bellmont suddenly fell. He hit his head on a table. He couldn't move. He still heard the piano music. Hedgecock fell too, into his vision. Before they passed out, they saw many of the others fall. But one man did not fall. He looked around and yelled out, "What is going on here!" The Chinaman with the knife ran at him, drew the knife out and hacked open his throat.

******

Bellmont awoke in the belly of the ship. Laying on the floor with a splitting headache. It stunk of must and dead fish. Other men were laid out beside him. The ship rocked with big waves. Telemore and Hedgecock were nearby still asleep or unconscious? Orientals walked among the 20-plus, downed men.

"Get up! Get up! We have work to do! Wake up!" They kicked at legs and torsos. "We are going to *Zhong-guo* and there is work to do."

"*Zhong-guo*?" a mumbling Dr. Henry Hedgecock said.

"China! Stupid dog. Now, get up. Up!"

Chapter 2
A Howling Wilderness

Camp Tasey, The Philippines, 1900

Mornings were beautiful. Quiet, but for the blue and white waves thrashing. Cool breeze. Johann Gunther walked the beach of Camp Tasey, thinking about the beaches of Cuba and the Caribbean he'd walked in the last war. There was nothing like the thick, towering coastland clouds and the...

"HEEEEY! Help!"

"Help!"

Gunther could barely hear men yelling, some even screaming. What?

Across Tasey, up the beach, he saw some soldiers running to the waterline. He saw men leaving the "make-to" mess hall in the distance following suit. Then Gunther jogged north. There were several motorized, open boats speeding into the Tasey docks. The soldiers inside the crafts were waving their hats, and some their shirts.

He counted. There were four open boats with some 15

to 20 men in them, and as Gunther got closer, he could see they were soldiers.

"They killed us!" one yelled.

"They fell on us with machetes!" said another.

The soldiers dropped from their boats once near shore, stumbled and blabbered, some were even wounded.

Lt. Felix Jefe Cocoy, Gunther's military aide-de-camp and intrepid Filipino scout dashed from their barracks toward the disturbance.

Gunther grabbed a wide-eyed sergeant by the shoulders. "What happened?"

"I…saw, I saw…Sgt. Martin. Seated in his mess table, leaning forward…clutching his spoon and his head was cut off…completely."

He was in shock and dropped to one knee. Jefe helped him up as Gunther approached another man, this one a corporal.

"We were hit, Major," he said. "We were eating breakfast. Outside. Our rifles stacked. And the insurgents rushed us, sir. They came with bolos, splitting heads and…and bodies. And spears. Then rifles. In a wave. A wave of death. A surprise attack."

The man sat on the beach and Gunther knelt beside him.

"We fought back with anything, Everything. It was hand-to-hand, Sir. Or, or hand to knife. Private Degraffen was throwing rocks at their heads. We, we here, regrouped. Us. Got to our rifles. We shot, but we couldn't stop 'em, sir. The wave. We fought our way back to the boats, and…"

"How many dead?" Gunther asked.

"Maybe forty. Captain Cornel, Lieutenant Rampus, and Major Griswald. Dead. They're dead, sir!"

The Camp Tasey commander, Captain Brookmiller

rushed out of the ragged Tasey headquarters building to investigate the commotion.

"What the hell?" he bellowed. He looked around at the chaos.

Gunther approached the captain.

"*Cappen'*, there's been an ambush. Insurgents at Malangiga. They swept in on them at breakfast."

"Why? Why?" Brookmiller said, puzzled. "This...all this, is all almost over."

There had been peaceful times of late with the people of Malangiga. Times marked by extensive fraternizing, lots of palm wine drinking among the soldiers and male villagers, baseball games and Filipino Arnis martial arts demonstrations. There was also a new and growing feeling of peace throughout all the islands.

"Have all these men checked for wounds, and then all of us in the briefing room. Now!" Brookmiller demanded to the officers around him.

"Gunther, ready the Pittsburgh and Company G," Brookmiller ordered.

Though Major Gunther outranked Captain Brookmiller, Brookmiller was put in charge of Tasey, and Gunther was there only to help out and represent General Jacob Smith.

"Yes, *Cappen'*," and Gunther and Jefe took off for the docked coastal steamer the Pittsburgh, with Gunther shouting over to the first man he saw in Company G with these new orders.

The doctors and aides looked over the survivors, treated them and amassed those healthy enough into the briefing room, some in wheelchairs and even stretchers. They were each handed a bottle of beer to calm their nerves. Some sat on chairs and some on the dirt floor. Once present, Gunther,

Brookmiller, the other command staff, and the curious enlisted crowded in to hear the horror story.

Jefe walked in, in battle gear, carrying Gunther's equipment also. Another aide brought in Brookmiller's equipment. Krag-Jorgensen rifles, pistol belts held Remington revolvers, canteens, bullets in loops and a bayonet. Gunther's belt held two short-barreled pistols, a "habit" left over from his Texas lawman days.

"It's Philippine General Vicente Likban," a surviving troop said. "He's behind this, and I saw the local police chief help in the attack."

"We're going in," the captain said.

"I'll go back, sir," one said, seated on the floor.

"What's your name, son?"

"Corporal Warren Lafaber, sir."

"From?"

"Kansas, sir."

"Corporal, we need a man who's been there, to show us every corner of the camp. Thank you."

"I'll go too, sir," another said, his head, neck and arm bandaged.

"The hell you will, son. You've seen enough. And I need you here to help guard this base. In case they try something here. We'll be ready for them, thanks to you."

******

In one hour, Company G, and support personnel, some 50 men boarded steam Screw Ship Pittsburg, a small to mid-sized steamer that ran the coastlines and was often commandeered into military service. Captain Brookmiller read his plans to his officers and NCOs in the ship's wardroom.

"It's a cutthroat re-entry into our camp," he said. "As we get close, I want men scanning the base with binoculars. We will set up lines of fire and will cover the dock as we disembark. It is a weak moment, and we need cover fire. I want 10 riflemen up on the bow under Sergeant Uvalde. You men will have the height and are *essential*. Then 10 riflemen at the end of dock in front of the ship. Sergeant Powell?"

"Yes, sir,"

"The dock? Yours. We will, under said cover fire if needed, charge the camp. Our mission is to reconnaissance the camp and collect the dead."

"Are we staying, sir?" Sgt. Uvalde asked.

"I don't know yet, we'll see when we get there," Brookmiller said.

Gunther cut a glance over at his new and best friend Jefe, attached to the US Army. Jefe's attention hung on every word from Brookmiller. Jefe was the son of the Spanish born elite society nicknamed the *Ilustrados* of the Philippines. They were the middle class and upper middle class who were educated in Spain and exposed to Spanish liberal and European nationalist ideals. He'd graduated the University of Madrid with a degree in economics. While there he belonged to a student group called the *Los Indios Bravos*, a collection of mostly men absorbed by any and all aspects of the American West and "cowboys and Indians". They shot "cowboy" guns and rode horses, "Western style". One of Jefe's original goals was to make his Philippines more like the image and ideals of the United States, and to bring higher quality education to his homeland.

One year earlier, in Manila, when Jefe met Johann Gunther and learned the tall German was once a lawman from Texas, from his *Los Indios Bravos* hobbies, he simply had to become this "cowboy's" best friend. Jefe used his influence and became Gunther's aide-de camp. He quickly turned into an excellent solider. He was also a lifelong hand, stick and knife Arnisador. As a result, he taught much close-quarter, survival fighting to Gunther. In the numerous battles across the Filipino islands, they had saved each other's lives, sacrificed much, and become blood brothers. Gunther influenced General Smithe to promote the college grad, Jefe as a lieutenant in the Army's Philippine Scouts.

Gunther looked at his friend's profile and once again worried for him. If he were ever taken alive by the rebels, the Moros, or any such group as there were so many enemy tribes, Jefe would be deemed a traitor and slowly tortured to death.

"To your posts, gentlemen," Brookmiller said.

It was mid-afternoon when the Pittsburgh neared the Malangiga docks, usually a fairly busy little commercial area for local trade and shipping. But a binocular scan of land revealed no life, no movement in the still, muggy heat. Gunther couldn't spot a soul in sight.

The 10 men assigned to cover left on the ship from the bow raised their rifles as the others jogged down the wide gangway and on the even wider docks, bound for the campgrounds.

Captain Brookmiller, Gunther, Jefe, and Corporal Warren Lafaber joined in the landing. Ten men took up positions, spread out, rifles up, once on land near the dock entrance. Gunther kept his rifle on his shoulder sling and drew one of his revolvers.

Brookmiller and 20 men, guided by Lafaber began searching the outskirts of the area. Sergeants took other small teams into the surrounding, dilapidated buildings in the distance. Gunther scanned the village. Not a sign of life anywhere on the field, the buildings and even the neighboring, usually busy, village. No movement except for the Philippine eagles and the Cinereous vultures ripping apart and feasting on the American dead.

"They came at us first from the church," Lafaber shouted.

And some of the men advanced on the church.

Gunther, Jefe, and an Army physician looked over the bodies.

"Dead."

"Dead."

"Dead."

The doctor went through the chopped, often headless remains of the soldiers, scattered among long tables and chairs out in the field. They'd been stripped of weapons, belts, knives, and boots. And the rotting of flesh under the hot sun had begun. Upon close examination, the hungry birds were not alone. The bugs were at work too.

"Dead."

"Dead."

"Dead." And he went on with the count.

Six men grabbed the bodies and dragged them into lines near the boat.

Jefe, with his bayonet affixed on his rifle, probed the dead Filipinos, poking them and turning them over. He studied the tattoos, clothes, shoes and sandals, skin tones, gear, and facial compositions. He looked over the dropped spears, guns, bolos, knives, and their handles. There were even ceremonial shields.

"What do you think?" Gunther asked.

"They are all from around here," Jefe said. "This island. Islands very nearby. To me, they have 'run amok'. 'Juramentado'."

Juramentado. Gunther knew the meaning of his term. He nodded. It referred to a male, Moro swordsman who attacks and kills occupying and invading police and soldiers, expecting to be killed himself, a martyrdom undertaken as a form of jihad, and considered a form of a suicide attack. This was often bolstered by drugs and tightly tied off body parts to restrict the flow of blood once wounded.

Captain Brookmiller and his contingent returned to the center of the field. He listened to a report from the doctor and from Jefe.

"What now, sir?" a lieutenant asked.

"I can't leave a company of men here as their larger numbers here were already overrun. Maybe two companies in a few days? But this place is no longer important to the peace movement. This camp would have been abandoned in a few weeks anyway! My God! Why! Let's get the dead aboard the ship and leave this place for now. I'll await orders from General Smith. What do you think, Major?"

"Good plan, sir," Gunther said. "This place is a ghost town of the dead."

Clicks. Odd, barely distinguished, clicking sounds came from the dense tree and brush line by the water and docks. The nearby soldiers who heard it first turned to see the Insurrectos emerge, maybe about 50 of them, some were trying to work the actions of the Krag Jorgensen rifles they'd just stolen. Others opened fire with their usual weapons in the direction of the captain. Others, swinging bolo-machetes and swords, charged. Some wore long pants, or pants to the calves or short wrapped pants like underwear. Some, no pants at all! Some wore hats, some not. Some barefoot, some not. Those that could not work the new rifles, dropped them, and pulled swords and knives, or pistols.

They overran, shot, hacked, and spread into the line of riflemen standing guard at the dock, as Captain Brookmiller yelled, "FIRE!" The few survivors of that dock melee stumbled off in an ambush confusion, retreating and firing.

Some soldiers on the grounds did not drop to a prone position as Gunther and Jefe did. Gunther slipped his rifle off his shoulder and hit the ground firing. They could see a line of men running down the dock, to the gangway, yet the soldiers in the front bow of the boat were so busy shooting down onto the attackers on the field, they failed to see the dock attack coming.

"THE DOCK!" Gunther yelled out. "They're after the ship!"

But no one could hear him over the gunfire and savage yelling. Gunther and Jefe exchanged glances and nodded at each other. Gunther got up, slung the rifle over his shoulder and pulled both pistols. He shot and charged the dock area, blasting an opening path of bloody humanity to the dock. Jefe rolled several times to the right and laid a line of fire at the dock to help, picking off the rebels as they climbed the gangway; but his angle made it difficult.

Right gun, left gun. Right gun. Left gun. Gunther methodically shot down anyone in his path to the docks. As he reached the dock, he could see the tops of a few soldiers over the rail on the bow of the ship, shooting into the field.

"BEHIND YOU!" Gunther shouted.

A soldier looked down at him and squinted as though he

could not hear. Gunther violently pumped his hand to the center of the ship. The soldier turned and fired. The enemy was now aboard.

But not all of them; a screaming mad man with a sword charged Gunther. He swung the blade at Gunther's arms, as Gunther leapt back and back again. He fired his brace of pistols into the man's chest, the last two hasty shots in his handguns, but even with his erupted bare chest, the wild swordsman was not done yet. Gunther turned, holstered the guns, and ran to land down the dock as fast as he could. He pulled his bayonet from his belt on the way, and near the landing, he spun.

The man reared back for a slash and Gunther whacked his weapon arm with the long bayonet. Wounded, he did not drop the weapon. He tried to stab Gunther, but Gunther again smashed his bayonet down on the gashed-open arm and this time the sword fell. The Filipino stood there, gasping for air, unarmed. His eyes wide, mouth open.

Gunther faked low then went high and chopped his long knife across the front of the man's throat. The rebel clasped his neck. With the man's hands up, Gunther went low and slashed his left thigh open in a powerful, deep blow. It was deep, cut muscle and the man dropped to his knee. Gunther cracked the man's skull with the pointed pommel handle of the bayonet with a powerful, downward, hammering motion. The man tumbled into the shallow, blue, clear water below.

Then Gunther dropped to one knee, put the knife on the dock and started reloading his revolvers. He looked up to see two men with machetes were racing toward him up the dock.

"Good God!" he mumbled.

Closer, closer. Bullets in, bullets in. He could go for the

rifle on his back but unslinging it might take more time. Bullets in...in...

He slammed the revolver's cylinders closed and opened fire. The rounds smashed into the first man's face. He too tumbled off into the water. The second man behind him was now fully visible. He stopped. He shook his head side-to-side, dropped the machete and leaped into the water. He struggled to run in the shallows of mud, then when deep enough, he was a fast swimmer and took off to deeper waters.

Gunther dashed up the gangway to the deck of the Pittsburgh. He charged the bow of the ship and saw the soldiers in hand-to-hand combat with natives. And losing. Four groups of 2 in close-quarter, hands-on fighting. Gunther approached the closest duo and shot the enemy in the face. He moved to the next one and shot that enemy. And so on, until he killed all six of the attackers.

The Americans aboard were dead, injured or stunned. They gasped for air. Some dropped to their knees.

"Get up!" Gunther ordered. "We've got the high ground up here. Get your guns up and shoot! Shoot!"

The six surviving men got themselves together, snatched their dropped long guns up from the deck and stood tall by the ship's front. They began shooting the enemy below on the field. Gunther watched their backs, loaded his revolvers again, with occasional peeks onto the field. Jefe was still down on the grass, firing away.

Finally, the shooting subsided. Only the groans and moans of the wounded remained. The men with him stopped shooting. Gunther stepped to the railing of the ship, waved to Jefe, then he spotted a wooden deck chair and sat down, wiping his brow. This whole event took only a matter of minutes. Just minutes, but he was exhausted.

"Don't..." he had to clear his throat, "don't get too comfortable, men, stand your guard. Stand your watch. Watch over them. This is the high ground." He coughed. "Napoleon Bonaparte said the most dangerous time in battle is right after a victory. Your guard is down. There might be...(cough)...be more trouble."

He took a mighty draw from his canteen. It was hot water cooked from the sun. After a few minutes of men yelling to each below, Gunther stood and took a serious look at the ground below.

Americans and Filipinos laid dead or dying. A nightmare, mess. A rifleman near him, a new private, vomited.

"You did good, son. You held your ground. You did your job, even with that bastard there," he pointed to the faceless attacker on the bloody deck. "You did good. There is no shame in throwing up. There's always time to vomit...later. I'll probably vomit later myself."

The kid just grimaced, too sick to respond.

Gunther took a good look at all of them.

"By God, you all are privates! All of you. Well, you all are corporals tomorrow. Tell your paymaster that Major Gunther told you so."

"Thank you, sir," several said, not sure this was good or bad news, given this experience.

Gunther walked off the ship with shaky legs, down the dock and back on the field. Jefe sat cross-legged on the grass near where he laid shooting. Gunther sat down next to him.

"I saw all that, but I could not shoot to help you. Too many soldiers in de' way. Bad angle."

"I know," Gunther said.

"It looked very bad," he said, then smiled.

"It was bad, but…you couldn't shoot to help me, but you did help me, with all your knife training."

"Ahhh, de' Arnis. Yes."

"So, you did help me."

"Okay," Jefe said.

Gunther leaned back, stretched out his legs and leaned on his elbows.

Captain Brookmiller walked up to them.

"Comfortable?"

"Yes, sir."

"I saw what you did. You probably saved the ship. Their plan was to cut us off from escape," Brookmiller said.

"All those kids up there in the bow? They all need to be promoted," Gunther said.

"I will see to it, Major."

"Thank you, Cappen."

"What of the buck sergeant? Uvalde, we left in charge of them?"

"He's dead, sir," Gunther said.

"Oh no."

"What was all that metal clicking noise?" an aide, next to Brookmiller asked.

"They cannot work de' bolt actions on Krag-Jorgensens. It is tricky to them. Unlike what they are used to," Jefe said.

Brookmiller offered a hand to Jefe and pulled him up and afoot. Then Gunther.

"Now," Brookmiller said, "let's all get the hell out of here."

******

Back at Tasey, Gunther showered in an outdoor stall and put on a clean uniform. He cleaned his 2 Remington pistols and put them in his holsters. Gunther had cut off the flap tops of the military style holsters, for a faster, quicker draw. That and his old police chief in Texas, once a Paris, France police detective, told him to use shorter barrel pistols for a faster quick draw. A military armory sergeant cut the barrels down for him. The Frenchman knew from the Paris criminal element, and Gunther knew from his Texas lawman days, how fast one might need one's guns up and out, and the time involved with opening the flaps and drawing out long barrels, was too much. He put on the customized guns, belt, campaign hat and tan uniform and walked to the headquarters building. A red sun was setting over the ocean. An evening breeze blew through the campgrounds, flapping some of the tent sides and shifting the palms on trees. Jefe was outside talking with some men, saw Gunther and joined him.

They entered the building and members of the command staff were arguing, shoving papers around and marking up maps on the wall. Brookmiller had not changed out of his muddy, sweat-wet uniform, and he was marching around upset with papers in his hands."

"Gunther, General Smithe has declared revenge," Brookmiller said when spotting him in the room. "He wants to turn the whole island into a 'howling wilderness'. His exact words. He wants us to kill every male over 10 years old."

Gunther was speechless at first, then said, "Ten? Are you sure?"

"We just got his orders. Can you talk to him?"

"I don't think that's possible, sir," a staff member interrupted them. "Major Gunther has a new assignment..."

"Yes?" Gunther said.

"We have rather immediate and urgent orders for you, sir."

"You do?" Gunther said.

"Yes, sir. It says that you are to report to the Subic Bay for a transport ship direct to San Francisco. There you will be met by a Colonel Westways. You will be billeted at the Presidio and be escorted to a special briefing with the vice president. Class A uniform required."

Gunther grabbed the orders out of the private's hand and looked them over.

"It's authorized by Vice President Theodore Roosevelt, sir. Do you know the president?"

"I...do...Cuba," Gunther said, still reading the paperwork.

"You are to meet with the vice president. I am to take you immediately to Subic, sir."

"And Lt. Cocoy?" Gunther asked.

"The orders are just for you, sir. You are to proceed alone."

"Well, I'll need him as far as Subic then," Gunther said, wanting to get Jefe out of any revenge bloodbaths of 10-year-olds on the island.

"Of course," Captain Brookmiller said. "He's your body-guard. He'll help get you to Subic alive...for the vice-president."

"And...at least...I will get a message to General Smithe about these revenge plans," Gunther said.

"Thank you, Major."

"Let's pack," Gunther said.

The two left for their quarters.

"What do you think this is about?" Jefe asked.

"I know Roosevelt. I did things for him in Cuba."

"Things?"

"Things. Missions. He...trusts me. They were not routine assignments. Not at all. And no doubt he needs me to do something not routine. I will get you to stay in Subic. You don't want any part of the mayhem around here. If I can, are you willing to help me in any Roosevelt plan or mission?"

"Yes. Will it involve going to de' United States?" Jefe asked anxiously.

"I have no idea. There is no telling what he wants me to do."

"Well, okay. You can count me in," Jefe said.

Chapter 3
To China with Me

Two weeks later...

**Subic Bay to Hawaii to San Francisco
to the Presidio to the executive suite, Palace Hotel.**

Major Gunther and Colonel Westways in their class A dress uniforms, of hat, jacket, pants, and boots, approached the two armed guards at the room door. A soldier saluted them, knocked on the ornate door and said,

"They are here, Mr. Vice President."

"Bully!" they heard Roosevelt say.

And the guard made a motion to let them in.

"I am to wait out here, Major," Westways informed and stopped.

Gunther's eyebrows propped up, and he turned, swept off his campaign hat, and entered the suite alone. He found quite a number of men and women sitting and standing around the lush surroundings.

"Johann! Johann!" Roosevelt said, jogging up to him and shaking his hand. He did not let go, and pulled him by the hand into the center of what was the suite's den.

"My friends, this is the man of which I spoke. Major Johann Gunther and I, when he was a lieutenant, were in Cuba together. Rough Riders! Now he's a major! And we faced many ferocious moments." Teddy threw a hooking punch through the air. "I asked many things of him, tough things, and each time he showed great resourcefulness and fortitude. I…I saw a lot in him. Yes. West Point! He's with us here, fresh from the Philippines."

Gunther did not anticipate such a spotlight. He turned the hat in hands held down in front of him.

"Major, this is California Senator Mr. McCormick Melaney. This is Mr. and Mrs. Bellmont, Mr. and Mrs. Hedgecock. Mr. and Mrs. Telemore. And this is Anna Hedgecock, their daughter-in-law, and Hedgecock grandson, Timothy."

Gunther nodded and shook hands even with the five-year-old boy.

"And this, is Suzannah Crippler," Roosevelt said, of a woman standing by a bay of windows across the sitting room. She was tall, thin, in a long brown skirt, a white, long-sleeve blouse with a brown leather vest. Her long thick brown hair fell far over her shoulders.

She walked in among the gathered group with an extended hand.

"Hello," she said.

"She's a real *rootin', tootin'* firebrand from Nebraska," Roosevelt declared with a massive smile. "Miss Crippler owns several businesses in St. Louis."

24

Gunther smiled and shook her hand.

"Have a seat. Have seat," Roosevelt said, pointing to a big wing-backed chair.

"Drink? Anything?"

"Ahhh. Coffee. Barefoot," Gunther said.

"Haa!" Roosevelt chuckled. "Roselyn? Black coffee for the major." He looked at the people present and explained, "Barefoot is…is the ol' cowboy way of saying black coffee. Major Gunther here, you see, was once a lawman in Texas."

"You're so young," Mrs. Telemore said.

"I've had a very condensed life," Gunther thought to say quickly. She liked that answer.

A woman appeared from the kitchen with a mug of coffee, no saucer.

"And what might I do for you all?" Gunther asked. He sipped coffee and crossed a right ankle over a left knee.

"Senator?" the vice president said.

"Major, I and my colleagues are trying to pass some enforcement laws on some of the problems we have on the San Francisco docks. Are you aware of the shanghai problem, sir?"

"Well, vaguely, sir, from the newspapers," Gunther said.

"We have a James Keleton, better known as "Shanghai" Keleton here. Or, or… "Red" Keleton. He is an American crimp…"

"Well now, tell the boy what a 'crimp' is, McCormick," Teddy said.

"A crimp is a shanghai, about shanghaiing, to…to shanghai or conscript men and women, as sailors, or servants against their will. Forcing them to work on ships. A crimp is someone who does this."

"Crimp. Like a pimp," Gunther said, quickly regretting it,

due to mixed company.

"Yes. All over the world, taking them, stealing them off, enslaving them all over the world. Keleton has a red beard and had a fiery temper to match. A criminal figure around here. Keleton is known for his gift of supplying men to understaffed ships. Women for other things."

"I see," Gunther said.

"He has a boarding house in San Francisco, reported to be on Broadway. He runs a number of bars including the Boston House at the corner of Davis and Chambers streets near the waterfront. And on dock, he runs the most nefarious, Red Keleton's Chinese Restaurant. He uses these places to collect men. He has party boats, we are told. One is the Goliath and announces a big party and free drinks and, and ahhh, yes, free women. He invites 'candidates' to the parties that he thinks ship captains in the bay will pay for, or anything anyone would pay for."

"Like slavery," Gunther said.

"Like slavery. Yes. The picked men, the selected men…

"He calls it a 'booze cruise,' and we are told that the targeted men…are eventually served opium-laced whiskey, knocks the hell out of them from it – pardon me – (he nodded toward the ladies) and then offloads them to ships in the mouth of the bay needing sailors. We have heard stories that they are sent to England. Japan. Australia. China."

"You seem to know a lot, Senator. Is this not a matter for the San Francisco police?" Gunther said.

"Ha! Ho! No, my boy," the senator said. "They will do nothing because the cases, the cases you see as they call it, have no complainants! The complainants are gone. Usually those that disappear, well, they are travelers, tourists, even sailors from other ships, and they just…disappear! And there is no one left to complain to the police, locally to care."

"I see."

"And someone is getting a little money at the police force to cover over this! Well, my colleagues and I wish to…to do something about all this," the senator said.

"And…and I…what do you want me to do?" Gunther asked, looking first at the senator, then at the vice president.

"Find my boy!" Mr. Bellmont declared impatiently from his seat on the couch.

Gunther looked at him.

"Find our boys. Find my boy, and his two friends."

The group leaned in, now involved in the discussion.

"They had just graduated medical school," Mr. Bellmont said. "They told their other friends that they were going down to the San Francisco docks to eat Chinese food. A celebratory meal! We were all there at the graduation, but they wanted to celebrate alone. Then, that night they never returned. The three of them are missing!"

"And you think that Red Keleton whisked…them off."

"Yes! There is no other explanation," Mrs. Telemore said.

"But whisked off where…to?" Gunther asked.

"CHINA!" she said.

"China? How do you…"

"Major Gunther," Mrs. Bellmont now spoke up. "A church group here in San Francisco contacted Mr. Bellmont and myself. We are from Sacramento; they contacted our Baptist church with a very strange story. They said that they heard from a missionary…there was this missionary from here in

Oakland who saw the oddest thing. He was delivering food and medical supplies to China. And this missionary delivered the goods to a Chinese military headquarters..."

"Boxers," Mr. Bellmont interrupted. "The Chinese Boxer headquarters."

"The Boxer's headquarters, in...in...Peking. And he said that he saw many wounded men in hospital there..."

"They are having a revolutionary war there, you know. The Boxer Rebellion," her husband interrupted.

"And he said he saw three young men..."

"And a woman," Suzannah Crippler added.

"Yes. Americans. Working on the wounded Chinese people. Acting, you know, like, like doctors, working on people and telling other Chinese women and men what to do to treat the wounded."

"China," Gunther repeated.

"Peking," she added. "And, at one point, one of the white doctors whispered to him his name, his friends' names and asked for help."

Gunther looked at the vice president and Teddy nodded.

"Do we know who this missionary is?"

"Yes, we do. We had him come in to see us and speak with us," Mr. Bellmont said.

"Did he see any photos of your son? Your sons?"

"Yes, he did. The three of them," Mr. Hedgecock said. "He looked at the most recent pictures, graduation pictures taken from the day before they disappeared, and he said, those three were the Americans he saw in Peking."

"And..." Gunther looked at Suzannah Crippler when she spoke up, "my sister Ethel. She is in the family business.

She and her husband Jacob were in China to develop…to meet with international shippers. We lost touch with her one month ago. The wires just…stopped. This was very unusual. She is very prompt."

"Has this missionary seen a picture of her?" Gunther asked.

"Yes, her wedding pictorials. He said Ethel was the woman he saw."

"Her husband, Jacob?"

"The missionary did not see him."

"Can you find them, Major?" Mrs. Telemore begged. "Can you find them? Can you bring them back home?"

"And we're having a pill of a time on the docks, Major Gunther," the senator said. "As you pursue this, can you help us out, any which way you can, on this ugly shanghai business?"

Silent and wishing he was not in the room, Gunther took another sip of the coffee.

"Yes, he can," Roosevelt said. "This is the type of problem my old friend is capable of solving."

"Well, I…yes, I can…try," Gunther said. He took a deep breath and examined the despairing faces in the room, settling in on the other younger woman on the couch.

"I am Rose Telemore. Jason's wife," she said. "This is our son, Jacob."

Gunther nodded with her presence painfully explained. A new family, a new career and life, gone.

"This is a very complicated situation," Gunther said. "A military mission. First, I would need to meet with this missionary and learn more details."

"Of course," Roosevelt said.

"I need a team of people."

"Of course."

"Boats. Guns. Ammo. I need…"

"Of course," Roosevelt said.

The room fell silent. The families and the senator could finally witness that Vice President Theodore Roosevelt, somebody, anybody, was actually doing something tangible with this dilemma.

"And now, my friends, thank you for coming. Thank you," Roosevelt said, "and now I will get these solutions going." Roosevelt stood, which signaled all to stand. "My staff will be in contact with you."

The guests thanked the vice president profusely. He bobbed his head up and down and grinned at each one. Then the parents shook Gunther's hand. The mothers held his hand with their two hands as they passed, imploring him to rescue their sons.

Mr. Belmont was the last parent.

"Bring my boy home," he said.

"I will try."

"If you can, you will certainly be rewarded."

"I thank you, sir, but I am in the Army and my pay is my pay."

"I know, but you won't always be in the Army."

Gunther had no answer for that remark.

Then they all thanked the senator. They finally filed out of the door. The senator said goodbye also and winked at Roosevelt. The vice president winked back.

Suzannah Crippler was the last. She approached Gunther with a cold, questioning expression, eyeing him up.

"I'm going with you," she said solemnly.

"I…I haven't even drawn up a plan to go…I…"

"I am going with you."

She shook his hand and left the room.

"Major, whoa, stick around," Roosevelt said.

Crippler, the parents, and senator finally left, and the guard shut the door.

The V.P. lit up a cigar. "Cigar?"

"Sure, sir."

He handed Gunther a cigar and they sat on the couches, facing each other. Gunther charged up his cigar.

"Cuban!" Roosevelt belted out.

"She says she is going with me?" Gunther said.

"Suzannah Crippler..." he took a big draw on the cigar, "Suzannah Crippler is no ordinary woman, Johann. She is a rodeo star and sharpshooter competitor. A champion. She's been running cattle and hogs since she was 8 years old..."

"Well..."

"She's been in many a gun fight on the Nebraska range wars. She and her dad run a huge meat business and a number of restaurants in Kansas, Missouri and Nebraska. She's fit as a fiddle, and...she has to go."

"Why?"

"*BECAUSE*, well...her family and my family go back a longways. She is my godchild. Her missing sister Ethel is my godchild. Ethel and her husband were there in China, there on family business. And, she just has to go, Johann."

"What kind of family business?"

"That is a business secret."

"A...secret?" Gunther said.

"Yes, and if she tells you, if she decides to tell you, well she'll tell you. I am not at liberty to explain her business."

Gunther nodded for the moment but figured that later he

could think of a way to get shed of her.

"Johann, I want you to go do this, but not as a representative of the Army. Not as a major. Or any kind of US soldier. I think you can accomplish more that way. Hell, the Boxers are trying to kill all foreign soldiers. President McKinley has a plan on his White House drawing boards to send 5,000 American soldiers there. Protect the Americans there. Lots of businesspeople and missionaries. You can get around a lot more not being an official soldier." He puffed the cigar. "Go as a...a soldier of fortune...a...a... mercenary. A missionary! You be someone else. This can't be an official army mission."

"Why not, sir?"

"This is a favor, Johann. It cannot be an official mission. It is too long and complicated to explain right now. There are many diplomatic things happening with China and this would just twist things up. Have you been well?" Roosevelt asked.

"Well, as...as the mud and jungle war can let me be."

"I see," Roosevelt grinned, infectiously, and Gunther had to smile back. "No fever. No problems from Cuba?"

"None, sir."

"Amazing as it struck so many. Did you hear that a Major Walter Reed has proven that the mosquito bite is the cause of these terrible fevers! We thought so; but by golly, he proved it. Those damn little bastards."

"I covered up all the time. We had a whole class on this at West Point. Doctors all over the world since about 1850 suspected the mosquito bite delivered the fevers. But the militaries all over the world ignored their advice."

"Well, that's why we wrote the 'Round Robin' letter and told McKinley we all had to get the hell out of Cuba," Roosevelt said.

"But the little bastards still bit me all over."

Roosevelt shifted in his seat and said, "This, this Philippines thing. It's a battle I did not start, but I will, by God, if I am still around, get any more power, I will finish."

Roosevelt stared at Gunther with a small smile. Admiration. Gratitude. It was clear that Roosevelt was glad to see him.

"Sir, as to the Philippines, General Smithe seems to have lost his mind. He has issued a command to Camp Tasey to kill every Filipino male over 10 years old on the island of…"

"Over 10!"

"Yes, 10."

"I will look into it, my boy. Right away. Right away."

"Please stop him, sir. We can't order this crazy thing. And I would ask you, as I need men for this China trip. A team. For starters, I have an aide in Philippines, a Lt. Felix Jefe Cocoy, Master Philippines Scout. He has been indispensable to me. Saved my life as I have saved his life. A real fighter. Hands, sticks, knives, and guns. Graduate of the Madrid University in Spain. Arnisador."

"Ohhh-hooo, Bully for him," Roosevelt said. "Arnis…Arnisador. Yes, yes and they do that stick fighting." Roosevelt swung his arms in the air. "I am going to do that someday."

"I can arrange that. He is a guro…"

"Guru?"

"No Sir, guro, with an 'o'. Means teacher in Tagalog."

"I see. With an 'o'."

I would like to take him with me on this. He looks a bit Chinese and can speak some Mandarin. He had a second in Oriental languages in Madrid University. He might be very helpful in this matter."

"I see. I see. Of course. Of course. I will cut the orders. You say his first name is…is…Jefe? Like 'captain' in Spanish?"

"Middle name. First name is Felix. Yes, sir, he's a lieutenant in the Scouts, Jefe translates to "captain" in Spanish."

"You know, I once knew a man named Terry Majors. He became a major in the Marines. Major Majors! HA! I know…I know from your lawman past, and by God from Cuba, I can count on you Johann. You're a Rough Rider through and through, for life. Leather for a heart. They are gone now and there were only a few of us Rough Riders left. You are forever one."

"Thank you, sir."

"Through *and* through! And forever my friend. You'll leave in a few days for China."

Teddy stood. It was time to leave.

"Oh, take this." He handed Gunther a file. "This is not to leave the Presidio. This will explain more in detail, photos and you know, intelligence."

"Leave in a few days, sir?"

"Yes…yes. Listen, my boy, there's one more thing you can do for me. Another complicated favor."

"What's that, sir?"

Roosevelt wrapped his arm around Gunther's shoulder as they slowly stepped to the suite's door.

"This *tawdry, tawdry* operation on the San Francisco docks," he sneered, "just…just bedeviling the law down there. This hijacking of human beings! This shanghai business. American citizens disappearing! Can you *imagine*! This ain't right, my boy. No! It's just not right! I fear for every able-bodied man and woman that walks the popular piers!"

Gunther nodded.

"This Red Keleton and his operation. I...I want you to go down there and stop it. I mean stop it! Put a damn stop to it! Any way you can. End it."

"End...it, yes?"

"Between you and me. End it, as much as you can. Kill the disease. Kill it off. As much of it as you can."

"I see, sir. I think I understand what you are saying."

"That is why, this...this whole thing cannot be an official Army operation. No, no. no. The San Fran docks. China..."

"I think I understand, sir."

"I think you *do*," Roosevelt said. "As a favor to me and the senator. It's always good for a vice president and a senator to owe you one. Right?"

"That it is, sir," Gunther said. He had to laugh at that one.

"A *big* one," Roosevelt laughed back.

"About a team, sir..."

"Team. Yes. Now, you're staying at the Presidio. And your contact man is Colonel Westways waiting outside. You know. Damn fine officer. He brought you here today. We'll get you to Naval Station, Hawaii. Honolulu. Then some damn island or another next and then on to China. Peking, China! For a team. Well, you know I love my boats. My ships. You will have at your disposal, the S.S. Rio Lobos."

"Rio Lobos. That's..."

"...that sounds familiar? Yes. I know. Made in Spain. We confiscated it in Cuba. It's a gunboat, Hell, it's a refitting war-ship now. You should *see* the bully firepower. Mighty machine guns. Swivel cannons. Navy calls 'em guns. But BIG cannons. Two 18-inch (450 mm) torpedo tubes. *BUT*, for this, for you my friend, it is disguised as a Chinese merchant ship to get you there and back. Steam. Steel screw. Faaaast. Over 30 knots. She seaworthy and also built for river patrol too. Oh, I love her." Teddy threw another hook punch on the air. "You're going to love her. And her crew? They are Chinese Americans from our Navy! Dressed up like Asian merchants. Oh, her captain is named Hoon, once of the Chinese Navy! He immigrated over here. We found him in Portland. Now he's one of ours and they say he is crazy mean. She has an American captain too, named Delane because I had to make the Navy happy with an American captain too. But the Hoon fellow is a bully of a warrior. That's your team."

"And Lt. Felix Jefe Cocoy, sir?"

"I remember his name. Yes, I'll have him meet you in Honolulu."

"Yes, sir. And General Smithe's order to kill every male over 10 years old?"

"Yes, yes! I remember! Yes. And we have Chinese and Americans along the way and there in China to help you. Westways will also brief you."

"And of the Boxer Rebellion, sir? I…"

"What of it?"

"I can't very well stop that, sir."

Roosevelt beamed. Giant teeth abounded. "Not so sure about that! But of course not. That's a war unto itself. Just get those doctor boys back and my godchild Ethel back, huh? Get 'em back! Make the parents happy. Tonight at 7 p.m. you will meet this missionary who spotted them. Tenderloins Steakhouse. It's a great place for steaks. Colonel Westways will take you there. This missionary can tell you directly when and where he saw our missing boys and girl. Dress tonight? Civies. Get him to go back with you to China. He does not need to know what you are. Soldier? Mercenary? Spy? Tell him only what you think you must to get them onboard. Money? Promises? You have my full support."

Gunther gave Roosevelt a quizzical expression.

"You don't trust him to know about me?" Gunther asked.

"Weeelll, not yet. Not just yet. Oh, and my Alice will be quite upset when I tell her we had this meeting. She still has *quite* the crush on you, you know."

"Tell her hello for me, okay?" Gunther said a bit abashed, but he noted the quick topic change off the trust subject. Roosevelt's daughter Alice always liked spending time with Gunther.

"I will! Ha! She'll like that. But...but now you look here! Look at me, boy, I don't want you for a damn son-in-law. You're too *damn* crazy!" More teeth.

They reached the door.

"I am off for Washington DC. With a stop in Denver. When you come back, we'll go hunting in Wyoming again, huh? These guides of mine? Ohhh, oh, they know all the good places and where all the good game is. And we'll sit around a *roaring* campfire in the mountains...and...stars, my God, Johann, the stars. The Rocky Mountains are closer to God and the stars, you know. And you can tell me *every* step, step-by-step, you took in the Middle Kingdom to pull this magic trick off because I want to know."

He ushered Gunther close to the front door.

"Oh, on, now, remember my little favor. San Francisco docks."

"Yes, sir."

"Then China with you, my boy!"

He opened the door and Gunther left the room. The door shut. Westways, seated on a velvet bench, looked up at him from an open newspaper.

"To China with me," Gunther whispered slowly to himself. Aghast.

Chapter 4
The China Runners

In his officer's-quarters hotel room, Gunther removed his dress uniform and put on civilian clothes, a tan shirt and Levi's pants. He opened the curtains and lifted the room's one window to see the three-story high view, surrounded by pine, cypress, and eucalyptus trees, and to feel blessed with cool, bay breezes. He poured a glass of water from a pitcher, dragged two chairs near the window and sat in one and put his bare feet up on the other. He reached for the file Roosevelt gave him from atop the dresser. He looked over the maps and intelligence information and paid particular attention to the typed biography of...the Chinese "Boxer".

"The Society of Righteous and Harmonious Fists, known by foreigners as the *Boxers*, or "Ye Magic Boxing", was a secret society founded in the northern coastal provinces. The Boxers consisted of local farmers, peasants, and other workers made desperate by disastrous floods and widespread opium addiction and blamed Christian missionaries, Chinese

Christians, and the Europeans who colonized their country. Missionaries were protected by a treaty. The Boxers called foreigners "Guizi" which translates to demons. They condemned Chinese Christian converts and Chinese working for foreigners.

The Boxers, armed with rifles and swords, claimed supernatural invulnerability toward blows of cannon, rifle shots, and knife attacks. The Boxers believed that through training, diet, martial arts, and prayer they could perform extraordinary feats, even such as flight. They claimed that millions of *spirit soldiers* would descend from the heavens and assist them in purifying China of foreign influences.

The Boxer beliefs were characteristic of tribal movements, like the Native American Ghost Dance, another practice of a society under stress.

The early years saw a variety of village activities, not a broad movement or a united purpose. Like the Red Boxing school or the Plum Flower Boxers, the Boxers of Shandong were more concerned with traditional social and moral values, such as filial piety, than with foreign influences. The goal was to "Revive the Qing and destroy the foreigners".

******

Six hours later, Colonel Westways, dressed in plain clothes, guided Gunther through the crowded Tenderloin Steakhouse. Gunther wore a brown suit, white Stetson, bolo tie and cowboy boots, and there before them sat the guest missionary in a booth by a back brick wall.

"I will leave you two gentlemen to it," the colonel said.

Gunther sat, tossing his hat on the seat, and the missionary man smiled at him. He had a stylish, oiled haircut, a trimmed beard and wore a suit and tie. In his late 40s, he looked tanned, trim and overly coiffed for a priest.

"Erasimo Mendante," he said, with an extended hand. Smooth. No callouses. Several rings.

"Johann Gunther. Should I call you Father? Doctor? Reverend? What?"

"Oh, eh, Erasimo is just fine. I am but a mere servant of God."

A waiter approached immediately, asking for drink orders.

"Floradora," Erasimo said.

"Some brandy would be fine for me," Gunther said.

"This place smells terrific," Erasimo said, rubbing his hands together.

"Yes, it does. What is your religion, Erasimo?"

"I am a Christian."

"And your church?"

"Saint Lucas, San Luis Obispo."

"And you hail from where?" Gunther asked politely.

"Ohio."

"Do you go to China frequently?"

"Yes, yes. Back and forth. Food. Medicine. God's work."

"Where exactly did you see these three missing men and this woman?"

"There is an old building in Peking, well, just outside of Peking. Chinese opera. Big as a warehouse. It's one of the big headquarters of the Boxer Rebellion armies. If you can call them an army."

"Where exactly is that?"

"I can't say exactly. Many side streets. Unmarked. You could say it is an opera house. I know how to get there. But the names of the streets and avenues? Too foreign sounding and you just can't read their scribble-scrabble signs."

The drinks arrived. Steaks were ordered.

"What did you see exactly?"

"Mr. Gunther, I thought it was strange that, that, so deep into Peking, to see three white men were there treating the sick and the wounded Chinese like doctors in an emergency hospital! I mean there are many white people in China there now. Businesspeople. Dignitaries. Missionaries. Soldiers, sailors, Marines." He sipped his drink. "But none in with the Boxers like that. Fixing them up. They want to kill us now, you know."

"What was the woman doing?"

"She was helping them. Like a nurse. It was just odd. Which is why I started to ask about them when I got back." He shrugged his shoulders.

"Did you talk with them?"

"Yes. I got very close to them several times. We had medical supplies to pass out and move around. One of the doctors came over to help us. It was Bellmont. He said, he whispered their names to me. He said, 'Tell my family we are here.'"

"Did they seem…free? I mean, tied up in any way? Guarded?"

"No. They were very busy running around the beds. Free. They had Chinese nurses with them too. I think they were nurses. Doing things. Following orders."

"That's quite the fashionable drink these days," Gunther said. "Floradora."

"Oh, oh yes, it is I suppose."

"Was this a hospital?"

"A converted hospital…area…I guess you might say. Part of the building. It had a stage. People were doing things all over the opera house. There was no theater seating. Big. Open. The men were working on the shot and stabbed Chinese Boxers in the open center."

"And you were…"

"I was there with medical supplies as we treat all the sick and dying under God."

"Hmmm."

Gunther sat back and sipped his brandy. There was another man several tables away and alone, who would not stop looking at them. He cut his eyes away when Gunther cast a wandering eye his way. He had no food on his table, only a coffee cup before him. He was stocky with a thick neck and long, shaggy, somewhat curly, reddish, brown hair with very thick, mutton-chop sideburns.

"When I returned to the States, I told a few people about this odd sighting and what the man said. Just gossip to friends. Word got around I guess, about what I saw and heard…and somehow…I was contacted by a man from Bellmont Industries. They had heard the gossip, from churches they said, and they asked me to his offices. I met 'Daddy' Bellmont."

"You looked at photos…"

"Yes, Mr. Bellmont had photos of his son and the other two men. It was them. Unquestionably. Waiter! Another Floradora!"

"When did you see the photo of the woman?"

"They have a group in San Francisco, a group called the L.L.O., 'Lost Loved Ones'. People looking for those missing from the docks, and the woman's sister is part of them. I looked at a lot of pictures and portrait paintings that Bellmont and the L.L.O. had collected. The woman looked like the one in wedding pictures."

"That Miss Crippler had?" Gunther said.

"Yes, yes that was her name."

"When will Saint Lucas send you back to China?" Gunther asked.

"When we get restocked from contributions. Mr. Bellmont has offered to give us quite a contribution to return to China in the hopes of securing his son. I guess with you along? Tell me, Mr. Gunther. You walked in here with that Westways man that looks like a soldier. He sounds like a soldier. You look like a soldier. You are two…?"

"I'm not a soldier," Gunther lied.

"What, or heaven's sake, are you then? Your skin is like leather from the burning sun. I've seen that before."

"I am…I am a soldier of…fortune. Misfortune. I was once a soldier, but now I do things for money. Sometimes the military needs something done, and I do it. Others need things done and I do that too."

"Ohhhh, I see. And I presume that Mr. Bellmont is one of the others? That he has hired you to get his son back?"

"You might presume that."

"The Crippler woman is very rich," Erasimo said. "Her family owns big steakhouses all over the country, the L.L.O. people told me."

Gunther nodded.

"Sooo, I see," Erasimo said, "a…soldier of fortune. Just. Well. Would…then…could then, you add one task atop another task then? Since you are a man of money? Of money concerns? Atop another?" Erasimo asked.

"Who's that man over there?" Gunther asked, changing the subject.

"What man?"

"That man."

The stocky man quickly turned away when they both looked at him.

"Oh, I...don't know, I..."

Gunther half smirked. He slid out of the booth and stood. He wiped his hands on his napkin, walked to the table of the lone man, and grabbed his coffee cup.

"HEY!" the older man growled.

Gunther walked back to the table with the cup. The mutton-chopped man had no choice but to follow.

"Sit."

Mutton chops sat. Gunther pushed the cup over to him. The man had one long scar down his left forehead, over his eye and all the way down his face, and even under his chin and down his neck.

"Is this another servant of God?" Gunther said, once resuming his seat. "Your guardian angel?"

Erasimo did not answer and looked embarrassed.

"Is he an angel watching over you from Saint...Lucas? You do know there is no Saint Lucas, just a Saint Luke. What's the scheme? This concern for money? This would-could," Gunther said with exasperation.

The two men looked at each other.

"If the scheme is about money?" Gunther said, "I can produce two or three times, whatever money you think you can make on your scheme. My hand is deep down in Bellmont's pocket. And the pockets of the other three families."

Erasimo's eyes widened. He smiled.

"They are paying me to bring back all three of those doctors and the woman. I have an unlimited budget."

"Un...limited?" Erasimo repeated with a sigh. The two men exchanged glances again and this time with smiles.

"Guns, Mr. Gunther. We sell guns to the Boxers. We can't go back there without a...a...contribution of...guns," Mutton Chops said.

"Rifles?"

"Rifles, pistols. Explosives. Ammo."

"And you did actually see these three people over there? The woman too?"

"Oh, yes. We absolutely did," Erasimo said.

The other man nodded.

"Your real name is Erasimo?"

"No. I use the church story to get in and out of China. It always worked before. My name is Ernest Parody. But it's a good idea to call me Erasimo in case anyone around is listening in. 'Ernest' was in a bit of trouble. There's a whole slew of people that don't like Ernest Parody. And Erasimo sounds like Erasmus. Kind of biblical? You know?"

"A nom de plume," Gunther said in a sigh. "Hmmm. You?"

"Collin Small."

"Real name?"

"Real name."

"One time military?"

"Nope."

"Where *ja* get that big-ass scar?"

"Picking apples. Working on a farm. *Cuttin'* branches on trees."

Gunther grunted, picked up his hat and slid over to rest his back on the brick wall in the booth. He put his boots up to stretch out, which hung over the booth seat. He looked the two of them over. He put the hat sideways on a knee.

"Where you from?" Collin Small asked Gunther.

"Texas."

"Look I can do this and pay you enough to never do any of this criminal shit again. No more guns to China."

"Ahhh…we ah, we also run one more thing."

"Run what?"

"Opium back from China," Erasimo-Ernest-Parody quickly added.

Gunther shook his head. What was he getting into?

"No more opium from China. Think of a number that might make you retire. For good. I will not supply the Boxer Rebellion with guns that eventually shoot our boys."

"Our boys?" Erasimo said. "I thought you were a mercenary."

"They are fucking Americans. And hey, I still have friends in the Army and some of them will come and work with me in the future."

"Oh, okay. Okay."

"And I will not bring opium back from China."

"No?" Small said, a little shocked.

"No. Think of a number and then quit."

"Quit," Small repeated.

"And I mean *quit*. Or…I'll kill you myself."

The two orders of steaks came. Gunther slid his plate over to Small and sat straight up again.

"My man Westways knows how to contact you?"

"Yes," Erasimo said. "He is putting us up in a hotel and

we were told to wait, meet you and make plans."

"Well, you did. WE have. It's on, and like the betrothed say, for better *er* worse. Think of a number. I think we will leave in two or three days. How do you two normally get to China?" Gunther said.

"We take a cargo ship from Samoa," Erasimo said.

"Do the Boxers know the ship? Or can we make the China shore on any ship?"

"Oh, they don't know or care how we get there. We just get there. We contact our men on the coast. They reach Peking. They come get us and we deliver in a caravan."

"We will go by US Navy ship, disguised as a merchant ship."

"The Navy? With our guns?"

"Stolen…guns? Are they stolen?" Gunther asked.

"No, no we buy them. Legal. But giving them to the Boxers is an international …problem. A law problem."

"You mean a crime. Well, not for me. Not this time. How much money do you need to buy these guns?"

"$6,000," Erasimo said.

"That's such a nice round number," Gunther said. "My man will contact you within 12 hours. Get the gun deal ready."

Gunther slid out of the booth and stood. He pulled out a 20-dollar bill and laid it on the table.

"See *ya*," Gunther said quietly as he put his hat on and walked away.

Once outside, Gunther walked toward Westways and their parked auto. The colonel stood by it.

"Major, how did it go?" Westways asked.

"Ohhh, okay, I guess. As seedy as expected."

Gunther leaned on the side of the 1900 Oldsmobile horseless

carriage and cupped his hands. The colonel took up the same lean on the other side.

"Tell the vice president this is going to cost more. A lot more. Thousands more. Tell him his gut feelings were right; the missionaries are not really missionaries. They are gun runners for the Boxers. They ain't at all what they appear. We need to buy guns to get us over there and get inside the Boxer building to find the doctors and the lady. We need to pay these cutthroats a lot of money to help us and make them quit doing this for good. They run guns over there and they return with opium."

"Opium in China. It's usually acquired from England over there," the colonel said, running a hand over his shaved head.

"Who is this Crippler woman? Are you in contact with her?" Gunther asked.

"Yes. She's tucked away in another hotel. I am supposed to put her and those two boys you just ate with on your ship to Hawaii when you're ready to leave."

"I worry about taking her along."

"She's a real pistol."

"That's what I hear," Gunther said.

"You might need her. She's an amazing shot. Cowgirl since crawling out of her crib. Rodeo champ. Has killed a rustler or two, so we've been told."

"Yeah, yeah. Let's get something to eat," Gunther said.

"Eat? No Tenderloin steak in there?"

"No steak. I couldn't eat with those two snake-oilers. But we need them. Let's get a steak or pork chops somewhere else."

"Your wish is my command, Major."

"Yeah, and then to the Presidio. My sleep is still on Manila time, and I feel like hell."

"I understand."

"And tomorrow and the next night, I need this auto again. And you."

"As I said, Major, your wish is my command."

"I've got a little something to do...on the docks."

Chapter 5

A China Vessel of Misery and Horror

The next night, Colonel Westways and Gunther parked the Olds on a cobblestone street with other cars, carriages, and horses. It was dark out and the air moist at about 10 p.m. Gunther, sans the big white hat and in a street-common, black derby, black suit, in regular tie and shoes, and Westways garbed about the same, slowly wandered the dock areas and piers notorious for tourists, sailors, merchants, as well as theft, robbery, prostitution and even murder. Yet, not well known to the average public was the continuous kidnapping, abduction and human trafficking for international shipping operations, sex, and slavery. For those that suspected as much and even knew about the human trade, some still frequented the area. Gunther assumed they all thought, "well, it will never happen to *me*."

After a brief walk, they saw the infamous Red Keleton's Peking Duck restaurant. Through the windows they could see it was full of men and women, chowing down with an excessive clamor given to more of a rowdy bar than an eatery. Uproarious laughter. Drunken, hand-waving and back-slapping. Even well outside, they could discern the muted piano and the *erhu*-a Chinese violin, and the *dizi*-the Chinese flute. They took note of the men and women, all races, walking with a purpose or strolling up and down the wide boardwalk of this commercial dock area. And then, not far from Red's, down one pier, Westways spotted the Goliath. They walked closer, leaned on the dock railing, and looked over large boat.

A man, in his late 60s or perhaps even 70s, also dressed up for an evening out, in gray suit, fluffy shirt and big bowler hat walked up near them, rested on the dock rail also and lit a cigar. Gunther and Westways took a few glances at him. His face, under a sparse, grey, wiry mustache was quite lumpy and rugged from old age.

"Gentlemen," he said in a very gravelly voice.

"Evening," Gunther said.

"I see that you two have an interest in the Goliath over there."

"Oh, just looking over the bay and the boats, sir," Westways said.

"Hmm," the man said with a low grunt. "I would whole-heartedly suggest that you stay shy of that particular ship."

"Oh?" Westways said.

He moved a bit closer to them.

"From the looks of you two, spying all around as you have. Such…serious faces. You might as well be writing in a notebook or having binoculars in your hands."

Gunther smiled at him.

The man smiled back in a crooked, sly sort of impatient way.

"Marines? Army? You've got the look."

They didn't answer.

"Navy perhaps. There's a lot that goes on, on the boat. The Goliath. Men and women kidnapped. Taken off to the four corners of the world. Europe. Asia. Africa. China. Many to China."

"Is that so?" Westways said. "And you? You know this?"

"That I do."

"Why then, haven't you done anything about it? Reported it?"

"HA!" the man said with a bellow. "Report it? To whom, sir? The local police? Oh, there indeed was a time, once, I would have done something, Mister..." He stuck out his hand.

"Westways. And this is Mr. Gunther."

"Clay Alexander," the man said.

They shook hands.

"So why haven't you done anything about it, Mr. Alexander?" Gunther asked again.

"There was a time when I fixed things, solved problems, for a price. But not anymore. I will be 72 soon. I ache in my bones. I can't sleep at night from coughing," he shook the cigar in his hand. "My legs are bowed like a wishbone from riding a horse all over the West, solving...problems. I have been shot over and over again. And stabbed! I have been jailed and almost hung. And that is not the half of it."

He stared out over the bay waters, but continued after a moment. "I...have...killed many a man. And in doing so, I've decided quite some time ago that while I could not solve all the problems of the world, as they are around... every...single... corner of it." He looked back at them. "But I could...I could solve some of the ones I was hired to solve. And I...I foolishly did some things for free."

"I see," Gunther said. "As...a...mercenary of sorts? A gun fighter of sorts?"

"Of sorts. I started out in the Civil War. The North. We won the war. We lost the restoration. But I became more of what you might say a...detective? But looking back, I don't exactly know what I was...exactly. Remedies was my business, one might say."

"Remedies," Gunther repeated.

"Remedies, gentlemen, and remedies don't always follow the letter of the law. Remedies may follow a higher calling."

"Higher than the law?" Westways said.

"The law. The law twists like an innocent man at the end of a rope, Mr. Westways. You can take daily bets on if the rope will snap? Choke an innocent man? Or a guilty one. Daily bets."

Then all three stared out over the bay.

"I no longer have the energy or the heart to worry about things like The Goliath, or the man who owns her. That boat there, the Goliath is owned by a Red Keleton," Clay Alexander said, not looking at them, "who also owns that Chinese restaurant over there. He is a vessel of misery and horror, and THAT..." he pointed to the Goliath, "is the actual vessel it starts on. I have lived in San Francisco for 30 years, off and on. I am close friends with many good and bad people. And with Chinamen here, and I can tell you two boys that Keleton is a ruthless bastard and a life destroyer. And if I were younger, I probably would do something about it. But I don't have the energy or the heart."

He pushed off the railing, stood erect and sighed. He shook his shoulders and his knees a little bit, like getting them all back into place. For the first time they noticed he had a fancy cane.

"Energy and heart, gentlemen. By the looks of you two? I think you possess both," he said as he looked them up and down.

"When there is a preponderance of ships waiting out there?"

he continued, lifting the cane and using it to point out of the bay, "Like tonight. Like this ending of this month's business in the bay, the start of next month, that is when they need so many sailors...crew...worker ants, and that's when Keleton starts playing his catch-and-sell games."

Gunther nodded.

"I stay at the Carlton Hotel, gentlemen. Almost always downstairs at the restaurant for breakfast at 8 a.m. If you should ever want any advice from an old man."

"That's a far piece away from here, old timer," Westways said. "Would you like a little company on your return walk? I don't like the looks of this area around here."

The man smiled. He pulled a small pistol from one coat pocket and stuck it back in, and then a two-shot, derringer from the other side pocket, and dropped it back in. He winked.

"I always travel with the company of two old friends as it is."

"Goodnight, Mr. Alexander," Gunther said.

And the man touched the corner of his hat brim and walked off, using that cane now and then as they detected a limp from within those bowed legs.

"There is probably a sword inside that cane," Westways said. "I'll bet. What do you think?"

"Probably," Gunther said.

"Interesting old codger," Westways said.

"*Yeees.*"

They turned their attention to the restaurant.

"Shall we?" Gunther asked.

"Lead on."

******

And the pair entered the establishment. Not a table was empty, and the place had a unique smell of Chinese food, beer, a touch of urine, and embedded, musty, old, wet wood. The tablecloths, dishes, glasses, and cutlery appeared clean and new and the food and drink upon them voraciously consumed, looked delicious.

There were open stools on the right side of a horse-shoe-shaped bar, and they took two of the perches.

"Good *ebening*!" an oriental woman said. "What would you like to drink?"

"Two Anchor Steam Beers," Westways said.

They watched her draw the beer from a keg on the wall. The keg was in full use of the waiters and waitresses.

When she returned, Gunther asked her, "So, who is the famous Red Keleton?"

"Oh, he is over there," she said and pointed to a big man standing by a table with his hand on the shoulder of one customer.

Red had a head full of long, red, hair waxed back. A full, straggly, red beard. A short-sleeve shirt revealed two forearms full of, what seemed from the distance to be naval tattoos. At one point he walked over to a gaunt Chinese man with a long mustache, long black and thick strand of a ponytail with a red satin tie-off on the end.

"He never, ever stops talking!" the bartender said. "Talking, talking, talking. But you know, good for business."

"And now we know who the famous person is," Gunther said. "Thank you."

Before they sipped the beer, they stopped and looked at each other.

"I guess, it's okay," Westways said. "It came from that keg and she's using it a lot."

"I think so too."

They drank and watched. Red worked the tables, helping the wait staff and the clean-up crew. They drank their beers, paid, and left.

On the way to the Olds, Gunther decided to ask of Westways, "You obviously know that the vice president has asked me to find these missing doctors in China?"

"Yes."

"And do you know he has asked me to…to…'clean up' this mess on the docks…related to the missing doctors?"

"Yes, I do."

"Are you aware to what extent, this 'cleaning up' means?"

"It means using the dynamite, the pistols and the knife you asked for last night."

"It does," Gunther said.

"Yes."

"Well," Gunther said, "like Clay Alexander said earlier, I can't clean up all the dock crime and kidnapping and shanghai, but I can at least clean up this one."

They got to the horseless carriage.

"Tomorrow night, I need your help. I'll need 4 sticks of dynamite. Long fuses. I have the pistols and knife I'll need. I had other plans…smarter plans…but I must get to China, and I have no time fool around. Are you with me?"

"Your wish is my command, Major."

******

The next night, midnight...

As Clay Alexander noted, the docks were full and the boats and ships in deeper waters were in abundance. Was this to be another night, the next night of a major shanghia? Gunther and Westways were dressed in black clothes this time. Black pants, shoes, socks, shirts, and jackets. They both wore the black, knit, skull caps of common seamen and could have passed as area workers. Gunther had a dark gray scarf around his neck. Under his jacket was a dark pistol belt with his two, short-barreled revolvers and knife. In the inside breast pockets of his jacket – 4 sticks of dynamite. The men sat in their Olds in a service area nearby the dock that overlooked from a distance, the Chinese restaurant and oversized party boat, the Goliath.

The party continued hardily inside the Chinese restaurant. Few people walked the docks. Gunther stepped down from the Olds and with hands in his pockets walked down to the pier of the Goliath. He lingered with a look over the bay like a tourist, then strolled onto the pier. He pulled the scarf up over his face. He made a hard and fast turn right onto the Goliath gangway.

Once aboard, he saw no one, scanned the landscape of the open deck and thought no one spotted his entry. He stepped inside a double door to the interior, pulled one of his short-barreled pistols and in a fast pace covered the halls and rooms of the big boat. One door led to the hull, and he looked over the hull of the ship. There were dozens of woven mats on the floor, obviously where the knocked-out victims would be dropped. The stench of urine, feces and death swirled up the stairs and passed through him via the draft of the open door. He returned to the hall and quietly shut the portal.

He jogged through the engine room. No one there. He swept through the helm. No one. He heard two voices down a second hall from the helm. The banging of some pots and pans. The galley. Gunther stepped to the door and peered in. Two Chinese cooks were at work. He opened the thin metal door and entered.

"Hey," Gunther said quietly.

They turned to look. Gunther pointed his pistol at them and cocked the hammer.

"Go. Leave. You understand?" he ordered. "Now." He moved the barrel to the door.

Wide-eyed, the two men had to approach near him and the one doorway to escape. Gunther stepped aside but followed them out. They started to run and so too did he. Up on deck. Across the gangway. Gunther stopped following them once on the dock.

The Goliath's bow was facing land. He holstered his gun and walked to the rear. He pulled out a stick of dynamite. He lit the fuse and tossed it aboard the rear of the vessel. It landed near some seats on the stern, sizzling.

Midway, he lit and tossed another.

At the bow, and the large-covered party area, he lit and threw the final two sticks, and he walked off. The two cooks had dashed into the restaurant and in seconds, none other than Red Keleton himself appeared in the doorway with a meat cleaver, beside a large oriental holding his own meat cleaver. The two ran to the dock.

"What the hell do you..." Keleton shouted, well ahead of the second man.

Gunther walked slowly forward on the pier.

Keleton, his face enraged, got closer and reared back that cleaver. Gunther pulled his pistol and shot him from the hip, blasting a .38 round into Red's weapon-bearing shoulder. The knife went flying into the darkness. Gunther charged in the last few feet, shooting again and again into the Red's chest, rippling, and tearing the plaid flannel. Keleton's expression disconnected with his brain. His jaw dropped. Gunther's next shot twisted him sideways and right off the dock.

He pulled his left-handed gun and shot the second incoming man. Head. Neck. Chest. He too, fell too lifeless into the bay.

The first stick blew. The concussion rocked the air and water. Wood and metal flew apart and into the air some 25 feet high. Gunther walked off the dock. The second one blew, gutting the right side of the boat, the starboard infrastructure blowing out and up, and across the dock. Flames. Smoke. Smell. The wooden dock caught fire.

The final two erupted as Gunther, once on land, turned back to the service area, customers of the Keleton's Chinese restaurant poured out, shocked, and Gunther saw the glowing, pulsating red, yellow, and orange flash across their faces and the establishment. The chaos was distorted in the reflections of the front, glass windows of the shops along his walk. He peeked to the left to spy on the hellish scene behind him, He thought for a second of looking like an innocent bystander would and turn around and watch the Goliath disintegrate but decided to keep walking.

"There! There!" he heard.

Gunther looked over his shoulder. One of the boat's cooks appeared from a side service door of the eatery to see three men pile out, as the cook told them what had happened and how that man in black scared them off. Gunther had not yet reloaded his guns. He started with a jog and then a full-out run up the boardwalk to Westways and their auto. He looked over his shoulder again to see the three big men in pursuit, holding clubs and swords in their hands, some 40 feet behind him. He knew he couldn't reload at a dead run like this. He had two shots left in his left-hand pistol. Four men, two shots and he could not count on two pistol shots stopping and killing two of the men.

But he did stop, turn, and shoot. He hit the lead runner in the torso who grunted and clutched his chest. He did not fall, but his charge was certainly interrupted. And, as Gunther had hoped, the other two dove upon the ground, fearing more bullets. He took off again at full speed for the service area.

While the third stumbled, the other two men jumped afoot and continued chasing. They cursed.

Gunther saw the Olds ahead. He saw Westways. The colonel stepped from the vehicle, lifted a rifle, and started shooting. Bullets zipped past Gunther. Methodically and at a rate needed to produce cover fire. Slow enough to save ammo yet do the job. Gunther got close and Westways pitched the lever action rifle to Gunther. Westways got behind the wheel of the car. Gunther caught the gun and turned with it to see two of his four pursuers down. The Oriental they saw the night before, with the long mustache and ponytail, held a sword in his hand, still charged.

"Forget it!" Gunther yelled.

He did not forget.

"Stop!" Gunther added.

He did not stop.

And Gunther shot him. Chest. The man forgot and stopped. The fourth man was sprinting back to the restaurant.

Westways had cranked the Olds ignition back when the first dynamite blew, and the engine was running. They drove off, just as another huge explosion caught the ship's fuel and ripped the Goliath into a final splintered end. Gunther removed the mask from his face and took in several deep breaths. The two said nothing to each other as Westways steered their path back to the Presidio.

Gunther thought of the man he shot that gave chase. He'd held nothing but a club. Keleton and his friend held only meat cleavers and of course, were still very dangerous. He had to remind himself he was *not* in Cuba or the Philippines. This was San Francisco! And what would his old Paris, Texas police chief, Gustav Henri think of all this mayhem? This violence?

******

A dapper Clay Alexander sat down for dinner the next night in the Carlton Hotel Café. A waiter brought him a glass of sherry and the evening edition of the newspaper.

"Thank you," he said as he unfolded the paper.

"Ha!" he uttered in a quick grunt, then the right corner of his mouth curled up in a half smile as he read the headline and the subsequent story.

"Party Boat Explodes in the Bay Docks," reported the headline. "The boat, the Goliath suffered a series of explosions last night and sank at the Livingston docks. The owner of the vessel and the Peking Duck restaurant, Red Keleton, as well as several other dock area motels and businesses, is missing, presumed at this moment dead in the explosions. An employee of the Peking Duck was also wounded by gunfire in a related incident. The police and fire department are conducting an investigation..."

Clay Alexander began his meal with a bowl of clam chowder soup.

Chapter 6
To a Burning Hawaii, to a Bloody China

The next morning after the unofficial "remedy", problem-solving on the docks, Gunther was drinking US Navy coffee, carried topside from the galley of the SS Regulator. His forearms resting on the starboard railing of the ship as it cut through the waters of the Pacific Ocean. The warship with a crew of hundreds of sailors departed the Presidio at 6 a.m. sharp, as though it was waiting like a racehorse at a starting gate for Colonel Westways' mere notification to speed off.

Gunther hadn't slept, he just packed and departed. Breakfast aboard, he planned on a long rest in the coming days of sea travel. He felt as though he was escaping California like a fugitive, leaving Westways to cover over any leaks and clues to their bayside deeds. But he knew there could be no other "justice" brought to bear on Red Keleton's shanghai operation than the kind he had just laid down in a few explosive minutes.

"Good morning!"

Gunther turned to see his two, gun-running, opium-smuggling, new "partners", Erasimo and Small walk up. They were dressed in long black robes, pants underneath, and Catholic collars.

"Yeah," he said. "Good morning, Fathers."

"We are finally on our way," Erasimo said. "We've been on this ship for a day waiting just for you to show up. This whole giant ship sat waiting for you. Just for you. You put your second foot on this deck and the ship took off. Come on, you must be an admiral or something?"

"Or some kind of general," Small said.

"Or nothing. I am but a pawn," Gunther said.

"Ahhh, but 'I am a pawn in *your* chessboard'," Erasimo offered, "said once by female medical missionary, Mary Ann 'May' Harriet Allen."

With that quote, Gunther looked at Erasimo's profile, shook his head and looked back out to sea.

"You know, you don't need those disguises until we dock in Peking. No one here cares who or what you are. You get all those guns?" Gunther asked.

"Yes, we did, Your obviously militant friend Westways set us up with a driver and a small truck...an escort...and we made our rounds. We bought rifles, pistols, ammo, we have belts and backpacks. Duffle bags. And medicine. Medical supplies. He drove us around. We purchased. He paid."

"What's next?" Small asked. "No one will tell us anything."

"Well, Father Small, we are bound for Naval Station Hawaii. Then we change ships to one dressed up as a Chinese merchant vessel, The Rio Lobos, which is actually a helleva small warship I am told, not as big as this one. And then we head to Peking."

"We've never been to Hawaii," Small said fancifully.

"Have you two come up with a figure that you might retire

64

on? Wait, don't tell me now," Gunther held up his hand. "I don't know how this is going to work out, and I might have to give you a raise, if you live through it."

The fake priests smiled and nodded.

"A raise? Westways said that if you die on this trip, we need to return to see him and he'll pay us," Erasimo said.

"Oh, he did."

"Yes. But the idea of a raise? Hmmm. My friend, the good Reverend Small and I will do everything we can to keep you alive."

"So, I have accidentally picked up two bodyguards."

"Yes, you have."

"Will there be time in Hawaii," Small asked, "to maybe see some of the legendary island girls? I have read so much about them."

"Not in those clothes, but who knows. Maybe. The islands are full of missionaries and priests, *converting* anyone they can."

"You are such a cynic," Erasimo said.

They watched the waves.

"Who is Mary Ann May..." Gunther had to ask.

"Harriet Allen," Erasimo finished. "She was an English missionary. Most of her work was in Africa. She is famous, in the missionary business. One of my heroes."

"Missionary business? Hero?" Gunther said.

"Yes, sir. We always bring more medicines and medical supplies with us than guns, Mr. Gunther."

"You can call me Johann."

"The people of China need modern medicine," he continued.

"Have you heard about the medicines of China?" Small interrupted. "It's...it's mysterious powders and chopped animal parts and…and smokes and needles and rituals. All kinds of mythologies. Like our Indians."

"No. Never been to China. But I can imagine."

"Western medicine is almost outlawed," Small continued, "and illegal in places. But we deliver some of our goods to a hospital outside of Peking, to very young Chinese doctors and pharmacists."

"For free?"

"Yes, for free," Small said.

Erasimo half laughed. "We are not just gun-running devils, Johann. And so many of the people who need medicine are not Boxers. Not fighters fighting. They're just…people. Regular people."

"And the opium you bring back?"

"We sell it. Yes. Usually to the rich here in California. They pay us and we keep this little back and forth venture going."

"Uh-huh," Gunther said sarcastically.

"What do you think the US government is doing?" Small said.

"It's the same and yet bigger and in a different way?" Erasimo said.

"I am not always sure the government knows what the government is doing," Gunther said.

"We are not criminals, Johann," Small said. "Well, not…not completely. We have some dirty business. And we help out too."

"And you didn't tell me this at the restaurant the other night?"

"No. First you told us you were a mercenary. So…no. We thought you were just a criminal so then we needed to be criminals too."

"And you still sell weapons to the enemies of our country."

"Yes, but!" Small said. "There was no Boxer Rebellion when we started. We didn't expect it. China just lost a war with Japan, not the USA. You know, now all this Boxer business started up and we've made only two runs since. They were dangerous runs."

"What can you tell me about this new Boxer Rebellion?"

"So, happens, I have this placard, this printed flyer to show you," and Erasimo pulled a folded piece of paper from his pocket and handed it to Gunther. He took it.

"It's in Chinese," Gunther said.

"You can see the Chinese Boxers in the photo."

"Uh-huh. They look crazy as all hell."

"Let me read it to you."

"You can read this?" Gunther handed it back.

"Yes. It says, 'The foreign devils. Everywhere they are starting missions, erecting telegraphs, and building railways. They do not believe in our sacred doctrine, and they speak evil of our gods. Their sins are numberless as the hairs of the head. The will of heaven is that the telegraph wires be first cut, then the railways torn up, and then the foreign devils be decapitated'." Erasimo folded the paper back up. "Want it?" He offered it to Gunther.

"No thanks. I think I will remember it. Even the hairs on your head are numbered. Luke, not Lucas," Gunther mumbled a rare line he knew from the Bible, staring out at the ocean. "So, missionaries are not popular in China," Gunther said.

"It started with a missionary named Sidney Brooks from Australia. They tortured and killed him. And about the same time, two priests from Germany. Sometime in 1899," Erasimo said.

"The Boxers hate all foreigners," Small said. "But they know we two are not missionaries. They think we are gun runners in disguise, helping them."

"Which you are."

"But it is getting very dangerous getting back and forth from the port of Tongku to Peking now dressed like this. They send their best Boxers to escort us."

"We can't play this part again. Maybe not even this time. The Boxers will eventually kill us," Erasimo said, "just for being Americans. I would say, so far, they have killed several hundred foreigners and several thousand Chinese Christians. They usually torture them to death. One thing they do is pull out your teeth, one by one, with pliers. That's one thing."

"Why are they called Boxers?"

"We, the foreigners," Small said, "call them "Boxers" because they do their...Kung Fu boxing and their calisthenic rituals. They call themselves the Chinese secret society *Yihequan* which means, "Righteous and Harmonious Fists"."

Gunther turned around, his back now on the rail and he viewed the landscape of the mighty ship. On an upper deck, quite a ways away, he saw her, a tall, slim figure, her long brown hair swishing around in the wind, her long jacket wrapped tightly around her.

"There she is," Gunther said.

"Huh? Who?" Small said, and the two turned around also.

"Suzan Crippler," Gunther said.

"Not Suzan. Suzannah. She's beautiful," Small said, scratching his curly sideburns. "She strikes a beautiful figure up there," Small said, "like a painting, or a...a...Greek statue, or a newspaper ad for a beauty salon."

"Hummm," Gunther groaned. "They tell me she is a rodeo star and a sharpshooter."

"Wow!" Small said.

"Wow," Gunther repeated with much less exuberance. He finished his coffee.

"Well, I am going to bed. Maybe I'll see you at dinner, or breakfast."

He walked off.

"See *ya*', Admiral," Small said.

"See *ya*', General," Erasimo said.

"See *ya*', pawns," Gunther said.

******

Days later, Gunther stood beside Captain Woreshamy on the bridge of the Regulator. The day of arrival. They knew they would soon see Hawaii on the horizon, but they first spotted black smoke pluming in the sky.

"What the hell is that?" Woreshamy said, "That can only be a massive fire."

"I still can't see any fire. Just smoke," a helmsman said, his face behind heavy duty binoculars.

"Try the ship-to-shore radio."

A sailor sat behind the new device in Navy development, which looked like a giant, metal church organ on the bridge, connected to much larger equipment in the next room.

"Not in range yet, sir. Nothing."

They paced. They looked. They waited. 20 minutes. 40 minutes.

"Keep trying, Dillion," Woreshamy said to the radio man.

"Aye-Aye, sir."

Static.

"SS Regulator to Naval Station, Hawaii. SS Regulator to Naval Station, Hawaii, come…"

"Naval Station to SS Regulator, we read you, over."

Captain Worshamy, Gunther and some crew crowded around the radio.

"Naval Station we are approaching you, requesting permission to dock, over."

"That is a no-go Regulator. No go. We have a crisis here. Repeat no-go."

"We have a mission to…"

"Regulator, you are to set to anchor 2 miles out. We are aware of your mission. Commander Merry has ordered a transfer of personnel and cargo 2 miles out. The Rio Lobos is already 1 mile out waiting, with tugs to run the transfer."

"Naval Base this is Captain Woreshamy," he said, lifting the microphone. "What is your emergency situation? Can the Regulator be of any assistance?"

"Bubonic Plague. Captain Woreshamy, this is Commander Merry. This coast is smitten with the Bubonic plague. Honolulu started burning down houses and hotels of the sick and dead. But the winds whipped up and has set most of the city on fire. Our station has been on a lockdown for three weeks. We are conducting all business, such as yours, at sea. The Rio Lobos has been waiting 2 weeks for you out at sea. Reach them by ship-to-ship radio for coordinates. Over."

"I understand, Commander, over."

"I can only suggest that you conduct the transfer and leave immediately. Get to a safe harbor and await further orders.

How are you on fuel? Over."

"We need some, as we do not know yet where we will go. We will check our charts, over."

"We can deliver coal by tug…"

The radio conversation continued. Gunther nervously wandered to the bridge windows. Honolulu looked like a burning city at war. He imagined the chaos. He worried about Jefe. The Bubonic plague! He knew to be patient and not ask about one man over this radio transmission.

"God bless you all, over," Woreshamy finished.

"SS Regulator to Rio Lobos, come in," the radio operator resumed control of the mike.

"This is the Rio Lobos, Regulator. We have monitored your discussion…"

Gunther walked out to the bow of the ship. Many sailors stood there aghast at what they saw on the coast, now much closer.

"The Bubonic plague," Gunther shouted to his shipmates. "They tried to burn it out and they lost control of the fire. The naval base is okay, though."

"The plague!" many shouted and repeated.

"You are not going ashore. The Regulator will go somewhere else after dropping some of us off at sea to another ship. You men will not stay here. You'll leave as soon as possible."

They got the Rio Lobo's location and headed to the rendezvous. It only took about 30 minutes to have her in sight.

As the concerned gossip among the sailors picked up, Gunther spotted Erasimo and Small at the rail. He stepped over to them.

"I guess…I guess," Small said, "we won't be seeing any exotic, island women, huh?"

"Not without very strong binoculars," Gunther said, "or a cure for the plague."

The good ship Rio Lobos sat in the harbor. It looked like a sleek, military warship, except for the wooden disguise on the sides. It was a three-mast ship but without sails at the moment. Gunther knew little about the workings of ships, sailing or warships, despite his immigration from Germany to New York's Ellis Island in the 1880s, and his military journeys. He'd been just a mindless passenger, biding his time. This time would be different.

The fires on the Hawaiian horizon spread. It took the rest of the morning and early afternoon, but the secret cargo of guns, gear and medical supplies were loaded by cranes onto smaller boats. Then these boats slipped over to the Rio Lobos. The last tug across was for a few remaining crates and for four humans. Suzannah Crippler, Gunther, Erasimo and Small.

It was a choppy journey and Gunther kept his eyes peeled on the Rio Lobos' deck as they closed in, trying to spot Lt. Jefe Co-coy. There were a lot of smaller boats and canoes in the distance, seemingly headed their way from the shore. A crane swung out and over the small cargo boat. The crate ramps were attached and the four climbed aboard the boxes with their personal luggage. Sea spray and wind half-spun and rocked them on the long way up to the deck level. Gunther noted that Crippler rode out every bump like she was on a barrel horse, swaying with each turn and twist with a great and easy balance. She smiled at the ride and Gunther caught a glimpse of it. It was the smile of a pirate that could steal your heart. The crane turned and lowered the load on the deck. The four jumped down on deck.

Jefe, in a suit, tie, and short-brimmed hat, stood off to the side with some Oriental sailors, all in common clothes. Gunther half grinned and walked up to him, stuck out his hand and then as a prank yanked it back, as though Jefe was contagious.

"Of all the places you have sent me," Jefe said, "you have now dispatched me into *de* Bubonic plague."

"Yeah. Bad timing. Feel okay? How long have you been waiting?"

"Only one day. Out here at sea. I left Subic and got here. I never walked on land. They kept me out here. Where are we going?"

"China. Peking."

"Peking? I read in the Manila newspapers that *de* Chinese are killing all foreigners."

"Not all Chinese are killing all foreigners," Gunther said.

"Just *de* ones we will meet," Jefe said.

"I...ah, afraid so."

"This way, gentlemen," an Oriental sailor interrupted.

They all followed the seaman. As far as Gunther could predict, the Rio Lobos did indeed look like a Chinese merchant ship, in slight disrepair, which made the overall look even better a disguise.

"Help!"

"Help us!"

"*Kokua*!"

As they walked, Gunther and his troupe looked over the rail to see some small Hawaiian boats and canoes rowing nearby.

"Take us to the next island! Help!"

"Take us away!"

"Hawaiians were trying to escape the fires and the plague. We cannot help them," the guide said over his shoulder. "We cannot mix with them, and they cannot escape in those small boats."

They walked through a portal into a galley area of tables. The big room smelled of Oriental foods.

An older, stout Asian man, in classic Chinese clothes stood beside a very American man in a Victorian suit.

"Hello, Mr. Gunther," the American said, aware not to reveal Gunther's rank. "I am Captain Willis Delane, and this...this is the real captain of this ship," he pointed to the Asian next to him, "Chung Hoon."

Erasimo, Small, Jefe, Crippler and Gunther introduced themselves to the pair.

"Sit, sit, sit...sit, gentlemen and lady," Captain Delane said. "Coffee and tea please!" he shouted to the workers in a steamy kitchen. "I am familiar enough with your rescue mission, Mr. Gunther..."

"Call me Johann," and he cut his eyes to Jefe, as much as to announce 'no ranks mentioned', Jefe caught on with a barely seen nod.

"...and we will supply entry and exit for you in China. All of the men you see on this ship are Chinese and Chinese-Americans. And half of them were in the Chinese Navy. Chung Hoon was a ship's captain in China and is really the captain of the Lobos. I am only a political figurehead, an appointed, figurehead Caucasian to make various commanders in the US Navy, well, happy. They told us back in Honolulu that you would brief us more on the details when you arrived."

Chung Hoon, stocky, grey-haired, folded the thick fingers his calloused hands on the table. He smiled, displaying green-stained teeth, and said in perfect English, "I was an immigrant to your country. Working in the shipping industry in Portland and someone in US Navy heard of me. They recruited me for your mission and for future assignments. After we ensure your safety, the Rio Lobos will return to China, strip off the merchant disguise, show our guns, and help the US Navy patrol the Yangtze River. And the men you see all around you? Recruited from the Chinese community on the West coast, from Vancouver to San Diego. Most were in the recent Japanese and Chinese War, as was I."

"We are very, very lucky to have Chung Hoon," Delane said. "We have some of the newest, biggest guns on this ship, all hidden inside wooden crates on the deck. One rope pull, and the sides fall away and...Boom! We have many Maxim machine guns disguised all around the ship. The hull is made of the strongest materials. It looks like wood, it is only paint on thick metal, as we must often look innocent."

Jefe looked at Gunther, wondering, "what has he gotten me into?" Gunther knew well that look and started to explain the rescue mission to all of them.

They all felt the ship suddenly "push off" powerfully underneath them.

"My mission, our mission is to..." and without revealing his rank, the US Army or Roosevelt's name, Gunther told the group of the enterprising and ambitious goal. By now, Erasimo and Small must have known this was an official United States mission of some sort, but it behooved Gunther not to say the source nouns out loud.

Chung Hoon sipped his newly arrived green tea and then said, "This is very dangerous, you understand. The Chinese Army, the Empress Dowager is now, slowly siding with the

Boxers. You cannot count on the Chinese Army. They are both killing more and more Christian Chinese and one-by-one killing foreigners they catch. Very soon, they will be in a full war on you, the French, Spanish, English, Russia, anyone there that is not Chinese. People are gathering like refugees into Peking, into the legation city, where all the embassies are. It has all the embassies, shops, residents, eateries. It is walled off in sections as we Chinese like to wall things off. The British have the best walls. The United States embassy legation is less safe. The people are fleeing there and into churches, and out into the countrysides, hunted."

"Our military there?" Jefe asked.

"Yes. Some. But not enough. There are small military units there from each country. They cannot stop the Boxers. They certainly cannot stop the Chinese Army if they completely join with the Boxers."

"Dressed up, disguised as we are, we can get you to the Taku Forts, close in up the Bohai Bay," Captain Delane said.

"We will meet our contacts near the Taku Forts," Erasimo said. "They are…Boxers…wanting for our supplies and they will take us up to Peking."

"Where the shanghaied doctors are?" Delane asked.

"Yes, sir."

"They are killing priests now. You cannot go dressed like that. And you," Hoon pointed to Gunther, "are a white foreigner. Too tall. Blondy hair. You are a target also. You…" he pointed to Jefe, "not so much."

Suzannah Crippler hadn't said a word yet.

"You…are a white woman," Hoon said. "And you will also be in very big trouble."

76

"And you will go and will get back the same way? With the rescued parties? How?" Delane asked.

"That...we don't know yet," Gunther said. They all stared at Gunther. "We'll have to make it up as we go."

"If you are stranded in Peking?" Chung Hoon said, while lighting a cigarette, "you must escape to the embassies. The legation city."

"We know where that is," Erasimo said, waving his finger between himself and Small.

"It's defendable," Small said. "There's a lot of tall walls, like the Tartar Wall that runs the whole length of one side. But there is a canal that runs through the whole section and some open streets. We know how to get there once we are in the outskirts of Peking."

"We will wait in the bay for as long as we can," Hoon said. "Like those poor Hawaiians outside, there will be hundreds of foreigners and Chinese begging us to save them. So, we will wait out in deeper waters."

Hoon turned to some nearby sailors and said something in Chinese. One hustled off. Then Hoon turned back to the table. "Are you familiar with...the flare gun?" he said.

"Yes," Gunther said.

Jefe was, but Crippler not, and Erasimo and Small suggested they were not. Gunther did not believe them.

The sailor appeared with a thick red pistol and some shotgun-looking rounds and handed them to Hoon.

"It was invented by an officer named Very in the U.S. Navy in 1877. It is a short-barreled, 10-gauge pistol from which a flare-like bullet, like a firecracker...fireworks can be shot. It can be easily loaded into the breech and fired. The flare gun was first used by the Navy in 1882. It is an excellent signaler, especially at night."

Hoon opened and closed the pistol. He simulated loading it.

"I will see to it that each of you will have one. As we get to the China coast, I will show you where the Lobos will anchor and wait for you. Get as close as you can on the shore and fire it into the air. We will have spotters 24 hours a day watching for your flare. Best at night if you can. You will each have 5 shots. We will send sampans in to get you."

The four men and woman nodded.

"Our ship is very special," Hoon said. "It is just big enough to travel the ocean, and just small enough to run the rivers. If we need to get closer in, say up the river past the Forts, we can try. We have a man, a special agent waiting on the beach to help. A Mister Zin from the legations."

"So, we are off," Erasimo said, his palms open and down on the table, as though he was feeling the ship vibrate.

"Yes," Delane said. "It will take, depending upon the waters. About a week. A week and a day or two."

"All we have to worry about for now are pirates," Hoon added.

"Pirates?" Gunther said.

Chapter 7
Where is my China Hat?

Gunther, stretched out on the bunk of his private room, engrossed in *Ben Hur*, a book he borrowed from the ship's small library, which was really just a closet.

A series of ship's bells sounded, a very long ringing, and he heard the commotion of yelling men responding to the alarm. Gunther slipped on his shirt, pants and boots and opened the door. The sailors were dashing past him in the passageway.

"What?"

He heard a cannon outside!

"Junk!" one man responded to him.

"Junk?"

Gunther joined in the race to the deck.

Topside, he entered the sunny warm, sea air. There was another ship out there some 150 yards away.

"That is a Chinese pirate junk ship," a sailor told him.

A raggedy one as it had three dark orange sails and a brown, wooden curved hull with an elaborate, multi-level stern. Men in baggy Chinese clothes gathered on its deck.

They brandished rifles and swords. Some held them in the air and shook them, yelling. Laughing. Jeering.

Another cannon sounded from the junk, the round hitting the water near the Lobos.

Jefe appeared beside Gunther with his rifle in hand. Then Suzannah Crippler showed up with what looked like a custom-made hunting rifle, with scope.

"Come on," Gunther said, and the three ran up and onto the bridge.

Captain Delane was there glaring wide-eyed out through the bay of bridge windows. Hoon appeared next in the command center, buttoning a Chinese shirt and slipping on a coolie hat. He was as disguised as their ship.

"Pirates," Hoon told them, almost with a grin. "Those are warning shots to alert us. To scare us."

"Can we help? Can we do anything?" Gunther asked.

"No. Just watch," Hoon said.

Hoon left the bridge and took the stairs down, 6 at a time, holding the rails and swinging his legs into leaps.

In the distance, the pirates lowered two small boats, with about 15 men in each.

Once on deck, Hoon positioned eight men, in groups of two, by four stout covered railing posts. They unhooked and reached under a canvas atop their rail posts and worked on something inside the wraps still not visible. Then Hoon ran to the bow and shouted instructions to six men there.

The crew of the Rio Lobos watched as the pirates boarded small boats, about 12 on each one and they rowed the choppy waters to the Rio Lobos. The main junk got closer and closer also, turning to slice into the Lobos' path.

"*Xiànzài!*"Hoon shouted, moving his hands like an orchestra leader. Gunther could only assume that translated to...

"NOW!"

The men up front by the crate pulled a large cable and four of the crate sides fell off. Then two men yanked off a canvas revealing a modern cannon. The sailors manned it, swiveled the giant barrel at the junk.

Meanwhile the eight men pulled the canvases off their railing posts, revealing four Maxim machine guns affixed on metal pivots! With two men at each, they further primed the weapons.

The pirates in the small boats saw this and a few readied their rifles to fire, but to no good end. Two machine guns off to the pirates' boat right, opened up with some 500, high caliber rounds per minute, machine gun fire. The two guns to their left were assigned the other boat and they too pounded rounds into that closer vessel. The small boats and occupants were blasted to red guts, sea mist and wooden splinters in about 10 seconds, just as the heavy cannon up front fired and rocked the Lobos, shooting a round at the big junk. The shock wave blew the coolie hat right off Hoon's head. The round hit the junk starboard side of the pirate ship like a big bomb.

Again, the cannon. Again, the cannon. The small boats between the ships were now in a shredded debris, so the Maxims lifted their firepower across the splattering water and up onto the junk. Between the cannon and the Maxims, the enemy ship and men seemed to virtually disappear, piece by piece, big and small, melting into the Pacific Ocean.

Hoon stood on the deck, shaking his fist in the air, laughing, and smiling. The firing stopped and where there was once a ship and two boats, and people, was now a thin pile of debris, like a floating layer of rubbish. The pirate ship and crew...disintegrated.

On the bridge, Gunther and Jefe could only look at each other, astonished, then back out to sea. The whole destruction took less than two or three minutes.

"I think..." Gunther said, "I think, that was...the most amazing thing...I have ever seen."

Jefe could only nod.

Hoon suddenly appeared beside them back up on the bridge, shouting orders.

Jefe leaned in to translate, "He said to search the horizon, as pirate ships are often not alone."

Gunther and Crippler nodded with the news.

Sailors used telescopes and binoculars to scan the horizon. "*Nàli!*" one pointed.

Off in quite a distance and closing in was another junk.

Hoon turned two latches on a bridge window and shoved it open. He yelled orders to the bow cannon men. They could not hear him, their ears diminished from the blasts, but sailors, half-way on the deck ran to them and gunmen soon looked up to the bridge. Hoon shouted more orders and pointed to the incoming junk.

The cannon swung into position. The men calculated the shot within one minute and fired. The ship was too far away, and the round exploded into the sea. The junk made a risky maneuver and turned sideways to escape, but still too far to hit.

Hoon nodded at the helmsman.

"*Qiánfang quánlì yi fù!*"

"Full steam ahead," Jefe translated in a whisper.

The Rio Lobos revved up and took off. Everyone on the bridge rocked with the surge. In a moment, the ship was cutting through the water like a hungry shark with great speed. Gunther, Jefe and Crippler regained their balance. They reached out and grabbed for more secure handholds. The chase was on, and the Rio Lobos was quickly gaining.

"These junks," Delane said, "are often not just sail boats, but also have engines. We'll see if they do, but they won't match this queen."

And the back-up pirate ship was no match for the Lobos. Once in reasonable range, the 15-inch guns fired two in succession. The second one hit.

More Chinese orders from Hoon.

Jefe translated, "He said continue to fire."

And they did. The closer they got, the more they shot until the junk was almost as decimated as their other partner ship.

As the Rio Lobos got even closer to pass them, they could see the remains and a few survivors clinging to wreckage.

"Should we…" Captain Delane asked of Hoon.

"No, let them die," Hoon said.

Hoon shouted orders to one of the Maxim gun teams. They opened up on the few floating survivors.

"They are criminal baggage that we need not, and we will not carry," Hoon said to Delane. "They will become spies against us. Against our mission."

Gunther sat down in an empty chair. He was feeling exhausted. Jefe and Crippler stared out the windows.

Hoon touched the top of his head with his palm, looking around with a puzzled face.

"Where is my hat?" he said.

Chapter 8
The China Invasion

Three days later, with all the machine guns covered over again, the crate up front rewired to cover the front cannons and again resembling a mere big box of cargo freight, the Rio Lobos cut its engine and pulled up sails and coasted in toward the busy China bay as might any other merchant or fishing ship.

But, once within range, they heard distant gun and cannon fire. Hoon and Delane walked to the bridge radio. An anxious Gunther, Jefe, Erasimo and Small stood by. Hoon took charge of the microphone and began contacting various people in Chinese. Their static-ridden voices sounded stressed, and fever-pitched at times. Hoon sounded angry and shouted back at some of them.

When finished, he scratched a match across a door frame, lit a cigarette and came over to them.

"Very bad. Things are very bad. There are battles starting up everywhere. The Boxers attack in many places. And with help from some of the Chinese Armies. Very confusing. Battles in the bay and up down the Peiho River. The Chinese have laid mines out. There are Men of War gunships anchored in the bay from…from Russia, from France and Germany. America, Austria, Italy and Japan, all off Taku." He took a long drag of his cigarette.

"Every country," Delane said.

"Yes. A land and sea battle for days now. The legations in Tientsin and Peking are in need desperate for help. And now… our men are landing…right now! And advancing on Fort Taku. There will be a bloody battle there. But the forts will fall, as they did in 1860. When the forts fall, so will factions of the Qing government and the Boxers will take greater power."

"Mr. Erasimo, where will you meet your contacts? Exactly where?" Delane asked.

"A bit north of the northern most Taku Fort, in a street pharmacy in a village. It is run by Boxer sympathizers. We walk in. They contact the Boxers for us. The Boxers show up in a day with wagons and horses. Then we ride up to a small city outside of Peking."

"I see," Delane said. "And your missing doctors and the lady are there?"

"I hope so. It is a Boxer headquarters. They were there two months ago," Small said.

"So, you will contact the sympathizers today," Delane said, "and return to the Lobos for tonight. We can get you to the shore and back in small sampans. Then tomorrow you will go back and find out the travel details. Then at that time, we will unload your cargo on the shore, and all of you on our small sampans. And from there, we will leave you all to your own devices."

They were interrupted by the roar of huge guns in succession out on the bay.

"You two cannot go as Christian priests," Hoon said. "They are killing them now. Killing them slowly. Torture. Wear local clothes. Get rid of the collars. Try to blend."

Small pulled the white collar from his neck. Everyone noticed that the scar on his face, ran under his chin and down his neck. Jefe knew this was a sign of torture, not an accident. Erasimo also disconnected the collar from his neck.

"You, Mr. Gunther cannot go on this first trip today," Hoon demanded, eyeing him up. "You are tall, you have blond hair and white skin. And a stranger. It is too risky for no reason."

"I will go," Jefe said.

"Good," Hoon said. "You look good."

Erasimo and Small agreed with Jefe over Gunther. It was risky enough for them. There was no need for an "Anglo" Gunther to make this first meeting.

"Of course, Miss Crippler you need not go for this first meeting," Delane said.

She nodded.

"Once on shore," Hoon said, "you will meet our very important contact, *Lonziasheung*...well...Mister Zin. Okee-dokey?"

The Americans chuckled at the odd colloquialism coming from Hoon.

"Mister Zin is very important to us," Captain Delane said. "He works for the American legation. He is Chinese of course, but very loyal to us, loyal to an idea of a modern, international China. He will help you."

"Tonight, we will fix you up, Mr. Gunther. Your hair is very short now. Good. Skinned on the sides. Good," Hoon said. "A hat will cover your head. We will get you into Chinese clothes. Perhaps the Boxers will think you are giant freak of Asian nature? Let me show you. Walk around like this…" and Hoon demonstrated a funny, hunched-over strut.

Despite the predicament, they all laughed at his theatrics, and Hoon was pleased.

"I had a *very,* very tall friend named Stinky back in Texas. I will mimic his walk," Gunther said.

"There is an old Chinese proverb," Hoon said, "reshape feet to fit new shoes. Huh? Ha! You reshape yourself to fit Chinese clothes."

"And we have one proverb in Texas somewhat similar, Captain," Gunther added, "those are mighty big boots to fill."

******

The Rio Lobos turned their sails northward, away from the land-sea battle, away from the mines and to the north side of the Taku Forts for their clandestine mission. Gunther had spotted a powerful telescope device up on a post outside and atop the bridge. He and Crippler exchanged curious glances and they climbed up the metal ladder and onto the lookout area, she with that rifle slung across her back. Gunther examined the telescope apparatus. He wheeled it to the left and looked in the lenses. He adjusted the clarity. He scanned and searched and there it was…

Fort Taku of Tianjin. A series of interconnected forts. They looked much like coastal forts around the world, he'd seen in the U.S., Cuba and the Philippines. High stone and cement walls. The ramparts. Cutouts for machine guns and riflemen. There were men in different colored uniforms, different nationalities, and armies, attacking the forts, shooting, climbing, and dying in the smoke and fire of a siege. He could hear off in the distance the explosions, but not the cheers, the orders, the grief, the dying. Soon it all disappeared into blur of smoke.

"What do you see, Mr. Gunther?"

"Oh, hey, call me, Johann. I see…war, Miss Crippler." He stepped away from the telescope.

"Call me Crip," she said, and stepped over to look in the device. "Everyone calls me Crip."

"And what is our family business, Crip? One that put your sister and her husband in danger?"

She stepped away from the scope. Gunther noticed for the first time she had a single pistol, gun belt under her light brown jacket.

"I'd rather not say, Johann."

"I see."

"There is much business spying…"

"I think the new term for it is industrial espionage, as I understand it from reading the *Wall Street Journal*," Gunther said.

Her eyes widened with the mention of the Wall Street Journal, suggesting she might be a tad impressed with his reading material. She positioned herself so that she could look at him and not have the sea wind blow her long thick hair onto her face. They were alone, just inches apart and he could see her face completely, framed by a distant red and yellow explosive battleground behind her. Her face was heart-shaped with dark eyes, he…

"And I hardly know you," she said. "You could turn out to be a spy. For money. You might slip and tell those two, gun-running, fake preachers, even by accident what I do. Best you don't know."

"That's a beautiful rifle."

She pulled it off her shoulder, handed it to him and said, "Huskvarna."

He took it. It was a bolt action. The metal was engraved with the hunting art of roving deer and bear. The wood was also carved with cattle and horse designs. The scope was expensive.

"It's a show gun. I shoot in a lot of competitions. For money. Against men and women."

"So," Gunther said, raising the stock of the weapon up to his shoulder and aiming the gun out toward the sea, "shooting is your secret business?"

"No, not at all," she said with a wry smile. "Shooting is a hobby. My…sport. I am *very* good at it. You? What is your hobby?"

"Well, I guess I don't have one," he said, handing the rifle back to her. "Reading maybe? I am very busy though…"

"Men are always busy with wars. Finding them. Making them."

"Another form of shooting, however unpleasant. If things get rough in there, are you going to shoot people with that rifle? And that pistol?"

"I have shot people."

"Okay. You have?"

"Nebraska range wars. Cattle thieves."

"Okay."

"I was very young, with my father and our crew."

"So, you rode the range, as they say?" Gunther asked.

"I did."

The ship slowed, then stopped. They heard the spinning wheel of chain drop an anchor. They watched Jefe, now dressed as what the Asians call a "coolie", climb aboard a sampan on the back deck as sailors connected it to a crane. Then Erasimo and Small joined him, followed by four men. Jefe looked up and spotted Gunther atop the bridge on the observation deck. Gunther held his hand up in the air, thumb up and out and pointy finger up, in the configuration of a pistol. Jefe nodded his head and opened his new, dark red, silken jacket, flashing two pistols in two shoulder holsters and two more on his belt. The crane lifted a sampan off the back deck, over the side and down on the water out of their sight. Within minutes it appeared to them again, asea, heading for the coast. It had a single mast for a sail, but the mast remained naked as the four extra men were rowing.

"*Goooood* luck, my friend," Gunther whispered.

Chapter 9
Showdown at China Pharmacy

Late afternoon. The sampan waded in toward the shoreline. They were miles away and north of the land and sea battles at the forts. Jefe spotted a lone man, his hands crossed inside the big sleeves of a Chinese jacket, standing in the mist on a mostly rocky, flat coastline.

"Mister Zin, there," a sailor advised.

As the small boat reached near land, the 4 sailors dropped their oars and stepped off the craft and walked the sampan in the rest of the way. Then, Jefe, Erasimo and Small climbed out.

"Mister Zin?" Jefe asked when approaching the man.

"Correct! Yes, yes, this way, gentlemen," and he guided them over to a larger rock outcropping for safety, cover and concealment. The four sailors continued to drag the sampan and carried it near their meeting place.

"I am Mister Zin, easy to call me that. I work for the embassies, the legations in Peking and Tientsin. I go back and forth. Supplies. Goods. Goodwill. There is much trouble in both places. They are under siege by the Boxers and sympathetic

Chinese soldiers. Tientsin is about, oh, less than halfway to Peking and to the south. To the left. Very bad there. But Peking will soon be worse."

"We need to get to a pharmacy in this village," Erasimo said.

"Okay. Okay. Follow me. Do you know most of the way?"

"Yes," Erasimo said, "it's that way."

"Correct!" Mister Zin said.

They left their sailors and the sampan among the rocks.

"See you soon, I hope," Jefe said with a smile.

The four men walked off the sand and rocky beach area into the outskirts of a small seaside village/city. The streets were oddly deserted.

"Everybody run from the war. You are part Chinese?" Mister Zin asked Jefe in Chinese.

"No, Filipino but I studied Chinese in college," Jefe said back to him in English.

"Ahh, ohhh. I see. I must tell you, Mr. Jefe, I have learned of your mission here from our Western agents. Very hush-hush."

"Yes."

"But, Mr. Jefe. Listen to me please. Please. We need help. The families in Peking. From all the different countries. Chinese Christians too. They will all be slaughtered in Peking very soon. I am now a Christian. The Boxers call Chinese Christians, 'secondary devils'."

Jefe listened but noticed that not only was there no pedestrian traffic in the village, almost all the shops and restaurants were closed. Most of them with windows and doors sealed off with wood and metal caging.

"Mr. Jefe, the people in Tientsin? They are near the river. Near the soldiers fighting. They will soon be rescued. But

Peking! No! Peking! Way up. They are surrounded. They are inland. Oh my God, Mr. Jefe, they need help. We need help."

"What kind of help can I offer?" Jefe asked.

"I am hearing, is it true? I am hearing that you are bringing medicine. Guns to trade, with the Boxers," Mister Zin said, and he stopped walking in front of Jefe.

The three men stopped with him on the pounded-flat dirt village street.

"Our people in Peking need guns. They need the ammunition. They need medicine."

Erasimo, Small and Jefe exchanged glances.

"Please!" Zin begged. "My family. My wife's family is in there."

"This is not our mission," Jefe said calmly.

"You *cannot* give these guns to the Boxers. They will kill everyone with them."

"I cannot make such a decision," Jefe said, stalling. "I understand your situation. I do. But *de* people in charge, are back on *de* ship. Out there."

Jefe started walking again and Erasimo stepped out front, guiding the way.

"Will you explain to them our problem?" Mister Zin asked.

"I will."

"Will they listen?"

"I don't know."

"Every day, at 3 a.m. the shooting begins there. The snipers begin. And then the cannon fire. The legation people are eating the horses and dogs now for meals. It is horrible…"

Erasimo turned the corner and jumped back, surprised and gasping. Jefe hustled over to him, touched one of the pistols under his jacket. All he saw was another lifeless street, but then Jefe looked down at Erasimo's feet to see three bodies strewn before him on what would be the sidewalk path. Two dead Chinese men. One Chinese woman. Rotting. Stench. Their clothes ripped apart, their chests and stomachs ripped open, and their guts were hauled out all over them and the road. The woman was beheaded. A dead baby was in her arms.

Mister Zin and Small turned around the corner. Zin shook his head in disgust.

"Christians," Mister Zin muttered.

Jefe gave Erasimo a slight shove, and they continued down the street.

"Around this next corner," Erasimo said.

Then they did hear some shouting ahead. The laughing and loud words of men. And when they turned that next corner, they saw six soldiers walking their way and too close. Four were dressed in red and yellow trimmed uniform, red headwraps, the other two in what looked to be Mongolian furs. They had rifles, pistols, and swords.

"Oh no, Kansu Braves," Mister Zin whispered.

"Friend of foe?" Jefe whispered back.

"Either, or," Mister Zin said. "They are Muslim soldiers, loyal to Qing. But Boxers too."

The six braves approached and stopped the four.

"Who are you?" one growled in Chinese.

They eyed up the white skinned Erasimo and Small.

Before Mister Zin could speak, Jefe stepped in.

"Peace be unto you," Jefe said in Chinese, and he spoke with them. Their stern faces turned to normal expressions, even half smiles when it became obvious to them that Jefe was Muslim, as were most Kansu Braves.

"Who are they?" one asked of Small and Erasimo. "Are they Christians?"

"They are not. They are with me. We are on a mission here. Are you with the Boxers?"

"Yes, we are."

"Well, these men, and me, are trying to deliver some goods to the Boxers."

"Two or three of them circled Erasimo, Small and Zin, examining them for these "goods".

"What goods?" one examiner asked.

"Goods," Jefe said. "Supplies."

The leader raised his rifle a quarter of the way high and said, "What supplies, *Akhī*?"

Jefe sighed at the Muslim word for "brother", accompanied by the rifle display.

"Are they Christians?" another soldier demanded again. He and another pulled their swords.

"We are delivering medical supplies, and guns to the Boxers in Peking," Jefe said. "They are not Christian, because we are delivering guns to Boxers in Peking! Christians would not do this. They are not Christians." Jefe felt he needed to save their lives at the moment with the true story.

"Where are these guns?" the leader asked.

"On a ship out on the sea."

"What are you doing here, *Akhī*?"

"I am helping them. The Boxers. I am a soldier of fortune. A man for hire. I am a Muslim fighter, a Moro from the Philippines."

"Ahhh. Oooh," several of them said approvingly.

"These two men here," Jefe pointed to Erasimo and Small, "organized this for the Boxers. They are taking us to their contacts."

"Then we will go with you."

Jefe nodded and he gestured to Erasimo to continue on. This was not at all good.

Further down the street, Erasimo stopped at a street side pharmacy. It was open! The only business open on the lengthy, winding block. Two elderly workers sat on the ground, with a small table in front of them. Behind them were racks of some 50 glass and ceramic jars of powders and vegetables. Their eyes widened at the welcome sight of Erasimo and Small. Helping each other up, they stood and shook hands with both of them.

"What do *they* want?" a pharmacist asked Erasimo about the Kansu Braves milling around behind them.

Jefe tried to follow the conversation as best he could, but he knew the pharmacists were yelling at the Braves to leave them alone, that these men were here to help the Boxers in Peking, and for the Braves to get away from the store.

The leader argued back, and Jefe understood most of his simple language, "We need guns here! We need ammunition here! We need medical supplies here! Right now. Never mind, Peking. Here!"

A barefoot teenage boy emerged from a back room, apparently frightened from all the yelling. One of the pharmacists called the boy over and gave him some orders. Jefe listened in…

"…tell them the Americans are here with guns and medicine…"

The boy ran off.

"Hey! Hey! Stop!" a Brave called out to the teen, but the boy did not stop. He dodged down an alley and out of sight.

"The Peking Boxers will be told," the pharmacist told the Kansu leader. "Then you will see, when all the Peking Boxers come here. You will see to leave us alone."

Angered, the Kansu leader pulled his broad sword out.

"No, no need for this!" Jefe yelled and stepped almost completely between them. "We are on the same side. The same cause."

"When will they come from Peking?" the leader demanded.

"I don't know. I don't know until tomorrow," the pharmacist said, "and, many cable lines are down. Cut down by the likes of you."

"And you," one soldier said to Jefe, "where is your boat of guns?"

"Out on the sea," Jefe said.

"Take us to it."

"That will not work. You will be killed because it is not in the plan. It is a gun boat from the Philippines and if they see strangers, they will shoot you to pieces," Jefe said. "Believe me I have seen them do it."

The Braves stepped away from Jefe and the shop front. They discussed their own plan and Jefe could hear only pieces and bits of their whispers.

He overheard...

"We need those guns, and..."

"If we bring in guns...they will reward us...promotions..."

"...medicines from the West..."

"We would be heroes if..."

Jefe leaned against the outer tiled wall of the closed shop next door and looked over this mess. In less than one half hour since landing ashore, he'd seen four butchered bodies, one important guide begging for this shipment to go to the besieged Peking legations, a group of young Braves wanting to hijack the shipment for their local battles, and two angry pharmacists.

Erasimo and Small walked over to Jefe.

"That was quick thinking, and you saved our asses," Small said.

"Up to this point," Jefe said.

"We still have the goods, though," Erasimo said.

"Up to this point," Jefe repeated.

The Brave leader approached the elder pharmacist.

"We want to speak with the men who pick up the guns."

"That time will be set up tomorrow," the elder said. "When we hear from Peking."

"We will come back tomorrow and find out the time," Jefe interjected. He pushed himself off the wall as if to leave, and he made a head motion to Zin, Erasimo and Small to leave with him.

"No!" the leader said.

All his Braves turned to them and took commanding stances, their hands still down, but shoulders back and chins thrust out. They looked like a wild pack of Mongolian mountain men about to attack.

"One of you will stay! As our…guest. To ensure we can speak to these pirates who will deliver the guns."

The two pharmacists shook their heads and cursed under their breath.

Jefe, Small, Erasimo and Zin looked at each other. Who was that to be?

"I'll stay," Small said.

"I'll stay," Jefe said, trying to smile. He knew he had the

best chance to survive any surprises the Braves might try. He was to be their hostage.

"Then he is our guest, and he will stay with us, here," the elder pharmacist said, pointing to Jefe.

The leader considered, and wishing for this transaction to remain secret, then said, "He can stay here. Yes." He looked at his Braves, selecting two of them and said, "You two will stay here tonight with him."

Again, the two pharmacists shook their heads and cursed under their breath.

Without turning his head, out of the left side of his mouth Jefe said to his people, "Get out of here. Now."

They hesitated, but just for a second. They began walking off.

"Tell your pirate friends at your ship we would like to talk with them about these guns," the leader shouted.

The pharmacists waved Jefe into the store with big sweeping hand motions.

"Come, drink, eat," they said, as they grimaced at the two Braves ready to follow them inside too.

As Jefe expected, on the street, he saw two more of the Braves peel off to follow Small, Zin and Erasimo. Part of the soldiers' plan would be knowing in advance where the unloading zone might be. He took some solace in knowing that Small checked over his shoulder to note they were followed. Small, the quiet one, had so quickly volunteered to stay, and that scar...that scar on his face and neck. He was a veteran of something?

And part of Jefe's plan was also intact – he still had four pistols hidden under his jacket. Up to this point.

And Jefe also knew once this bad news hit the Rio Lobos? Gunther was coming.

Chapter 10
China Dominos

"The sampan is coming back. They are missing one," the sailor at Gunther's room door reported.

Gunther jumped up from his cot and followed the messenger out to the deck. The sun was setting. Captains Hoon and Delane were there with others watching the small boat approach.

Gunther counted heads. Not good, one short indeed, and as they got closer...

"Jefe," Gunther grunted between clenched teeth.

He started to pace. Hoon lit a cigarette. The boat was hooked and lifted by crane onto the deck. Suzannah Crippler joined them.

"He's okay! He's fine!" Erasimo shouted when in hearing range. "They are keeping Jefe until we return."

"Keeping? Who's keeping?" Gunther said.

The men jumped off the craft and began to explain what happened. Gunther listened intently and asked for details, his head bobbing up and down with every word. He grilled each man, Erasimo, Small and this Mister Zin with the same questions. Who? What? Where? When? How and why? Captain Hoon listened, vigorously puffed away on his cigarette.

"Then Jefe is a hostage," Gunther concluded.

"Yes, he is," Hoon agreed, "The Kansu Braves or Gansu Army...very dangerous. They are a unit of about 10,000 Chinese Muslim troops from the Northwestern Province of Kansu. They are joining the Boxers. This problem is a six-man platoon of the Braves."

"Mister Gunther, what do you think?" Delane asked, and all eyes fell on the Texan.

"I think...the Braves want the guns and the medicine, and from what you three overheard, they want to bring the shipment into the Katu Forts or the area Boxers themselves and get credit for it. Maybe even to sell them off? I don't know. But I suspect they will keep this a secret right now."

"I think we should return tomorrow and see what the pharmacists say about the Peking trip," Mister Zin said.

"I think..." Gunther said, "We should kill all six of them... and...you, Mister Zin, are taking me back there tonight. Right now."

Mister Zin gasped and stutter stepped back.

"You remember the way?" Gunther asked.

"Yes...correct...yes...but...I..."

"We'll go too," Small said.

"No, we need you and your connections alive, even though you are the white devil to these people."

"And you are a white devil too," Delane said.

"Yeah, but I am a killing devil."

There were seconds of silence after that description.

"And it's night. I won't be easily seen. Hoon, get this boat ready. Fresh rowers. Zin, get yourself something to eat. You shoot a gun?"

"I...ah...no...I...no!"

"I'll be right back," Gunther said and left for his room. Crippler followed right behind him.

"This is pretty risky, Johann," she said.

"I know."

"Maybe they all will have this meeting tomorrow, and..."

He stopped and turned to her. "They will probably take Jefe off to another location as soon as they can. We'll lose him. They'll say they'll trade the shipment for Jefe. Jefe is a Muslim as are they, but I am not sure they won't kill him anyway."

She understood. Gunther made for his room. She followed again. He put on a shoulder holster with a Colt revolver and his old Western style, two-gun belt. The belt also held a large sheath and Bowie knife. He removed two pistols with short barrels from his luggage and holstered them in the gun belt.

"Those are awfully short barrels," Crippler noted.

"Many if not most pistol fights are close. Short barrel, faster draw," he said as he slipped on a dark maroon, Chinese jacket. The jacket hid all the weapons.

He shoved an old, small telescope and two boxes of bullets in his pockets to support the ones in the loops of his gun belt. He put on the furry hat Hoon had given him earlier, a Mongolian/Russian style skull cap with ear flaps so that he could cover more of his face and head. Black pants, black boots.

Lastly, he pulled a short-barreled, lever-action Winchester rifle from his duffel bag and threw the weapon over his shoulder via a dark brown leather sling. One more box of bullets for the rifle. He stepped around Crippler and left.

******

Hoon readied the sampan for the return trip.

"These man? Armed?" Gunther asked about the sailors.

"Of course," Hoon said.

"They know where to go?"

"Wherever Mister Zin tells them to go."

"Ready Zin?" Gunther asked.

"No."

"Come on, I'll keep as safe as I can. Let's go," Gunther said.

Gunther, Mister Zin and four sailors got on the boat. The crane began to lift the craft.

"We cannot take on any prisoners!" Hoon shouted. "Remember!"

"*THAT*...is not a problem, Hoon," Gunther shouted back.

"I think I can see..." Hoon leaned over and commented to Delane, "why Vice President Roosevelt assigned Mister Gunther to this task."

"Me too," Delane said.

The sampan hit the choppy water, and the men rowed off to the shore. It was dark and the village on the coast had but a few flickering lamps. But, south by the forts, the sky still lit up like a lightning storm from artillery and raging fires.

"We are not landing where you landed earlier," Gunther said. "Take us north of there."

"Why?" Zin said.

"Because the Kansu are probably watching that spot for our return tomorrow. Small told me y'all were followed by them back to your boat," Gunther explained. "Tell these men to go north."

"I will. I must ask you now, sir. Listen. These guns. These medical supplies. We need them in Peking to *fight* the Boxers..." and he continued with the litany he offered Jefe hours earlier, "...if there is any way to get the supplies to the legations and not to the Boxers..."

Gunther was listening but did not look at him. Instead, he studied the upcoming land and interrupted the plea.

"Where did you meet the boat this afternoon?" Gunther asked.

"Over there. Right there," he said and pointed.

"Okay." He marked the large rock outcropping in his mind and imagined what it would be like, approaching it from the side, or rear.

Far enough out the sampan turned south and then after 5 minutes turned toward the coastline. Once again, the little boat floated near land, the sailors got out and walked it in. Gunther and Mister Zin exited. The man lifted the craft out of the water and up to some brush.

"Stay alert. Kill anyone that isn't us," Gunther told them.

Then the two, with Gunther in the lead, went inland a bit and walked north, slowly, and quietly. The nervous Mister Zin mimicked him. After 10 minutes, he knelt. Mister Zin knelt.

Gunther scanned the landscape. They could see the original large rock outcropping in the distance. Gunther removed the telescope from his pocket and for about 5 minutes studied the rocky and sandy beach. Off in the distance the flashes of light and red from the war fires reflected off the clouds and helped light the ground.

"Stay here," he told Mister Zin.

The guide sat down, worried beyond his control. Hunched

over, Gunther made his way to the rock outcropping. When he got considerably closer, he dropped into a crawl. The hiss and break of the waves on the beach offered him some sound cover.

Closer and closer. He saw two men in the red and yellow parkas on the land side of rocks. One started a very small fire. One started cooking something over the fire. Gunther picked his best angle to approach, one that either soldier could not see until the last moment. He undid his jacket and pulled the two pistols. He stood and started jogging in toward the men.

They did eventually hear him, but they did not see him. When he was about 20 feet away, he started shooting. Four rounds, Two from the left gun. Two from the right gun. Two bullets for the soldier on the left. Two for the soldier on the right. They tried to react, tried to turn, tried to get guns, and fight back. Tried to…but they just fell limp.

He ran into the rocks, turned, and knelt. He shoved their guns further away from them. The men were in some gasping death throes. He scanned the landscape in the case of undetected reinforcements. There were none. By this time, the two were dead. He kicked sand over the fire. He reloaded his guns, holstered them and one by one dragged the bodies deeper into the rocks. He removed their colorful jacket tops and turned them inside out, exposing only the inner gray, covering them like blankets. The Braves left no gear in their lookout spot except a metal cup that was heating up for a drink. Gunther threw the cup into the rocks. The two dead guards were as invisible as Gunther could make them for a while.

With an eye on the inlands, he ran toward Mister Zin.

"Zin, let's go!" he half shouted.

Mister Zin caught up with him and they walked onto a dirt road to the village. It was still as deserted as the early afternoon. One block. A turn. Two blocks, another turn and they passed the carcasses.

"Chinese Christians," Mister Zin told him. "It is just up here. One more corner."

When close, Gunther stopped his guide, walked point, and peered around the corner. This last street was also ghostly empty.

They walked on until Mister Zin said, "Here."

The pharmacy. There was a metal corrugated door pulled across the front. It was secured by a rope around a metal post to the left of the shop. Gunther pulled out his Bowie knife and cut the rope.

They listened. No sound. Gunther shook his head with all the bad choices that remained. Shoving that long metal door open would no doubt echo all the way down the street, least of all, alert any occupants inside.

"Tell them you are here and need to talk to them," Gunther whispered. He held the Bowie in one hand and a Colt in the other.

Mister Zin got close to the crack in the door and said in Chinese, "Hello! Hello! This is Mister Zin from this afternoon. I have news. I have some news...ahhh. Can we..." he quickly regretted saying "we", but not as much as Gunther did. "Can *I*...come in?"

Silence.

"Yes," came a very low voice.

Mister Zin pushed the door sideways to open it, enough to get in. It was screechingly noisy as expected and it echoed up and down the street. He entered the shop bound for the back room. Gunther eased in behind him. The shop was dark and empty, and a half open door in the far corner revealed a yellow, flickering light. Gunther sheathed the knife, pulled out the second gun, and with slow peeks he spied into the room. He finally saw Jefe, half-seated, resting on some rice bags. Jefe had one of his pistols on his lap.

"What took you so long?" Jefe said.

Gunther walked in and looked around. The room was big and dirty. With...four dead people on the floor.

"I had to have some supper before I left," Gunther said, looking over the bodies.

"What was *de* dinner?" Jefe asked.

"Lots of rice. Different kinds of rice. And some kind of turnip thing. You ahhh. You, do all this?"

Mister Zin stepped in the back room and gasped, "Oh, oh my Lord Jesus." He stepped around the bodies. "These two men here are the pharmacists! These two...these two are two of the Braves. Oh, my sweet Jesus."

"It was not good here," Jefe said. "*De* two old guys, *de* drugstore guys, started arguing with *de* two soldiers, about who is to gets *de* guns. Who wants *de* guns. So, underneath all their white robes, *de* old guys had Chinese pistols! They were standing there arguing, cursing at each other, and *de* old guys tried to pull out their guns."

"Un-huh," Gunther said.

"*De* one old guy, that one over there, shot one solider down. The other soldier got his pistol out and shot *de* two older guys."

"Uh-huh."

"Then, then I shot *de* last soldier."

"Un-huh! Like...fell one, two, three, four. Like dominos."

"I am not a very good hostage," Jefe said.

"That you are not."

"Well, what about the other two soldiers? Are they coming back?" Mister Zin asked Jefe.

"You mean the other four soldiers?" Jefe said.

"No," Mister Zin said. "No, he killed two of the other four..."

"Uh-huh," Jefe said, as it was his turn to comment.

"...down at the beach," Mister Zin finished.

"I'll bet he gave them no chance," Jefe said.

"No," Mister Zin said, "just..." and made his fingers into the shape of pistols and rocked them back and forth, as in shooting.

"Uh-huh," Jefe said.

"So then, why are we still here, amigo?" Gunther asked Jefe.

"They sent a teenager to meet their Peking Boxer contacts this afternoon. He is supposed to return with a time for *de* caravan up north. We need to know *de* pick-up time. We must wait for him."

"Well, what if those other two soldiers come back tonight."

"Then we kill them," Jefe said calmly. "I heard *de* men say they would return to check on us at about 9 o'clock."

Mister Zin just stared at him, then looked at the wall. A Chinese clock said it was 8 o'clock. Gunther looked at his pocket watch.

"Mister Zin..." Gunther asked, "is there anything around here that looks like...like coffee? American coffee? Or, I guess, tea, or something? And food?"

Mister Zin started looking around.

"And..." Gunther said, "we need four chairs, Zin. Look around and get us four chairs."

Gunther went to the lobby and hauled the noisy metal sliding door closed.

******

Jefe cooked rice and tea. Mister Zin and Gunther found four chairs. They set the chairs in a tight half circle, the backs to the room door. Then under Gunther's guidance, Mister Zin and Gunther lifted the first soldier off the floor and over to a chair. Gunther undid the big yellow and red jacket, removed it, and forced the body into the chair shape. Gunther put the jacket around the back of the chair, wrestled the dead man's arms into the sleeves and buttoned the jacket as best he could. The body was held upright in the seat by the jacket.

"There," Gunther said, proud of his work. He straightened out the hat.

They got the next soldier and Mister Zin was a fast learner. They quickly attached this Brave to the seat by way of wrapping the jacket.

"Very nice," Jefe said, stirring the pots and watching.

The old pharmacists were wrapped in Chinese robes. "Tying" them to the chair was more complicated, but sufficiently done. Their white garb was bloody but only from in their fronts.

Facing the four dead man, Gunther stepped back and looked at them. Four dead men in chairs. Mister Zin joined him.

"They look dead," Mister Zin said. "Their heads are, you know, slumped over."

"Yes," Gunther said. He walked around to the door to look at their back sides. Zin followed.

"They look a bit better from here," Mister Zin said.

"Yes," Gunther said. Maybe they are eating. Heads down eating?"

"Maybe."

109

"Anyway, they will only be seen for a few seconds. That's all the time we need."

Mister Zin was trying to guess the plan, and whatever it was scared the hell out of him.

"*De* rice is done," Jefe said, smelling his work. He dipped three food bowls into the rice. He handed Gunther and Mister Zin their bowls.

"I guess, no spoons huh?" Gunther said.

"Use *de* mano-mano techniques," Jefe said, and dug in with his fingers.

They ate fast, looking around the room.

"Look," Jefe said. "A music box." He put down his bowl, knocked the rice off his fingers by clapping his hands and pulled the box off a dusty shelf. He opened the top and cranked the crank. The spring turned a coil that hit metal strings in a harp-like melody.

"That will help," Gunther said.

An hour later, the two Kansu Braves turned the corner of the deserted street. One was pulling a small wagon, a bit bigger than a child's toy. They were talking and even laughing at times, their voices echoing up and down the avenue. The sounds were Gunther and Jefe's cue.

One stopped the leader and looked into a shop that foolishly left their glass storefront unprotected. He took his rifle and bashed the glass. It fell in a shattering roar disrupting the quiet. The two laughed. On a window display rack were rows of sculptured candles. He reached in and grabbed one shaped like a bird.

"Oooohhh, huh?" Since a section of glass still hung in the frame above, he quickly yanked his hands back.

The leader nodded.

The Brave carefully tucked the wax bird into the small wooden wagon beside the other items he'd stolen.

The pair was slightly drunk, reveling about the score of weapons and supplies they would soon secure for the cause, for the Boxers. Perhaps they would show up as heroes with it? Perhaps…perhaps they would sell the shipment? They would decide when they saw it. Either way the platoon would kill the Americans and the Filipino delivery men.

They stopped at the closed pharmacy, looking to confirm the location. The leader nodded again. He grasped the sliding metal door and with great effort slid it open. As they entered one at a time, they could see the back room. The door was open. The place smelled of food. The aromatic room was dimly lit by a small flickering fire, and they saw four men seated in chairs. They could hear a Chinese music box playing. They smiled at the coziness.

It was their last smile. The leader walked into the room first and noticed the men's slumped over heads, his smile diminished, and his brow furrowed. Jefe, flush against the wall, shot him once in the wrinkled brow. The second man, pulling the wagon was still in the store approaching the backroom door and stopped. Gunther threw back the canvas covering him in the shop and shot him in the head. Gunther turned to the front door. No one else. He took a chance and bolted to the opening. He peered outside. Nothing. He stepped outside. No one.

"No one out here," Gunther said.

"Excellent," Jefe said.

"You can come out, Mister Zin," Gunther said.

Mister Zin removed his piece of canvas with trepidation.

He'd been hiding in the far corner of the store front. He stood, walked to Gunther, and handed him Gunther's second pistol, Zin's last ditch, survival insurance. Gunther holstered the gun and smiled at him.

"You have been a big help, Mister Zin," he said.

"I am glad I did not have to..."

"I know."

He could only nod his head. His face was contorted like he suffered a toothache. He stepped inside the back room. Jefe was investigating the leader's clothes, pockets, and guns. He put the guns and ammo in a pile on the floor.

"Now, we wait for *de* teenager," Jefe told Mister Zin.

"His grandfather and his grandfather's best friend are dead," Mister Zin said. "He will scream from his heart."

"Yes. We have to make a plan."

"Correct," Mister Zin mumbled.

The three removed the four bodies from the chairs and laid them in a line along the back wall, then dragged the two Braves' bodies beside.

******

Gunther sat in one of those chairs just inside the front sliding door, in the dark, keeping watch on the street. The boy arrived at about 11 p.m. Gunther stood up, moved the chair, and let him pass. He was startled to see this strange white man there, but surely assumed he was just with the other white men and the gun shipment. The teen went into the back room and Gunther heard him scream. And scream. From the heart. Screamed in a painful, unusual, baleful way, then gagged and cried. Gunther heard Mister Zin talk with him. Then Jefe tried as best he could to speak Chinese with him.

Gunther thought back to his time on the Paris, Texas police department. How Gustav Henri, his chief, or his deputy comrade, the giant Stinky Moses would tell families about deaths. Deaths from accidents or crimes. Shootings. Meaningless murders. Odd accidents. He recalled their tenor, their caring and learned from them how to deliver such bad news to relatives and friends. But these skills were rusty after 4 years at West Point, the war in Cuba and the fight in the Philippines. Death in the field was so random, so impersonal, with no messages from him to families or friends. When his fellow soldiers died, colonels and generals wrote the letters or sent special officers to visit the homes. The boy cried out again. Gunther just had to listen, detached, and watch the street.

Jefe walked out to speak with him. "*De* caravan will be at *de* beach at 10 a.m. tomorrow morning. We have to do something for this boy."

"Like what?"

"He has no family left here. He has family in Peking. We can't leave him here."

"He knows too much already," Gunther said, "leaving people behind like him has not turned out well for me. Even children."

"We should take him to Peking with us. He is a Boxer at his young heart and believes in *de* Boxer promise. *De* mission. He wants to arm his Boxers in Peking. He should not be a problem."

"What does Zin think?"

"He agrees with me. We have no choice, Gunth."

"Yeah."

"We can take him to *de* city limits with *de* caravan. He

said he will go home by himself from there. He speaks no English. He does not know our real mission. He thinks we are on his side."

"Captain Hoon will not be happy with a new guest," Gunther said.

Jefe shrugged.

"Then let's get the hell out of here."

Jefe walked back into the room. Gunther stood. Mister Zin, Jefe and the boy emerged together. They left the shop and walked back in the dark, midnight chill of the village. They left the village outskirts heading to the beach, past the rock outcropping where more Braves lay dead in the rock crevices, and on to the underbrush where the sailors waited. They prepped the boats, all boarded and off they rowed for the Rio Lobos.

******

Suzannah Crippler was sound asleep on the metal observation deck, a railing post between her knees and her feet dangling off the side. She started her watch for the sampan hours earlier but grew so tired she simply laid back, her thick brown hair and hat as a crushed pillow. The grinding roar of the ship's crane woke her up. She was a little sore from the corrugated deck, but she'd spent many a night sleeping on the hard Missouri and Nebraska ground, and this was little different for her. She checked her watch. It was 2 a.m. She stood and watched the small boat hoisted on deck. She counted heads. Gunther, Jefe, four sailors, this mysterious Mister Zin. And...and a Chinese teenager? Captains Hoon and Delane were donning jackets and walking to the boat.

Gunther, Jefe and Mister Zin walked across the deck and Gunther was in a deep conversation with the Captains that she could not hear. Gunther looked up to spot her on the observation deck, but barely twitched his face in recognition. She barely nodded back. They walked into the bridge. She climbed down the ladder and followed them.

When she stepped inside, Gunther pulled his rifle from his shoulder and leaned it against a cabinet. Jefe stood like a statue of a soldier next to him. She heard a detailed account of what happened in the village.

"….so we leave in the morning. Well in advance to detect any new ambush." Gunther finished up. He looked to see if Crippler heard their departure time. She nodded.

"We'll have to tell Small and Erasimo," Gunther said.

"Will do," Delane said.

"We have to take care of this kid. This damn kid. He doesn't speak English. He thinks we are all gun runners helping the Boxers. We have to keep this story up, best we can. Isolate him."

"So, do you feel you have contained the Kansu Brave problem?" Hoon asked.

"I think so," Jefe said.

"Was our Mister Zin a big help?" Hoon asked, putting a hand on his shoulder.

"A big help," Gunther said, winking at Mister Zin.

Hoon told a sailor to take Mister Zin off for some food and a bed. They left.

"Zin…" Gunther started, "wants us to deliver our haul to Peking legations and not the Boxers. I can't say that I blame him, but I can't figure out how to do that and get the doctors…"

"And my sister. And her husband," Crippler added.

"And...your sister. Husband," Gunther repeated. He rubbed his hand on his forehead, forcing his furry China hat up and back. Then he yawned.

"Get some sleep," Hoon ordered, "all of you. Very tough business tomorrow."

"Yup," Gunther said.

The three left the bridge and headed below deck. Gunther stopped, turned to Crippler, reached out and held her upper arm. She did not retract. Jefe stopped too.

"The doctors will tell us about your sister and husband," he told her. "They can help us rescue them. Erasimo is ex-Army. Small...Small has to be also, but he won't admit it. You...you don't have to go and do all this with us."

Jefe nodded.

"You need me," she said, looking at them both. "I need to go."

"*Ooo-kay*," Gunther said with a sigh.

The three split up for their rooms.

Chapter 11
Crippler's China Nest

Dawn. Three of the four sampans were lowered by crane into the sea. Twenty men, one teenager and a woman. Twenty coffins full of rifles. Five big crates of ammunition and pistols. Five crates of medical supplies. Five duffle bags of clothes and other survival gear. The boats spread out. Jefe was in one boat, Gunther in another, scouring the landscape with binoculars for any possible trouble or ambush.

Mister Zin was in Gunther's boat and the Chinaman sidled up beside Gunther and Erasimo and started in on a whisper campaign again to deliver the goods to the legations and not the Boxers.

"Look, Zin, I can't do this. If I could, if I can, I would. I will! But I don't know what we will find when we get to the Boxer headquarters."

"What if…what if I went on ahead, went in first. Looked around. Announced you were coming and looked to see where these doctors are. Exactly where they are." He turned to Erasimo. "When you saw them, they were walking around free helping wounded Boxers! Right? Am I right? Correct?"

"Yeah," Erasimo said, not looking at him.

"Correct! Let me in first. Look around. If they are free, maybe they can sneak out, and we can leave with all the supplies and make a run for the legations."

"Go ahead by yourself? How do you know where to go? How will you break away from the escorts?"

"I...don't know. Will you think about it?"

"I'll think about it," Gunther said.

"You'll think about it? Yes?"

"Yes, but I don't know what we are dealing with, Zin. Boxers will be escorting us in a convoy right up to the headquarters."

"Yes...yes," Zin mumbled.

"There!" Erasimo yelled out.

They all looked to the beach and there was a fire with a long trail of black smoke fighting the sea breezes.

"Is this how they do it?" Gunther asked.

"Yes."

Gunther got Jefe's attention with a hand wave and gave him a thumb's up sign. Jefe returned with the same signal.

As the sailors rowed closer, they discerned five wooden wagons with a two-horse team for each, and about 10 brightly colored uniformed soldiers on and off horses. One waved a big red pennant back and forth.

"That's them," Erasimo said.

Within 15 minutes they hit the beach, and the sailors pulled the sampans as far up the sand as they could. Gunther immediately walked up the beach, then turned back to the meeting and made ready for trouble. Even with his Mongolian fur cap, it was easy to see he was not Chinese. Four of Hoon's armed sailors followed him.

Erasimo and Small recognized a few of the Boxers, but not all of them. Their greeting was quiet. The leader they did recognize looked over the unloading cargo.

"This is Commander Wunongee," Erasimo nervously announced to everyone in earshot.

The commander was huge. At least 6' 5", heavy set under a long colorful jacket. He had a classic Chinese mustache and a heavily scarred face. An Oriental pistol belt wrapped around his waistline outside of the red jacket, with a Chinese revolver in one holster and another one tucked in his belt line. His red hat looked almost like a Santa Claus cap. He snapped his fingers, and two men ran up, pulled knives, and opened some of the boxes. He saw the stacks of cloth-wrapped guns inside. He nodded in approval.

He half pointed at Suzanne Crippler.

"Dis, no good," he said in growling half-English to Erasimo. "Dis no good. No safe. Why...here?"

"She's the boss," the quick-thinking Jefe said in Chinese, stepping up to them.

Crippler was expressionless. She had a light, lever action rifle over her shoulder, a brown pistol belt and revolver under a short jacket, black pants, and boots. Her thick, brown hair flowed down from a brown Western hat.

"This is all her idea. She gets the guns, everything," Jefe said in broken Chinese. "She is the boss and she wanted to come this time."

"Who you?" he asked.

"I work for her," Jefe said. "California."

The leader looked at Erasimo, and Erasimo agreed.

"Him too? He nudged his chin toward Gunther a bit up the beach.

"Him too," Small said.

"Him?"

"Mister Zin our guide."

"You no need guide. I take you in. I take you out. Like always."

"I know," Erasimo said, "but sometimes we got stuck here waiting. You know this. And we thought…"

"And him?" He pointed at the teenager.

"He is the grandson of a dead boxer. Your man from the pharmacy was killed," Small said.

The leader's eyes widened.

"Who kill him, who…" the commander asked in Chinese.

The teen burst into a long diatribe about what happened the night before and how the local Boxers wanted to steal the guns. He started to cry. The boy pointed to Jefe and then to Gunther, explaining what they did to protect the shipment. The leader seemed pleased with the boy's story, and now it seemed like Jefe and Gunther were new comrades. He waved Gunther into the group.

"Stay here," Gunther told the armed sailors.

The Boxers loaded up the crates in the wagons. The commander issued a long, serious statement to Erasimo in Chinese.

Jefe tried to follow the fast Chinese and what he caught worried him.

"What?" Gunther said.

"He said," Erasimo translated, "he said he is pleased with what you did last night, sad for his old friend at the pharmacy. Glad you avenged his death. And…he said…that this was to be our last trip here. No matter what we did, what we do for the Boxer Rebellion, that we were now just more foreign dogs, ahhh…scum…invaders. Interfering. And if we ever come back here again, we will be slaughtered."

"Uh-huh," Gunther said calmly.

"And he said…that the woman, boss, or no boss, her coming here is a big mistake because they may just kill her anyway. Now. Right now. Kill her now. We have no future here after this trip. And…he also wants to know if we are Christians."

Gunther was staring down at the sand listening and slowly looked up at the commander. Jefe did not like the look on Gunther's face, a half-smile, a half, mean smile at that and Jefe dreaded what might come next. Jefe slowly flanked off to the side.

Gunther walked up the commander, not too close, but close. Close enough. He craned his neck up to look at his face.

"You tell this big, ugly, stupid-looking bastard, that I am no Christian, and that I am the *goddamnest*, fire breathing, devil-dragon on this Earth. And you tell him, that I may just kill *him* anyway."

They stared at each other as Erasimo translated.

"Every word!" Gunther demanded.

When Erasimo was done, the commander looked a little shocked. Gunther was waiting to see a hand go to those two pistols, which he would grab a hand, pull his own and shoot the big bastard. Everyone was so distracted by the English and Chinese threatening lingo that Jefe backed off unnoticed to a good, flanking, shooting position. Crippler slowly cocked out her gun-side, hip.

They stared. Then the commander let loose with an explosive roar of laughter. Spittle flew from his mouth. His head cocked back, and the end of his Santa Claus hat bobbed up and down. Then all his men laughed. The commander's laugh was so deep, it looked like it could hurt his chest. He stopped, gagged, and had to spit up some phlegm from it, and gasped for breath for a second or two.

"What name?" he said.

"Gunther," Gunther said.

"Grunda," he said, trying to pronounce it. He smiled. "Grunda...let's go." He turned, smiling, and made for the wagons.

Gunther stood there a bit perplexed. He looked at Jefe, who shook his head in disgust.

"I think," Erasimo said to Gunther, "he likes you."

******

Gunther, Jefe, Small, Erasimo, Zin, Crippler and the teenager climbed into wagons with their duffle bags, squeezing in wherever they could fit betwixt the crates and coffins. Crippler sat next to Gunther after hearing that tirade on the beach and what he did. She gave him a half a wink as she did.

The convoy stayed off major roads, but they could hear cannon fire in the distance and occasional gunshots much closer. The further they traveled, the more the closer and louder the explosions were directly behind them, like the war was closing in on them and they were escaping. Gunther studied the land around him. They passed odd little clay and tile houses and farms. Some of the land was flat, some hilly. The landscape looked very much like Eastern Oklahoma and east Texas to Gunther, except for some small, rocky, mountains, oddly shaped, and the swirling displays of water and rice in patties. If they came upon traveling villagers, the locals quickly jumped off the dirt road to get clear of the Boxers and wagon train. One woman carrying baskets of vegetables toppled off the road and fell screaming into a ditch to escape their path.

The wagons veered off the road and stopped. Gunther stood to see why. More Boxers and Chinese soldiers were marching south, marching past them. Some looking like they were bound for a grand parade, some looking like poor slaves. Some rode horses by them, at a trot. Gunther watched them and guessed about 200 men with 100 riders dashing by, followed by 10 or so wagons. Once they passed, the caravan continued.

There was no other stopping until the outskirts of Peking. There, Commander Wunongee stopped the procession and rode his horse back to the wagon that contained the teenage boy. They spoke. Wunongee pointed down some streets and the boy jumped off. He waved goodbye to Jefe and Mister Zin and left. Gunther was relieved to be shed of him.

When Commander Wunongee rode past Gunther's wagon he glared at Crippler. Not a single word had been spoken between Crippler and Gunther in the entire 5-hour trip so far. When the commander passed by, she looked at Gunther and raised her eyebrows. Gunther nodded.

The wagons took up again and they were soon surrounded by people and buildings. To Gunther it looked like any U.S. Western city of the day, large dirt roads, horses, wagons and business, houses off the main avenues. Except, it all had an Oriental flare, look and even smell. No signs of a war anywhere there. A long, dusty caravan of camels laden with towering supplies and walking caretakers passed them by.

Crippler smiled broadly at the sight and interjected, "Camels."

Gunther smiled at her smile. He had never seen a camel before either.

"Not quite Peking yet," Erasimo said, leaning over to Gunther and Crippler.

They passed under beautiful archways over the streets and spotted tall stone buildings with sweeping rooftops. But then they saw on a street corner, a pile of bodies. Chinese bodies. Stripped of clothes, torsos gutted. Some without heads. Some children poked sticks at the corpses.

They started passing soldiers, some resplendent in colorful Chinese uniforms and others more like the Kansu Braves. They stood in groups along the way, talking, idle and watching the streets. Then the wagons entered some open gates and a poorly fenced off open field area. The wagons stopped.

Everyone in the wagons front and back jumped off and Gunther and Crippler, their backs to the front in the wagon, finally saw what was up front. A unique tall building, half oval in shape, stood before them.

"It's a Chinese Opera house," Erasimo said. "We have been here before."

Commander Wunongee stood on the front steps and waved for them to follow him inside. They did and wagon masters lingered by their horses.

They entered the opera house. It was damp and chilly inside. The floor slowly degraded down to the stage. On the stage, military men conferred with what would appear to be well-dressed, Chinese citizens among a series of ornate tables and chairs. Due to the acoustics of the house, their voices echoed across the theater. On the floor, the pews of spectator seating were ripped out for storage of an assortment of supplies, boxes, and gear to the left. To the right – many wounded men, some in beds, some on the stone floor.

Gunther, Jefe, Erasimo, Small, Mister Zin and Crippler followed Commander Wunongee up the side, stage stairs and onto the stage.

"General Eeyung!" Erasimo said, approaching an older uniformed man. Small did too, and the three shook hands. The general remained poker-faced. He did not seem pleased to see them but was not displeased looking either. They started talking. Mister Zin and Jefe stood nearby, listening in. Gunther wandered over to the edge of the stage and he studied the emergency hospital side of the house.

There…they…were. Three white men working with the wounded, working bed to bed to bed. Gunther slowly walked off the stage and over to that area.

The three men stopped when they saw Gunther approach.

"Dr. Livingstone, I presume," Gunther said quietly when close.

"Bellmont," the doctor corrected.

"It's a joke," Gunther said.

"Oh, oh yes…yes."

"And Doctors Hedgecock and Telemore," Gunther added, minus any facial expression, looking instead at a wounded man.

They nodded, a bit astonished.

"I am here to rescue you. Don't shake hands," Gunther said, backing away from them. He dramatically pointed out the double doors and said rather loudly, "There are crates of medical supplies on those wagons outside." Then he whispered, barely moving his lips, "get them in and we'll talk."

Gunther quickly walked away from them as the doctors ordered some Chinese workers dressed in medical whites to follow them outside. Gunther noted their freedom of movement to come and go, at least in that area. Gunther wandered the beds and examined the wounded, he peered on the stage once in a while and saw Commander Wunongee watching him closely. Crippler joined Gunther on the floor.

"Is that them?" she asked.

"That is them. I don't see your sister or brother-in-law."

"Neither do I," she said.

The five crates were carried in and dropped on the floor. Gunther walked over to them, pulled his Bowie knife, and pried open the first crate.

Without looking at the three doctors, he said, "Are you guarded at night?"

"Not much," Telemore said. "They have grown to trust us and…and where would we go anyway?"

"Out of here," Gunther said. "I have a Navy ship out in the bay."

"My sister, Crippler, well, Ethel Halpren…and…and her husband…" Crippler interrupted.

They began rummaging through the crate, pulling things out.

"Ma'am," Belmont said, "Miss, they…they're…dead."

Gunther opened the second crate.

Crippler was silent. No expression.

"They killed her husband first, about a month ago," Hedgecock whispered with still lips, pretending to read a package of bandages. "Then they…they killed her about three weeks later. We thought that if she helped us, she would appear very useful."

"Who did?" she asked.

"The commander. The big one up there on the stage. We think he hates women. He abuses our nurses all the time."

"Rape?" she said pointedly.

"Ahhh, yes," Bellmont said.

"Where are your rooms?" Gunther said, handing them another package from the newly opened crate.

"Over there. Three bunks in that room." He barely nudged his chin to the far right, corner.

"Alone? Anyone else in there with you?"

"No."

"Locked doors?"

"No, we work all night. All hours. We hear screaming or a new group of wounded brought in, we run out here to work," Telemore said.

"Well, we are leaving tonight," Gunther said.

"To...night? How? When?" Hedgecock said.

"I don't know. Just get ready to go. What is guarded around here at night?"

"Some guards walk around at the field outside. Some guards at the gates."

Gunther left them and opened the third crate. He saw that Commander Wunongee was still watching them.

"Crip, walk with me," Gunther said, and he turned for the front doors.

She followed. They stepped out onto the field near the wagons. She rested her back against a wagon. She stared at the skyline.

"Crip, you can't kill him, unless we can kill him...safely."

"I know."

"WHAT was your sister doing here? What?"

She sat on the edge of a wagon bed.

"Spices."

"Spices?" Gunther said.

"My family is in the food business, Johann. Cattle. Pigs. Steak. Pork. We had an idea that we could also start a spice business. Maybe even Chinese food."

Gunther sat beside her.

"Spice, International spices. Flavors," she continued.

"Salt and pepper? You couldn't tell me back on the ship about spices?"

"We wanted to be the first big international spice supplier. The first big one. Really big. And I don't mean just salt and pepper. All kinds of spices. The Chinese have big vanilla farms…do you know how hard it is to produce vanilla?"

"No."

"Well, it is incredibly hard, and they have many other flavorings and spices here that would build restaurants. Famous…chains of them."

They sat quietly for a moment.

"We read that China was a booming place, a…a…place to do new business, and my father came up with the plan, this dream. We would open up the Oriental market of spices. Add it to our food business. Get cheap spices. Ship them home and sell them. I couldn't tell you or anyone because it is…it could have been a million-dollar business. It is an industry secret. We wanted to be first. Maybe the only one. How was I to know you wouldn't steal the idea. Or reveal it?"

"I guess it's a good idea," Gunther admitted. "But I will not steal your idea, Crip."

"I believe you. Now. My sister and her husband came here to make connections, to...to...open the market. Contracts. It was supposed to be a high-brow business trip. Diplomatic. The newspapers back home from St. Louie read like this was an amazing cultured new world. Full of opportunities. Magically."

"Instead, we have a savage little war here on our hands. We have to get out of here alive and get those doctors, home. YOU home."

She stared down at the ground.

He leaned over and looked at her face under her wide brim hat.

"You're *gonna*'kill him, aren't you?" he asked.

"Yup."

"What if I kill him?" Gunther asked.

"Won't be the same."

"And you have killed before."

"I told you I have," she said.

Gunther rubbed his face with his hands and sighed. "This has been one big nightmare from the start. Look, let's just see what happens, okay? It is possible that they won't let us leave here alive anyway, since they don't want us *Christian,* gun-running devils back again."

"You have a plan?" she asked.

Small and Jefe walked up to them. Six men carried two of the big medical crates back outside.

"Hey, the commander just said not to unload any more medical boxes," Small said. "Two of these wagons of guns and supplies have to be delivered tomorrow to some troops that were behind us. The fighting picked up as we left. We just got out of there in time."

Gunther rapped the wagon bed twice with his knuckles, turned to Crippler and said, "I think…I just got a plan."

"Oh no," Jefe said.

******

Evening. Outside the opera house, a cooking and eating area was set up under some massive pieces of canvas. Dinner of rice, pork and green tea began at 6 p.m. and after a long wait on a chow line, and under many hostile stares, Gunther, Jefe, Crippler, Erasimo, Small and Mister Zin collected their food on clay plates, sat on the ground in a small circle and ate.

"We are stuck up north here," Erasimo said. "We escaped the fort, coastal area in time. There is much fighting between here and the beach. "After a few days here, I don't think they will care about us anymore, and they'll forget the promise to return us to the beach. Commander Wunongee will have another assignment."

"The only thing that kept us alive in the past," Small said, "was the idea that we would be back again and again. If they don't want us to come back…"

"We are worthless," Erasimo concluded.

"You been paid yet?" Jefe asked.

"Yes. In Jade. It's their gold. They just steal it from the villages and hand it over to us. They'll probably kill us and take it back."

"I agree," Mister Zin said. "I also listened in on what the leaders were saying on the stage. They are worried about the legations in Peking and the advancing armies from the coast.

They are not thinking about us. When they do start to…"

"They'll kill us," Small said.

"They will kill me too because I am with you," Mister Zin said.

Gunther and Jefe exchanged glances.

"Then we must escape?" Jefe said.

"There is only one place to go. Peking proper. The embassies. The legations," Mister Zin said.

"How far is it?" Jefe asked. "Which way?"

"I know the way," Mister Zin said. "It will take 4 hours walking."

"Us? We? Walking through the Boxers surrounding the legations?" Small said.

"It is very strange, Mr. Small. The Boxers and the Chinese Army…they attack sometimes, very hard, and then they don't. They bombard. They shoot. And then they don't. To me, it seems like when the leaders excite them up, the men take action. Then get bored? Without a push? They stand around. They lob in bombs. They snipe a bit. Sometimes the Boxers and the soldiers walk up and talk to our men at the street barricades. There were Chinamen walking up sometimes and selling eggs to our people. The eggs were not poison, as we thought at first. The eggs were very good."

Gunther watched as the three doctors got on the chow line. No Chinese spoke with them, but they did not treat them poorly. They were ignored. Gunther also noted that other than some sneers and apparent words of gossip, their little troupe of foreign devils were ignored too after 10 minutes.

"Some areas around the legations have different Chinese Army and Boxer commanders covering them, and they fight differently. Some earnestly. Some, not. It seems like some of the Boxers hate the Chinese army more when they help the foreigners," Mister Zin said. "And they hate Chinese Christians very much. Extra hate, they…"

"We leave tonight," Gunther interrupted. "We know that they are delivering two wagons of gun and supplies to the Boxers south of us. We need to know where those wagons are stored."

"I know," Jefe said.

"And know where two teams of horses are kept," Gunther continued.

"I know," Jefe said again.

"And the smallest gate." Gunther said, "One ignored. Least watched…"

"I know," Jefe said.

They all looked at him.

"I walk around," Jefe said, surprised at their surprise.

"At 2 a.m., we sneak to the horses and the wagons and ride '*em* the hell out of here," Gunther said.

"What about the gate guards?" Small asked between big, sloppy bites of pork.

"We kill them. Miss Crippler, you are the ranch hand here. You get the horses and wagons ready with Zin, Erasimo and Small. Jefe and I will kill the guards."

"Just like that?" Erasimo said, still a bit shocked.

"There are several gates," Jefe said, "one in the back by the stables."

"Jefe will sneak up from one side of the front gates. Me the other. We'll stab '*em* all and shoot '*em* if we have too. You all run the wagons and any horses you can find to the gate. We get on. And we all get out. We go to Peking. To the legations."

"We'll be chased!" Small said calmly.

"We'll be killed," Mister Zin pleaded.

Gunther looked at Jefe.

"I like it," Jefe said.

"Oh, my sweet Jesus, I don't like it," Mister Zin said.

"You'll get your wish, Zin," Gunther said. "If it works, we'll deliver two wagons of supplies to your legations."

"I can certainly drive a wagon," Small said, finally wiping his mouth clean.

"Me too," Erasimo said.

"What do you think, Crip?" Gunther asked.

"I don't want to die here, and I would like to skin a few skunks here."

"Where are we supposed to sleep? Did they say?" Gunther said.

"No," Small said. "In years past, we slept anywhere."

"Good. If they don't tell us where to sleep, then they don't know where we are. Okay. Avoid the commander. Lay low. Be forgotten. Jefe, show them where the stables are and where the gate is later.

The doctors took their food off to a corner of the field by themselves.

"I'll tell them," Jefe said, motioning to the doctors. "You, a giant ugly American, will draw attention. I will get some green tea and sit with them."

Gunther nodded. Jefe, sitting cross-legged, "Indian style", was limber and athletic enough to stand straight up from the cross.

******

At 8 p.m., Jefe wandered the grounds in a slow stroll. Some Chinese soldiers even smiled at him as they passed him due to his ethnicity. He could almost pass as a walking guard. He got closer to a row of trees and bushes by the rear of the opera house. Some fires were lit across the field. The flickering red glare revealed parts and shadows of a rutted road. He casually walked that way and once on the trail saw it was indeed a well-worn, wagon-wide path separate from the surrounding patches of grass and weeds. It veered left into the trees. He walked on. He heard some voices. He did not follow the turn because it was too close to the voices, but rather kept going straight. There in glance to the left, he saw a back, double-door gateway! Solid wood. Like an old service entrance for the opera house, And four soldiers where there. Two standing and two stretched out in chairs. They barely noticed him walk by. He sure noticed them.

******

"I got a good look at *de* back gate," Jefe told Gunther later.

"Is it locked? Chained?"

"I don't know," Jefe answered. "I couldn't look at it too closely. I just walked by. It's wood."

"No matter what, we go out the back. There are eight soldiers guarding the front tonight. Torches. All lit up. We'll find a crowbar or something to break those back gates open."

"And it is closer to *de* stables of *de* horses and wagons."

******

Midnight. Most of the group laid awake inside the opera house, stretched out among the supplies. Mister Zin however, was sound asleep and snoring. Gunther and Jefe sat on some boxes up near the stage.

"Most of *de* Boxers are asleep on bedrolls under *de* big tents," Jefe said. "Some are walking around. They have green tea brewing all day and all night. I will go out there now, get some tea and take a last look around."

******

At 1:40 a.m., Gunther started rousting the group up. Jefe walked over the floor of patients and into the doctor's room. The three emerged in Chinese clothes and some colored canvas luggage that resembled large purses. They all congregated behind the mountains of supply crates and boxes.

"Horses. Loaded Wagons. At 2 a.m. sharp, slowly, as quietly as possible, ride to the back gate," Gunther told them all.

Jefe handed each doctor a revolver and a box of ammo from one of the crates. Hedgecock took it between two fingers like it contained the plague.

"I…I…ahh…as a doctor, I…" he said with a grimace.

"You…ahhh…what?" Gunther said, stepping up to him. "We are escaping. These people will kill you and your friends here eventually. Tear your tongues out while you watch. You want to live? Or want to die painfully? Or by God, do you want to die trying?" Gunther grabbed the gun with one hand, the doctor's hand with the other, and shoved the pistol deep into his palm. "I came all the way over here for one got-damn reason. To save your life. One! You fight for it. Till the end. I will."

Hedgecock looked at the pistol, then up to Gunther. He nodded. Gunther nodded.

Gunther took a hard look at the odd, ragtag group of gun runners, an Oriental guide, a Filipino scout, doctors, and a rodeo star. Will they make it all alive?

"There might be guards by the stables," he said.

"We'll take care of it," Small said matter-of-factly. He tapped a knife on his belt.

"Let's go," Gunther said.

With all their baggage and duffle bags, they walked out the back door of the opera house. The stable attack team carried Gunther and Jefe's bags. No one was in sight on the back field. Jefe went wide to the far right, Gunther to the far left.

The two watched each other get to the tree line. They advanced to the back gate trail and then closer to the trees on each side of the gate. No voices. No noise. No guards?

But there were, indeed, guards - two guards. On each side of the large wooden double gates. Two men in chairs. Stretched out. Arms hanging off the sides of the chairs. Asleep.

******

The other group walked single file across the grassy field to a stable. Small handed his bag off to Erasimo and jogged ahead. He pulled his long bayonet from his belt sheath. Once at the stable opening he peered inside. Some torches were posted on beams. One man lingered around the many horses. Another man laid on the ground asleep by the wagons. Small dashed across the opening. Slinked around the corner wall into the stables. He crept upon the sleeping man. The man's jacket was wrapped in a roll for a pillow under his head.

Small shoved his left palm on the man's mouth and with great determination cut his throat, getting both jugular and windpipe. Once done, he stuck the knife in the ground and put both hands over the man's mouth, shoved down, waiting for death, while watching the other guard across the stables, hoping the subtle, gurgling sounds of an open windpipe went unnoticed. It did.

Small slowly stood. His hands and lower arms were covered in blood. He unrolled the jacket-pillow and tried wiping them clean, but he was a dark red mess. He picked up the knife and held it behind his back. Then he clasped the weapon-bearing forearm with his other hand, and, as casual as possible walked out into the center of the stable and under the occasionally placed torch lights.

"Good evening," Small said in Chinese, strolling causally when close toward the second guard.

The man spun around and eyed him up. Small smiled. The man did not.

"How are the horses this evening?"

"You are the man with the new guns?" the guard said.

"Yes. Yes, and we are sending those two wagons south tomorrow morning to help out."

Small could see that the soldier was in his 20s. Filthy and unhealthy. He nodded at Small.

"You know..." Small started, then whipped out the bayonet from behind and with a neck-high, horizontal slash so fast it was almost invisible, he nicked the man's windpipe. Then Small charged in closer and grabbed the man's pistol handle in his belt holster. The man clutched his throat with both hands. Small hit the guard's head 5 or 6 times with the pointy pommel of the military knife handle. He heard the skull thuds with each blow and the man fell backward. Dead.

Erasimo was spying in from the open doors. He appeared in view, waving the others inside.

"Kill some of these lights," Small ordered.

The doctors went for the torches. The rest moved toward the horses and the wagons.

"Dead, general?" Erasimo asked.

"Dead," Small said, wiping the bayonet on the guard's pants.

Crippler overheard the word "general" as she selected the horses for the wagon.

******

Gunther and Jefe stepped closer with their knives drawn. Gunther detected the deep breath, and slight snore of a sleeper from his soldier. And he could see that across the gateway, the other guard's head tilted back too far for an awake sitter. Mouth wide open.

He and Jefe knew they were in position. They jumped out, grabbed the heads of their men, and cut open their throats, dragging the guards back into the lines of trees.

The crowbar Gunther absconded with from the opera floor that ran from Gunther's pants pocket all the way up to his armpit, remained tucked under his coat. He pulled it out, and the duo inspected the gates. A chain ran through large ornate handles. The gate was old, and much of the wood rotted. Gunther started prying on the plate that held the door handle with the crowbar. Within a moment, with some noise, it was cranked off. They opened the gates and saw a dark field out back with some scattered homes and a river. Jefe ran out for a better look. He was back inside in seconds.

"We can go right across a big valley. No river to cross," Jefe advised.

They heard the creaking of wagons and horse snorting. They stepped further in to see the teams approaching. Two wagons, everyone aboard. Crippler ran one wagon. Erasimo the other. And four saddled horses, two to a wagon were tied to the back ends.

Gunther and Jefe ran to them.

"I brought four horses," Crippler told Gunther and Jefe as they climbed board, "in case something…"

Something was happening. Two soldiers were walking across the field, carrying trays to the back gate.

They saw the wagons, the open gate and shouted out warnings into the night air.

Crippler cracked the reins across the team, and the wagon took off, with Erasimo's wagon right behind them.

A gunshot!

Gunther slipped his Winchester, lever-action rifle off his shoulder and watched the soldiers. The shouting soldier first fired in the air for some reason instead of at them, as an alarm, but both men dropped their trays and started shooting at the wagons. The wagons quickly turned the corner of the back wall and out of sight and range, with Gunther on foot chasing. Gunther jumped on a horse pulled by the wagon. Bellmont, in the bed, hustled over and untied the reins from the wagon, freeing Gunther's mount.

It was dark and they fled by moonlight. Mister Zin was

in the bed of the first wagon and crawled within earshot of Crippler.

"Turn here!"

"Turn there!"

The wagons left the few village streets surrounding the opera house and entered a vast, treeless area with an incline that steepened to a high crest with trees and rocky outcroppings.

"This is going to be a long, hard climb for the horses," Crippler announced. But she pushed on. The teams ran and ran and then naturally slowed from the increasing incline.

"On no!" Mister Zin shouted. "They're coming! They're coming. We are doomed!"

Everyone looked and under the cloudless moonlight they saw a tiny stream of riders exiting on horseback through the back gate down below them. Crippler went another 50 yards and stopped the wagon. Then Erasimo stopped the second wagon to see why she stopped.

She handed the reins to Jefe and jumped in the back. She opened her duffle bag and extracted a gun case, and from it that beautiful hunting rifle, with scope and a small bag.

"You all go on," she said, "I'll slow them down."

"It's suicide!" Mister Zin shrieked.

Gunther jumped off his horse too. He undid the reins of another horse from the wagon's rear.

"Go on!" Gunther ordered the wagons. "GO!" He ran the horses over to some bushes and tied them off.

"No!" Crippler said to Gunther.

"Yes," Gunther said to her.

Jefe and Erasimo got their teams moving back up the hill. The pair laid down behind some small rocks and Crippler readied her rifle. Gunther took his lever-action off his shoulder. The range was too great for his rifle.

Gunther pulled the telescope from his coat pocket.

"Eighteen of them, Crip. Maybe 20."

She nodded.

"Commander Wunongee is leading them." He knew what that meant.

She nodded again.

She took off her jacket, rolled it up and laid the barrel of the gun on it. The gun loaded, she ran the bolt action and looked through the scope.

Boom! A rider's head exploded in a red mist.

Bolt action.

Boom! Another rider hit in the chest and off the horse he went.

Bolt action.

Boom! Another rider hit in the chest and off the horse he went.

Bolt action. Another...

Then another...

Reload.

Repeat.

Gunther marveled at her precision. In about one amazing minute and a half, she took out 10 of the mounted soldiers.

The rest were getting closer, and Gunther lifted his rifle. He shot and missed. Still, too far out. He worked the action, guessed some compensation, and shot again. He hit a Boxer in the right shoulder, and he fell off the horse.

They could hear the men yelling now. And hear the horses' hooves. Crippler clipped away as the horses got closer and closer.

"Where is Wunongee?" she asked, not daring to move her scope and rifle too far from the central group.

"He is still coming. Still in the lead," Gunther answered. "But they are spread out."

Five or six riders were left, and they now shot back. With the closing distance, bullets were zipping by and dropping all about them.

Crippler reloaded again. Gunther tried some more shots and hit a few.

"There's a big drop that runs to left, if they get behind that, they have some cover for a minute and get closer and..."

"We can't see them..." Crippler added.

And that happened. Instinctively the survivors galloped into lower ground concealment. Gunther and Crippler could hear them but not see them. Gunther reloaded his Winchester.

Then some appeared in a charge. Very close.

Crippler hit one but they were now too close for the scope. Bolt action, she shot again without using the scope. Gunther's started shooting fast with his rifle while Crippler had to run the bolt on hers. It seemed all of the enemy were finally dead?

Then, to their left, a giant horse appeared, on its haunches to leap into their sniper's nest. Atop the enormous steed, was the enormous Commander Wunongee, pistol in one hand, a sword in another.

Gunther, shocked, dropped on his back, pulling both short-barreled Colt pistols from his belt, and blasted away, hitting the horse and rider. Twelve rounds. The horse did not stop, and it jumped at them. Gunther rolled off to escape the hooves. Wunongee fired his gun without aim from his injuries. Crippler fell back too, drew her pistol, and shot Wunongee four times from her side.

The magnificent horse, hurt and confused, stopped, and stomped the ground, whining and snorting as they rolled and dodged away from its unpredictable path. Then it lost the use of its front legs and its front end dropped, it pitched the wounded Wunongee forward to the ground.

"Reload!" Gunther ordered, but Crippler didn't. She stepped up, saw Wunongee's dying eyes look at her, and she shot him in the face.

Gunther watched the battleground before them for anymore survivors while shoving shells in his Winchester.

Crippler dropped to a knee and reloaded her pistol and rifle.

Way off down in the distance, they could hear the last wails of the few wounded men.

"That was amazing, Crip," Gunther said. "I would kiss you if I didn't think you'd kill me too."

She allowed herself a half-smile and a half-impatient expression at him.

"I got him, after all," she said.

"That you did. Let's go," Gunther said. They got up.

Wunongee' s horse was in a labored, moaning breathing, down on its side.

"I am so sorry. You *are* a beautiful thing," Gunther said quietly, "magnificent," and shot the horse in the head. Surprised, Crippler watched his sad apology and winced slightly at the gunshot.

They jogged over to the two tied-off horses behind them and took off for the wagons.

When cresting the hill, they turned to look back again. No one else followed. Crippler's nest had bought them time.

Chapter 12
The Bloody Peking, China Gauntlet

Within woods and rolling hills the wagons traveled at a fast, walking pace. The three doctors seemed to be in a state of shock in the open bed of one wagon. Small sat in the back of the rear wagon, rifle barrel resting the closed rear hatch. Gunther and Crippler trotted up to the rear wagon.

"Here they come," Small said.

"*Ya* get '*em*?" Small asked calmly.

"Every last one," Gunther said, "including that big bastard, general."

Small grinned.

Gunther and Crippler remained on their horses and rode on ahead. They hadn't spoken a word to each other since the nest, just exchanged glances back and forth.

"You should have seen Small at the stables," Crippler suddenly said quietly.

"Yeah?"

"He killed two soldiers. One asleep and tricked the second. Cold. Calculating. With a bayonet."

"Humm," Gunther said.

"Erasimo walked up to him right after and called him, 'General'," she said.

"General? Maybe a nickname?"

"It didn't sound like it," she said.

"He told me he was never in the military. My guess is he's lying. But a general?"

An orange-colored sun appeared to their right, behind some Chinese Red Pine trees.

"Ahead!" Mister Zin shouted out.

Gunther and Crippler waited a moment until the wagons caught up.

"Ahead. There. Is Peking. There are many city streets to cross through. There will be soldiers. Armies. But it is early morning. They will be eating soon."

"How do we get into *de* legations?" Jefe asked.

"There are street barricades. And legation guards. But the whole area is walled in. Giant walls or we would all be dead by now."

"How will we get inside?" Gunther asked.

"Well, I could ride up to *de* barricades and tell them to get ready for our wagons," Jefe suggested.

"You look good, Mr. Jefe," Mister Zin said, "but you will be shot by the guards. Maybe? Huh?"

Jefe looked to Gunther.

"I will go," Mister Zin said. "Only I can go? Correct? I will go in on a horse and I walk slowly up to the legations and slowly up to a barricade. Look at me. I am *fan fu*. A commoner. And look at my clothes. And maybe some at the barricade will recognize me. I don't know. They will not shoot me. Many already *know* me.

There are a lot of new legation soldiers there, French, Indian, Germans, but maybe someone there will recognize me? I will tell them to clear a pathway for wagons of supplies."

"That'll work," Small said from a wagon bed, still spying on the backroad.

"Give me, as you say, a 'head start'," Mister Zin said.

"I know the way in," Erasimo said. "Which avenue?" he asked Mister Zin.

"There are barricades at Legation Street. I will go there and tell them we are coming."

"I know where that is," Erasimo said.

Mister Zin got off the wagon and untied a horse. He mounted it like an expert.

"Give me some time, okay?" Mister Zin said. "Give me 30 minutes."

"You have it," Gunther said. "Tell them to give us support, cover fire when they see us."

"Correct!" Mister Zin said.

They watched him gallop off.

"Let's get under the canvas in the beds. We'll spread out the canvas over the whole wagon," Gunther said. "Jefe. Erasimo, you stay where you are. Drive the wagons."

"We'll just ride in, slowly at first," Jefe said to them all. "Not draw attention."

Jefe and Erasimo were dressed like Chinamen. Jefe was the right skin color and Erasimo had a full beard and big farm hat to help cover his Caucasian look. He would have to lead the way.

"If things get bad, then we will race in," Jefe added.

Erasimo nodded, and he turned to help spread the canvas over the whole bed.

146

Gunther and Crippler dismounted and tied their horses to the rear of the wagons. Gunther walked over to the wagon bed with the three doctors and leaned on the side.

"How ya' doin', Docs?" he asked them.

"The three still sat side by side on the bed.

"I...alright...I guess," Belmont said.

"This could go very well, or...not," Gunther said. "We may have to shoot our way in."

Hedgecock had his revolver on his lap, and he looked down at it.

"I reckon you're wondering what the hell you're doing here? Safer back at the opera house? Feel like you've been shanghaied yet again?"

They just stared at him.

"But we are here to free you. You can live back there like a slave. A slave doctor. You know this. Work with me and you'll see your families. You'll see the USA again."

"Crippler's sister's husband? Her brother-in-law?" Telemore said, leaning in and whispered so Crippler couldn't hear. "They killed him alright. Slowly. They tortured him. They pulled out all his teeth and his nails. They slowly cut him open. They..."

"Like the Commanch..." Small said with a sneer, pulling on the canvas and close enough to hear. "The Apach. They know special ways to kill slowly. Day by day, by day. Special ways to keep you alive day by day, to kill you slowly day by day."

Telemore nodded, "And when they were done with him? He was still alive. Somehow. There was nothing we could do for him."

"He was gutted," Belmont said.

"Her sister see all that?" Gunther asked.

"She did," Telemore said.

"Save a bullet, boys," Small said. "Save the laaassst bullet. Kill as many of these *mother fuckers* as you can, Put the last one right into your mouth up toward *yer* brain and say nighty-night, oh you cruel, cruel world." He glared at the doctors and walked off.

They looked back at Gunther. Gunther grimaced and nodded.

"These wagon sides and back are pretty thick. Pretty stout. Shooting starts? Lay low. Stay low. If we get stopped and have to shoot back? Lay your barrels on the side. If you can? Keep your head only eye level with the gun. Eye level! Do NOT stand!" Do not stick your head all the way up," Gunther said.

"I guess we should save that last bullet?" Telemore asked.

"I am," Gunther said and walked off to the wagon fronts.

Erasimo and Jefe were kneeling by the horses and Erasimo sketched a quick map of Peking, their route, with a knife on the dirt, should they lose each other.

"We will certainly be challenged when we make that last turn," Gunther said over their shoulders. "They will want to know why wagons are walking into the siege."

Erasimo stood. "Yes. It'll be a gauntlet."

"How long are your reins?" Jefe asked Erasimo.

"Fair to middling."

"Take a look at this," Jefe said, and he waved Erasimo to follow him. He pointed to the front of the bed of his wagon. "Look at this space from *de* front seat back to *de* crates of guns." He waved his hand back and forth over it. "We can't sit up top and be shot at. I think when can jump back here on the bed, stay low and still steer *de* horses."

"I think so!" Erasimo said.

"Let's go see," Jefe said, climbing aboard and testing the

length of the reins. Erasimo did too.

Forty minutes later, the two slow-moving wagons were on the smaller streets of Peking. They were not alone as the streets were full of pedestrians, carts, big and small wagons. Deeper in, the brick and stone buildings were taller, the old and new were a mix of bland and then elaborate, Oriental design. Erasimo's wagon was in the lead. Crippler, Small, Gunther and the three doctors laid flat in the wagon beds under the canvases.

Jefe's wagon followed. As they got closer to the Legation street, Jefe took stock of the war zone around him. Frightening. There were crowds of Machu and Chinese soldiery, infantry, cavalry and gunners in uniforms, tunics of vast colors and designs of dragons and swords. The Boxers were not so well adorned in mixed-matched and even civilian clothes. Banners and flags of all shapes and sizes. The Chinese were strengthening their positions, reporting to morning assignments, or… just standing around. There was gunfire of all calibers off in the near distance, and occasional cannon fire. A sports stadium came into his view down an avenue. It was on fire.

Erasimo turned ahead, and Jefe followed. Jefe saw the first English and Chinese Legation Avenue street sign! It was wide enough for many lanes of traffic, and bordered by some 50 small shops, stores, and restaurants. All closed, boarded, bashed, or otherwise reduced to rubble. They were about 50 yards away from the barricades. He saw four Chinese gun nests surrounded by sandbags, and numerous Boxers and soldiers milling around. The wagons slowly rode on.

About halfway, several soldiers stepped out in front of Erasimo's wagon. They started yelling at him, asking him what he was doing.

Some soldiers walked back to Jefe's wagon and Jefe smiled and said hello in Chinese. Nosy, one Boxer stood on his toes and peered over the wagon side. He reached in and pulled off a section of the canvas.

Gunther laid on his back, his two pistols out and across his chest. When the canvas went back, he looked up at the Boxer. The Boxer was a bit dumbfounded at the white man lying on the bed inches away.

"Good morning," Gunther said in English, and he shot the man in the face.

With the crack of Gunther's shot, Erasimo whipped the reins on the horses, and they took off as he jumped back and over the seat into the back of the wagon.

Jefe followed suit, jumped back, got low and smacked the reins on the team.

In a few seconds, the rain of fire began. Bullets pounded the sides and back of the wagons. Gunther prayed for the horses, praying for the common instinct not to shoot a horse. The wagons were still streaming smoothly down the flat dirt street.

Then an immense mechanical roar occurred. Gunther knew they were from heavy machine guns, and they did not match the sounds of the rounds hitting the wagons. They came from up front, and it had to be cover fire from the legations. Blessed cover fire!

Jefe, low and back to behind the driver's bench, saw the men at the barricades now, shooting rifles at the Chinese. At one high corner of a building, a man ran a machine gun on a tripod. The wagons passed the Chinese sandbag gun nests and Jefe saw the soldiers couldn't even peek over the top with the stream on incoming fire. For the first time, he thought they could actually make it!

The right side of the barricade slipped back, and Jefe could see men in uniform pulling metal bars and wood and general stockpile of mess back by ropes. The opening!

Erasimo made it through! He raced through the "gate".

Jefe followed at full speed.

Men inside cheered at their victory. Some soldiers in Italian uniforms, further in, guided the wagons into a left turn and out of gunfire.

Erasimo bailed off the wagon as Small and Crippler threw back the canvas and emerged from the bed, wide-eyed.

Jefe sat up on the crates and stayed still, catching his breath.

"Okay, Jefe?" came a muffled voice from the rear.

"Okay, Gunth. Come on out."

He did. The three doctors did too and stood up. Gunther and Jefe inspected them as they jumped from the wagon. Gunther also sat atop the coffins, ripped off his Chinese fur hat and laughed out loud.

"This is not funny," Jefe said.

That made Gunther laugh out loud even more.

"You did not see what we just did."

"I heard it!"

"But you did not see it. I saw it. It was not funny."

The wagons were surrounded by men in different uniforms, beaming and smiling. Women ran up, and some children appeared. They hugged and greeted Crippler, Erasimo, Small and the doctors. The doctors got most of the attention and gratitude. Jefe and Gunther remained on the wagon, dodging the fanfare. Gunfire still rang out back by the barricade, but it was diminishing.

The women, some finely dressed, yet some in rags, engulfed Suzannah Crippler and started to whisk her away down the street. She looked up at Gunther with wide-eyes and raised eyebrows up as much as to say "Where am I going?"

"Hold it," Erasimo said to them and retrieved Crippler's luggage from the wagon and handed it off to the ladies.

"Everyone is very happy," Jefe said, "but now we are all prisoners, captives of this siege."

Gunther slapped his knee and ignored the remark. "Well, I guess we'd better get off this rig." And he too jumped down.

Jefe shook his head and slowly crawled off the wagon, his legs a little wobbly.

Gunther looked over the horses.

"Not a scratch. Not a scratch," he said. "If they'd a shot one horse we all might be dead." He stroked their necks.

A distinguished gentleman approached Gunther and Jefe, followed by groups of international soldiers of some rankings. He had on a worn, dusty but once fine blue suit, an oily head of black hair like a swimmer's cap, eyebrows curled out like a wild bug, and thin mustache.

"Gentlemen," he said to Jefe and Gunther, "I don't know who you are or why in the bloody hell you are here." He was English and he shook their hands.

"Johann Gunther, USA."

"Jefe Cocoy, Philippines."

"The Honorable Roger Semitagold. British Military. Colonel. Retired. At your bedeviled service. I am the titular head, by vote, of this little legation of a mess here. Pray tell, do you have any news from the world?"

"We don't, Colonel," Gunther said. "We are here to bring

these doctors home as they were kidnapped from America."

"My God, Mister Zin told me. We need them here."

"I know. I know and they will jump right into it. When we left the coast, numerous navies were bombarding the Taku Forts. And in route here, we were passed by desperate Chinese troops going south to fight. Some of these...our goods here... were to be sent south, but we hijacked them for here."

"Our faithful messenger Mister Zin apprised us of your mission and dilemma. And we thank you for delivery. Even the horses. I am afraid many of us here, have taken to eating the horses. We have many mouths to feed, as a thousand Christian Chinese, refugees, have fled their homes and are hiding with us."

"How many acres here, sir?" Jefe asked.

He grimaced, "Oddly shaped, but about 1 mile wide by 2 miles long. I'm afraid we are crammed in. Legation people and soldiers. Our borders are...inventive...and guarded 24 hours a day by our best troops and civilians. Somewhere along the tenuous line of sand we have built, each day we are attacked in waves, sniped, and bombarded, and somehow we hold our own."

"A Chinese Alamo," Gunther said.

"Yeessss, if you insist."

Men had the back wagon gates down and were opening the boxes and admiring the rifles and pistols.

"Colonel Brickmire!" Semitagold declared, "Take an inventory and we will divide the shipment equally and appropriately."

"Laddies! You heard the man, now back off! Back yourselves off," the Brit said gruffly with a very serious face.

"How many days have you been here, sir?"

"Twenty bloody days. We are now on the street of the Russian Legation. But my men will see you to our British

Legation," he leaned in with a whisper, "It's the best. The American building is full of fleas, flies and mosquitos." Then he continued loudly, "We will have a dinner and some wine, and you can wash up and rest up. Our legation has over 3 acres, It's like a small city inside all this."

Just then a huge explosion hit across the street, blasting a building to smithereens. Everyone reflexively scrunched their shoulders and squinted, except for Semitagold, who stood tall.

"You'll get used to it. The bloody bastards slowly shell all day long. That's the Chinese bank building over there. Or...was."

Mister Zin called out and ran up to them with a woman and three children.

"Mr. Gunther! Mr. Jefe! Hello. Hello!"

He hugged them.

"It worked, Zin," Gunther said.

"Correct! We did it. Here...here...this is my wife *Chunhau*...here, here are my three daughters, *Chingching*, *Biyu* and *Changyin*!"

With a broad smile, Gunther shook their hands, kneeling down for the little girls. Jefe did the same. Jefe stood and put his hand on Mister Zin's shoulder. Erasimo and Small, their bags in hands, came over and shook their little hands too.

"They are very beautiful," Erasimo said.

"Correct!"

"Let's get you down to our legation house," a British sergeant said.

Gunther and Jefe pulled their duffle bags from the wagons. And they headed off, followed by numerous troops. A small victory was won. Fleeting hope was restored, despite another cannon round exploding a mile away.

Chapter 12

Nightly Serenades of China Rifle and Artillery Fire

Almost every day at 9 a.m., many of the besieged men and women gathered at Fu Park near the center of the walled community to share any news. This morning, some 500 people showed up, anxious to hear any news from their new arrivals. Gunther, Jefe, Erasimo, Small and the three doctors were in the crowd and were sized up by everyone. And then Crippler, in her same travel clothes but only cleaned and ironed, her hair expertly braided under a brushed hat, walked up in the company of some 20 women. She left them and strode over to Gunther, standing on his right side.

"Good night?" Gunther asked.

"Yes. You?"

"We ate well. No horse or donkey meat, and the Brits have wine. Did you have any wine?"

"I did! They fed me...bathed me and did my hair." She lifted her hands, "And nails! I don't do my nails, but they did. They must be *very* bored. They even polished my boots." She lifted her leg for a show.

"I, we…had no such treatment," Gunther said. "Ate, drank and slept. Well, you look just fabulous this morning, Miss Suzan and smell wonderful," Gunther just blabbed out without thinking.

She almost blushed, or her version of it. She looked Gunther up and down to see he was back in his American clothes. Brown pants, boots, tan shirt, thin tan jacket and wearing his beat-up tan cowboy hat. He was sporting his two-gun, pistol belt with knife and she suspected his shoulder holster under the jacket.

"You…*don't* smell well," she said. "Cleaner, but still stinky."

"Good morning, dear ladies and gentlemen," Semitagold said while climbing atop a wobbly, picnic table. He read off some supply statistics, announced three deaths of wounded soldiers and added eight more to the wounded list.

"And thanks to these gentlemen and lady and their courageous drive to get here, we now have 125 new rifles and 5,000 rounds of ammunition!"

The people cheered and applauded.

"And crates full of medical supplies! And not one mind you, but *three* medical doctors, who are already hard at work at our hospital."

"I think it's a miracle!" a man yelled.

More applause and cheers.

"Please…" and with a welcoming hand gesture, Semitagold made them step up one at a time and introduce themselves.

Gunther was summoned out front, and he offered up only his name and a shy wave. But a U.S. Marine also stepped out of the crowd. He was a captain and looked very familiar to Gunther and Jefe on sight.

"THAT…" he yelled, "is *Major* Johann Gunther, United

States Army, graduate of West Point, Veteran of Cuba and the Philippines. Served with him on the islands, just 2 months ago. And an old Texas lawman to boot."

The crowd oohed and aahhed.

"Well, hello, Yorkie," Gunther said. He was no longer on a secret mission at this point, and the revelation of his rank announcement didn't seem to matter.

Erasimo and Small smirked at each other, suspecting all along that Gunther's soldier of fortune bio was fishy.

"And that Filipino feller there with him is a top Army scout," Yorkie continued.

Jefe waved to him. "Hola, everyone. Lt. Jefe Cocoy," he said with a smile.

But Yorkie was not through yet!

"And THAT man there?" Yorkie shouted with a tone of disdain and pointed to Collin Small, "Is Lieutenant General Mortimer Swellen, US Army. AWOL!"

"Why is it that your American generals always have two last names?" Jefe whispered out the corner of his mouth to Gunther.

Small-Swellen looked at the ground and scratched an ear behind a giant sideburn.

"Oh yes. Yes! They call him 'Swoop'. Swoop Swellen. Indian wars. Indian war vet. And...a *helleva* Indian killer," Captain Yorkie said. "He...he swoops in and kills."

The onlookers did not know what to say or do, just mumble among themselves.

"Well then, we have three more military men," Semitagold said, rescuing the awkward moment, "and experienced, to say the least!"

Erasimo spoke but did not reveal his background.

The crowd dispersed after several minutes. Gunther and Jefe walked over to Captain Yorkie and shook hands.

"How long you been here, Yorkie?" Jefe asked.

"Just about three weeks. We barely made it in. It all shut down behind us."

A very stuffy British officer approached them.

"Captain Randolph Smithe." He offered no hand to shake. "I am the ranking military officer here under Semitagold. Senior experience. You men are to be assigned at my whim to military duties."

Yorkie, with a small grin, looked at all their faces.

"Of all these armies and high-ranking officers here, *Captain* Smithe? You are in charge?" Gunther asked.

"That I am," he said.

"That you are," Gunther said. "But if you are playing the card game of rank? I am a major in the United States Army. Which is, as you know, higher than a captain."

Smithe guffawed.

"I have been tasked to run..."

"That's fine," Gunther said. "I don't want to run anything. I also don't remember swearing any allegiance to the British military."

"This is a joint effort and we..."

"I will remain a rover."

"Well, then...I...I...you...I will assign you to the emergency team."

"Captain Smithe, that sounds just fine to me, you can assign me anywhere as I will continue to rove wherever the hell I want," Gunther said with a sudden smile.

"As for you..." Smithe turned to Jefe.

"He stays with me," Gunther interrupted. "He is my attaché. My bodyguard. My consultant."

"Humm! Very well then," Smithe said with an expression of disgust, "Ahhh, emergency it is." He briskly turned off toward Erasimo and Swoop-Swellen-Small to assign them somewhere.

Yorkie shook his head, as they watched him walk off.

"Aww, hell, he's okay," Yorkie said. "Bit stuff in the collar, that's all."

"Yeah well, right now, I don't feel like taking any shit from a stiff-collar, corn cobb," Gunther said. "I prefer to roam."

"Let's take a rove then. I *gotta'* get back to the Tartar Wall. That's our Marine assignment."

The three took off at a brisk pace.

"The Tatar Wall is about 43 feet high, and they say about 43 feet thick," Yorkie advised. "It's on the south boundary, that separates us from them on the south side. It's a long wall that runs way past the legations either way. We have barricades on either end. It's miles long. And every day or so, they make a run on it. If we lose this wall? The Chinese will shoot down at us unobstructed."

They stopped and Yorkie pointed to the far east of the wall and then to the far west of the wall.

"The ends of the wall go a-ways off and the Boxers get atop at the far ends. Then they encroach in on us. The Chinese get up by ladders and ropes and set up their own barricades on the wall. Then they move in inch-by-inch trying to get close enough to do us in. We have to push them back every few days. Anyone give you fellers a real logistic rundown yet?"

"Not a military rundown," Jefe said.

"Uh-huh. Well, we have us nightly serenades of rifle, and

artillery fire. The Legation Quarter here is about 2 miles wide and 1 mile long. Eleven countries represented. Twelve Christian missions. No one has counted them, but I think there are a thousand Christian refugees in here."

"A thousand?" Jefe said. "That's a lot of people in small space."

"Yup. I've heard that maybe five or six babies die a week from starvation. The Brits, we Americans, French, German, Japanese, and Russian military, we each took up the responsibility for the defense of their respective legations. The Germans help us with the wall too. The Austrians and Italians abandoned their original isolated embassies. The Austrians joined the French, and the Italians collaborate with the Japanese."

Within minutes they were atop the wall.

"We got us some bad news a few days ago," Yorkie continued, "we do have a few spies that run back and forth. They sneak in and out, like Mister Zin. They learned that the London newspapers reported we were all dead here. Tortured and slaughtered. We all think the newspapers killed off any rescue attempts."

"We didn't hear anything about that," Gunther said. "But surely our guys will invade deeper and deeper and check this place out."

"We hope."

Gunther and Jefe inspected the wall. Many sandbags, scrap wood, barrels and stacked furniture made two walls, one east and one west. Some 60 Marines and German soldiers kept watch at each sandbag barrier and peered over the edge of wall to the dry canal and houses and streets below. The partitions were not unlike the barricades down on the few open streets. The view was high, breathtaking, and vast of Peking.

"At first, the Boxers tried to burn us out. Smoke us out,"

Yorkie said. "They burned everything that surrounds us." They looked over the blocks of burned buildings outside. "They even burned an ancient Chinese historical library near the British Legation. All those charred remains you see out there, they did."

"Small. Ah, General Swellen," Jefe said. "What did he do?"

"He is a butcher. Real killer. We all know what dirty deeds were done with the Injuns. Back and forth. But Swoop hated them and killed them anytime and anywhere he could."

"Massacres?" Jefe said.

"Oh yes," Yorkie said. "Tale goes back that when he saw the butchered bodies of a family in Colorado when he was a lieutenant, he became obsessed with killing Injuns. Thinks of them as rattlesnakes."

"A tale more than twice told," Gunther mumbled, looking over the rooftops of the Chinese houses below.

"Swellen ran a fort in Minnesota. He was ordered by the Army to organize a treaty and he did everything in his power to interfere with its success. The Army found out. Gunth, he's AWOL!"

Gunther shook his head.

"Yup. *Yer* traveling companion is a wanted man. A big bounty on him. He told the Army that he would rather exterminate all Injuns than treaty with them. One day, he just changed into civvies and rode in a supply wagon to St. Paul. Disappeared."

"AWOL. What do we do about that?" Jefe asked Gunther.

Gunther shook his head again. No answer.

"This below us, outside here is dry canal," Yorkie continued with his tour. The three stepped to the wall and looked over. "It is dry most of the year, they tell us, unless there's heavy rains. You can see from up here there's another dry canal that runs through legations.

Something zipped, cracked and dug into the wall. It was directly followed by the sound of gunshot.

"SNIPERS!" a Marine yelled, and everyone dropped down.

"Okay," Yorkie said, "they are starting up."

A few more random shots hit around them.

Gunther peeked over the wall top.

"Where…could…they…be?" he mumbled.

"We usually see them on the taller buildings out there," Yorkie said. "If they can see us up high, they take potshots at us."

"Are they any good?"

"Some are, but some are not. They're 'hit and miss'." His eyes widened with the bad pun. Gunther grimaced. "Starts in the morning. Stops. Picks up a bit through the day. Sometimes at night."

Gunther sat down with his back to the wall and studied the buildings in the legation. He said, "I got an idea."

Jefe shook his head and said, "Oh no."

Chapter 13
China Sandbags of the Red Dragon

The British legation had one of the tallest buildings on their grounds, the elegant house, office and library of Henry Cogburn, a liaison secretary to the Chinese. Balconies surrounded the exterior of the building on each floor and the openings were covered in walls of sandbags. The Brits, knowing all suffered under the sniper fire and cannon fire in periods of time each day, instantly agreed with Gunther's "idea". His plan.

Around midnight, Gunther and Yorkie supervised the rooftop construction of various walls of sandbags atop the British building. Like all the hard work there, the heavy lifting was done by the Chinese refuges, "paying for their keep".

"Looks like Christmas," Gunther said, bedazzled by the artistic sandbags.

"About three weeks ago," Yorkie said, "the women of the sandbag committee began collecting every excess piece of cloth they could find. Some came from the shops outside before the Boxers set fire to everything. They began cutting it all up and making sandbags. They ran out of the excess and started chopping up their clothes."

Gunther watched as sandbags of every color and design, beautiful silks, linens, cottons, draperies, carpets, chopped up pants, shirts and jackets were stacked, squeezed into positions.

They set up a long line of carriers and hand-offs to the top, up the steep steps to the roof hatch and then onto the roof. In the darkness the roof team built four-foot walls around the perimeter of the roof, which already had a brick and stone wall. Gunther tried to imagine fields of fire from the roof and onto the roof. They created slots from which to shoot and to change over, slot-to-slot when detected. Yorkie was concerned that the Chinese snipers might be out of range.

"Not to worry, amigo," Gunther said.

"They sometimes climb trees off to the east over there. And they sit or lay on rooftops, over there. And they shoot from windows over there. They have what they call 'Jingal' rifles. The barrels are extra-long, shoot from afar and other Jingals...some are like the old blunderbusses - they shoot coins and nails."

Gunther took mental notes of the locations.

Yorkie and the workers left the roof a little after 3 a.m. Gunther used a sandbag as a pillow and there under a China moon and stars he fell fast asleep, until...

"Good morning!" she said.

Near dawn. Gunther looked at the opening roof hatch and saw Suzannah Crippler's head sticking out of the hatch.

"Is this your new home up here?"

"Welcome to my abode," he said.

"Very nice. Very colorful. I thought maybe you were opening a dress shop up here," she said as she climbed the ladder and appeared on the roof. Pants, jacket, boots, hat, and gun case. She didn't stand up straight but made her way near him, crouched over.

"This is it?"

"This is it."

Another woman's head popped into view through the hatch.

"Good morning, Major Gunther!"

"That's Agatha," Crippler said.

Agatha climbed up and out with a wicker basket.

"Tea and yellow rice," she said with a sympathetic face. "It's the best we can do!"

"Thank you, Agatha," Gunther said, as he opened the basket.

"I will leave you two, to the...you know...job."

She climbed back down the roof hatch.

Gunther unpacked a teapot and two cups from encircled towels and poured the tea. The rice was in a bowl, and he dished it out into two smaller bowls, all the while Crippler loaded her hunting rifle.

Gunther filled her in on the common problem areas as Yorkie reported.

"If they figure out where we are? They start shooting back," he said.

"I figured they'd figure that," she said unpacking her case.

"Then we'll have to move from roof to roof each day or so, when we need to, because they will start looking for us."

She nodded.

"We'll just see how this goes," Gunther said.

She just smiled at him.

It was a *very* big smile, as though catching him "preaching to the choir" and her wry grin caught him breathless for an instant.

"Okay, well," he said, "let's have some tea and this rice. Then have a look around and see what we can see."

Once the makeshift breakfast was done, with the binoculars they received from the Marines, they started scanning the red-orange dawn and the rooftops, high windows, and trees.

"We should only use those rounds for this job. You need to save them for this. This is very important."

"Yes."

They heard chanting, bells, and horns off in the distance, from all directions.

Without removing her eyes from the binoculars, she thumped Gunther on his shoulder. He looked at her and looked to where she was staring. Upon his close inspection, there were men wearing various uniforms congregating on a roof, rolling open gun rugs.

"Probably," Gunther said.

She put down the binocs and grabbed her rifle. She laid her forearms on the bags and Gunther softly grabbed her arms and pushed them back.

"Stay low, Suze, always stay as low and back as you can."

She nestled in, this time with the barrel on the sandbags.

"I had a boyfriend in 5th grade who called me Suze," she said, eyeing the roof with her rifle scope. "He was a very cute kid."

"Let's see who holds the rifle. Just shoot him. Save the bullets. Just shoot the assigned rifleman."

They watched.

"And was he the first boy who ever kissed you?" Gunther asked.

"No."

"Second? Third?"

"No and no."

166

"Okay, looks like he's the one," Gunther said. He saw three men laughing and one man setting up the rifle. Gunther shuffled to the left as he hurried and stuffed torn cloth into his ears from his pockets.

BAM!

"Get *'em*?"

"Got him."

Gunther regrouped with his binoculars to see the rifleman down and the other three men in a surprised panic. They flattened out on the roof. This had never happened before to their little morning parties.

"You are amazing," Gunther whispered.

"That's what those boys told me."

The three men gathered up the gear and grabbed the sniper by the feet, dragging him to a stairway door.

"We won't shoot our way out here, will we?" 'Suze' Crippler asked.

"No. We have to hope that, as the old saying goes, 'the cavalry comes'. I am worried about it. We'll give it a few days. A week maybe then we'll have to do something about the Rio Lobos. And we can't do this every morning from here. They'll eventually scope us out. And, we have to save your bullets."

"Look there," she said. "In those trees way over there…"

After three hours and some 12 snipers killed, the potential snipers stopped appearing on the horizons, not unusual for the daily timetable activity Yorkie suggested. Crippler cleaned her gun.

"You know I wasn't being rude," she said, polishing away.

"Rude?"

"When we first met. And the Lobos ride over. The wagon trip up here to Peking. I wasn't being rude to you, not talking with you."

"Oh well, that's…okay. I didn't think you were," Gunther said.

"I wanted to keep some distance between us."

"You did?"

"I had a feeling I did not want to…to get too close to you."

"Okay."

"I had a feeling I might like it too much."

"I…ahhh…"

"But it now appears, sir, that we are going to be very much closer anyway."

She packed up her gear, winked, smiled, and made for the roof hatch.

"Let me help…"

"No need," she said and descended out of view.

******

Gunther and Jefe made the rounds at the barricades and wall. They saw Swoop-Swellen-Small working with Marines, and they did not speak with him, still trying to figure out what to do with this AWOL fugitive, renegade general.

They found Erasimo standing around with the allies at the Legation street barricade.

"The very good Reverend Erasimo," Gunther said.

"Gentlemen," he said, nodding to Jefe and Gunther.

"Looks very calm here, but…whoa, it STINKS!"

"The Chinese are piling up their dead bodies on their

side of the barricades."

Gunther and Jefe exchanged glances. They could smell it, too.

"It's a good idea, really," Erasimo said. "Makes for more good barricade material and they don't have to remain close to guard it, and they know we will stay away too," Erasimo said. "It's craziness down here. Sometimes…sometimes the Chinese come right up and talk with us, maybe trade cigarettes. Sell melons. Sell eggs. Then, three hours later they are blasting away and charging the breastwork. Crazy."

"Yeah," Gunther said.

"Chinese cigarette?" Erasimo offered.

"No thanks," Gunther said.

"No smoke," Jefe said.

"Boxers or the Chinese Army?" Gunther asked, nudging his chin to the wall of rubble.

"Mostly Boxers. Then the Army comes in."

"Swoop…Swellen Small?" Jefe asked.

"Yes," Erasimo said. "*Ol'* Swoop." He put the butt of his rifle on the pock-marked concrete and cupped his hands on the barrel end, resting on the weapon. The Peking cigarette dangled from his mouth.

"Swoop," he continued, "has a different look at the world. Different blood. Bloodlines. You know, Swoop's grandmother was an Indian. Crow Nation in Montana. His great grandfather was a slave."

"A slave?" Jefe said, "He doesn't look like a Negro."

"No, no he doesn't. Nor Indian. Mixed marriages. Nobody knows this! The Army didn't know all this history. He joined up. Teenager in the Civil War. For the North. Became an officer.

Battlefield promotions. Then out West after the war. Moving up, up…up…" He pumped his thumb up in the air and drew on the cigarette. "But Swoop is…is an Indian in his heart of hearts. Indians you know…fight Indians. Always have. Long *running* hostilities. Tribal feuds. People…the Army…think he hates *all* Indians. Oh, no, sir. He is a got-damn Indian at heart. Swoop hates 'the enemy' Indians. The assigned enemy. *Hates'em.* Hate *'em* once? Hate *'em* always. There's something else going on his head." With that, Erasimo circled a finger around his own head.

"What?" Jefe asked.

"Point him at a group and say "kill". Hand, stick, knife gun, he's a blood-*spitten',* human Gatling gun in a fight. At some point, like a bear, it don't matter who, or what it is, he…he kills."

Gunther watched Jefe take this in. Jefe loved stories, and especially American history stories. Cowboys and Indian stories.

"How do you know him?" Jefe asked.

"He court-martialed me for stealing years ago. Can't say's I blame him, as I was stealing shit from the Army and selling it in Cheyenne. Years later, after Swoop went AWOL, we were both on a mule team in Oregon and we recognized each other. I looked up, I saw a grizzly old character and there he was, my *ol'*pain in the ass, lieutenant general."

Erasimo looked right at Gunther. "Course now, I couldn't tell you all this when we first met back in San Francisco. We didn't know who you were, and you didn't need to know who we really were. You might not have made the deal. There's bounty on Swoop's head. He's a hunted man. You mighta turned him in. Fornicated this whole trip up. And then…then we all might not have been stuck here in…in…"

"A China Alamo," Gunther said.

"Yes, the Alamo of China," Erasimo repeated slowly.

A few cannon rounds exploded here and there and there were several barrages of enemy gunfire through the day, but night fell, and things quieted down.

Gunther dragged his assigned shabby blanket from his sleeping spot on the stone floor in a second story office and decided to sleep instead up on the sand-bagged roof where a summer breeze blew free, and the sky was clear. This was to be his new abode, he decided. The rooftop. He took off and unslung all his guns and laid them out nearby. He pulled another sandbag over as a dusty pillow. This one was a soft material with a red dragon on it. Looked once to be a gown. Where had this 'pillow' been? A ballroom in London? A dinner in Vienna? A picnic in the Alps? Stretched out, he contemplated the moon's half face. He marveled that this was the same moon as the one over Texas. Where else did this moon go that he'd been? He had few memories of his childhood in Germany but no recollection of the German moon as a kid. For him, life began in the U.S. Army in Oklahoma and in Texas.

And anyway, who were all those boys kissing on Suzannah Crippler?

Chapter 14
Battle of the China Wall

9 a.m. The three doctors sat a long table, sleeves rolled up, eating some rice-based bread, and drinking green tea. Their long hair was a mess, but they seemed clean and rested.

"How are things, sawbones?" Gunther said, repositioning his rifle and sitting on the long bench across from them.

"We are as caught up as we can be," Bellmont said.

"Tea, Major Gunther?" asked a woman assigned to hospital kitchen duties.

"Well, yes, ma'am, thank you."

"No one died last night," Hedgecock said. "That might be a record."

"With the Boxers, the dead and dying never stopped," Telemore said. "And, we have four doctors here already to help us. And nurses."

"This is the life of an army doctor, eh, Major?" Hedgecock asked.

"'*Fraid* so, Doc. In a battle anyway."

"That man over there," Bellmont pointed out, "is a doctor

from Austria. He is here with his wife and two children. Hans Gruber. He said that every few nights he thinks the wall will be overrun and he and his wife renew their...their terrible promise. He said that if overrun, he will shoot her...in the head! And then the two children. If he is wounded first and she has their revolver, she is to shoot him, then...then both the children."

"As you told us getting here," Hedgecock said.

Gunther nodded. "Yes, fellers, this is not an uncommon promise in war."

"We've seen the Boxers torture people," Telemore said. "I guess I would make such a promise."

"I know we want to leave, but I hate to leave them...stranded. Stranded and without our help. We are needed here," Bellmont said. "And I mean the people, the regular people, fleeing with their lives. Hurt from the surrounding power struggles."

"Another common problem in war...regular people," Gunther said. "But, not to worry, we have no plans to leave for a while. Help is on the way, we hope. We think. We heard. I just hope our ship waiting off the coast will wait for us and not think we are dead in a ditch somewhere," Gunther said.

"You believe that help is on the way?" Telemore asked.

"This is a very confusing siege. They are out there trying to, wanting to kill us. I was told that two weeks ago the Chinese threatened to march 80,000 men in here. But they never did. And...yet the Chinese leaders communicated with Semitagold almost every day. They wish him well. They offer us a surrender..."

"They do?" Bellmont said.

"They do! They do while the bullets are pouring in. No one trusts them. Semitagold and his staff think we would

173

all be slaughtered if we marched out of here. Every man, woman and child."

The doctors grimaced and agreed.

"People in each legation have Chinese contacts, spies, friends on the outside. And the Italians are throwing rocks tied with messages over some of the walls. About a day or so later, rocks come back with news wrapped around them."

"Can they be trusted?" Hedgecock asked.

"Hell, if I know," Gunther said. "I think…I've been thinking, we are all hostages here until the battles on the coast are decided. They have to keep us here like one big poker chip. Keep us alive to barter with later if they need to. When they no longer need us? They'll send in that 80,000."

Bells rang in the park.

Gunther squinted, counting them. "I *gotta* go, men. Semitagold is calling an emergency military meeting."

Some 15 men showed up in Semitagold's British legations office. It was an ornate affair of paintings large and small and a fine furniture mix of Victorian and Oriental styles. There were leaders of the various armies, to include Yorkie, another Marine captain, and the stuffy Smithe. Everyone was in a uniform; even Jefe was wearing his Filipino Scout khakis. Gunther in civies felt like he was the Davy Crockett in the room.

"Captain Myers. For anyone new, he is the commander of the U.S. Marines here," Semitagold introduced the officer.

The Marine captain stepped forward.

"Gentleman, in the last 14 hours, the Boxers have made serious advancements atop the wall. They have been moving their barricades up and up. Closer and closer."

"Those ingenuous heathens!" Semitagold declared, slapping

a leather glove in his hand.

"Yes, sir. It was hard to see the increments at first, but it became obvious. We have tried to stop them, but to no avail."

"Throw firebombs on '*em*?" Gunther asked.

"THAT…is not exactly cricket, Major Gunther," Semitagold said.

"The only thing that's cricket is cricket," Gunther said.

"But we tried that!" the Marine confessed. "Their barricades are made of various pieces of wood, yes, but mostly metal. There is only one thing to do. Jump overs. Jump over ours and theirs and attack the invaders."

There were mumbles and nods. The Italians and Japanese received translations. The two German officers there were already working with the Marines on the wall and knew the problem. Those officers from India knew English.

"This is your best plan?" Semitagold asked.

"Yes, sir. A frontal assault. Another day and they will be in range to start sniping the legation grounds to pieces."

Semitagold and Smithe exchanged glances.

"So be it then," Smithe said. "And might I suggest a middle of the night invasion? Catch the buggers on the sleep."

Everyone agreed.

"We'd like volunteers, a few from each legation," Smithe continued.

Gunther and Jefe raised their hand, as the leaders did.

"Very well, then, we'll meet on the grounds of this institution at, shall we say 1 a.m.? For a 2 a.m. assault?" Smithe said.

******

Smithe sat in a wicker chair in the small park, in the dark, alone, in front of the main British building. It was 12:45 a.m. Gunther and Jefe walked up, looking around for the others.

"Captain," Gunther said.

"The Americans and Germans are already on duty on the wall. We are waiting for the others to show up."

The others. 12:55 a.m. Two Italians showed up.

One a.m. A few others from the legations.

Smithe stood and walked among them, asked what questions of them he could.

Then Swoop-Swellen and Smithe showed up.

"What should we call you now?" Gunther asked him.

He grunted and said, "Swoop. Call me Swoop."

"And you are AWOL? From the Army?" Jefe asked.

He pulled a cigar from the breast pocket of his jacket. Then some matches from his pants pocket. They noticed he'd acquired a Chinese sword, hung on his belt, replete with red tassels on the handle and sheath.

"I am AWOL. I walked away from my post. My fort. Just couldn't stand it all anymore. It's easier to hide away in the bigger cities. Other counties. Easy to use another name. Bounty hunters are always after me."

Gunther didn't quite know what to say about that. Then Smithe approached Gunther and Jefe interrupting their questions.

"Well, there is one or two from each army. That is, they tell me, the best they can offer. Damn it all. Shall we go?"

"Yes, sir," Gunther said, and the small group of men, totaling 15 made their way in the dark to the stone stairs up the steep climb to the center of Tartar Wall.

At the top, Myers, Yorkie and a band of Marines were waiting. Several German Marines stood beside them.

"This…it?" Myers asked.

"This is it I am afraid. A mere representative or two from each army."

The Chinese barricade was some 40 feet away.

"They asleep over there?" Gunther asked.

"Most," Myers said. "We'll all go over our top. I'll take these eight men and we'll creep over our side, crawl up to theirs and see what we can find. I'll whisper to Yorkie on this side for the next step. Hopefully, whoever we find over there will be dozing and we'll take care of *'em*." He patted the sheathed bayonet on his belt.

The legation barricade, like the Chinese one, was a mess of material, like a sunken, crashed ship all the way across the wall walkway, some 43 feet wide and about 6 feet deep of jagged junk. Myers and the seven Marines and one Russian started scaling the makeshift wall. Within a moment they dropped out of sight in the "no-man's land" between the walls.

And a hellfire of gunshots resounded that zipped through the air and pinged, punched into or bounced off the barricade. Gunther and the men tried to get a position to shoot back but the dark and the denseness of the barricade offered no purchase.

"*Cappen'* Myers!" Yorkie yelled out.

"We are okay. We got cover!" a voice yelled back, under the unceasing Chinese gunfire blasting away.

Then Gunther heard an odd shot from way off to his right. What? He looked north. Another one in a flash! It came from the legation rooftop. It had to be Crippler. She was shooting into the Chinese as best she could see them behind trees and a few buildings.

"We've got cover fire," Gunther said, though he could not imagine how she could see any Boxers on the wall from her rooftop angle.

The Chinese gunfire hit a lull, from Crippler's disrupting effort, or were most of them just reloading?

"Come on!" Myers yelled.

Gunther, Jefe, Swoop, even Smithe and the Marines hauled themselves over the top and across their wall, stopping only to shoot when they could at the enemy. They followed Myers and his team up and over the China wall. Before them on the enemy side were scattered debris, remnants of partial prior walls, some tents, and a few small campfires. Myers and the initial team offered some cover fire.

Gunther spotted a few Boxers slammed with rounds from their Marines and more flung down, ripped or shredded one at a time from Crippler's hunting rounds. The allies advanced. Gunther dropped his rifle to sling length and pulled his brace of pistols, blasting at the Boxers he could see.

Some Marines fell. Myers fell, crying out in anguish and cursing.

"Go! Go! Go!" Myers yelled, holding his leg. He could feel the energy of a successful charge in the night air.

The men dashed from debris to debris, clearing out the makeshift camp-like area and a little makeshift fort. The Boxers were running off now and they ran into an opening zone visible to Crippler. Gunther watched as she shot two right off their feet. The survivors disappeared down the wall, and it looked like they leapt right off the tall parapet!

Swoop began a wild man yell, not unlike the American Indians he reportedly hated so much. He pulled his Chinese sword and chased one of them. The Boxer did not turn around and Swoop hacked at his head and neck. The man's tall hat flipped off, and with the side of his neck destroyed, he stumbled and fell. Another Boxer, seeing the sword attack, and one who must have exhausted his ammo, and/or also so outraged, pulled his own sword and charged Swoop. Swoop and the Boxer began sword fighting! Ancient Chinese "Kung Fu sword" versus US "cavalry sword". They exchanged powerful clanging blows amid death cries in English and Chinese.

Gunther ran to the wall's edge to see a wide ladder leading down to the dry canal. His shoved 5 more rounds into his rifle. His first shot though was not at the fleeing Boxers, but rather at the dueling Chinaman. It plummeted into the torso of the nearby battling Chinese swordsman. The soldier dropped like a corpse in front of Swoop, who, in surprise, turned to Gunther and made a disgruntled, disappointed face. Gunther turned back to the ladder and took aim at the descending enemy.

"What?" Jefe asked as he caught up with him, while reloading.

"Those sons a bitches are getting away on ladders."

He shot a man on the top of a ladder. The Boxer gasped and shook but did not fall. Gunther shot him again and the man fell on the Boxer below him and then they both fell on the Boxer even lower on the tall ladder. All three dropped some 25 feet to the dirt below. The lower four men clung to the shaking ladder and hung on. Jefe and Gunther killed the rest of them, but about 10 or 15 Boxers with a head start ran away into the Peking night.

Swoop stepped around looking for wounded Boxers to stab to death.

"She shooting?" Jefe asked, catching his breath, he pointed to the rooftop.

"Yes."

"You tell her to?"

"No. She needs to save those bullets for snipers."

Other German and American Marines slipped and stepped over the mess of a barricade. Several rushed to Myers. The Marine captain was shot in the leg. Midway in the mess, Gunther saw a bleeding Captain Smithe, all 60 some-odd years of him, hat gone, hair a mess, surveying the scene, pistol still in his hand, hanging down at his side.

"You okay, Captain?" Gunther asked.

"Yes. I am all cut up from bloody barricade. I remain thus far, unshot."

His clothes were torn, and Gunther took a look at himself and then Jefe. Their clothes were torn also, and they were bleeding about their legs and arms, from the sharp-flying edges of iron, broken clay, and stone of the monster walls they crawled over.

"Rip that tent down and set up a line of fire up there!" Yorkie called out to a team of Marines. He pointed past the tentlike structures the Chinese had built. "Kill anything that comes this way."

Smithe walked up to Myers.

"Fine job, Myers. You are done for tonight. These men? To the doctors," he ordered the Marines near him.

Six Marines were dead, and only five wounded.

"You see those fellers shot way over there?" Gunther pointed out to them. "My sniper lady shot them. It must also be an opening for us to be shot at too. I'd rig up this monster wall down past that."

"We're *gonna* move our barricade up to there, sir," Yorkie reported to Smithe. "This space, all of this space is now ours."

The men carefully hoisted Captain Myers and the wounded over the ragged barricade. Then Gunther and Jefe followed suit.

Jefe started to limp. Badly. By a freshly lit torch, Gunther kneeled and looked at Jefe's right leg. His pant leg was ripped to above the knee.

"That's a bad one, amigo," Gunther said. He pinched at the open flesh slit that ran from the knee down to the ankle. "Stiches. You need some stitches. Get to the hospital."

Gunther shouted to some of the Marines walking the wounded off.

"Hey! This man needs stitches!"

Jefe was disgusted at himself for being wounded. A German Marine ran up, and Gunther spoke in German about Jefe's condition. The Marine grabbed Jefe's torso with one arm, and he too joined the march to the infirmary. Some random incoming fire started up from the grounds outside, and a Marine extinguished all the torches.

Staying low, the allies began setting up the new wall from their hard-earned space.

******

Within 20 minutes, Gunther crossed the grounds, entered the British legation, and received an ovation from the men and women there who remained awake, too nervous to sleep. Crippler was not among them. He climbed the steep stairs to his rooftop. The hatch was open. He stepped up through it and saw Crippler sitting on the rooftop, her back to the sandbags, her hands clasped before her face. She stood when she saw him and ran to him.

"What...you...you..." Gunther tried to speak.

She threw her arms around him and kissed him.

Shots rang out in the distance and they both dropped to the floor, he on his back, her atop him, still in their embrace.

"You were supposed to save those bullets, we need..."

"I know," she said. "I know, but when I heard about your mission. I had to help you. I had to do something."

"How many did you shoot?"

"Twelve."

"Twelve," he repeated. "Twelve rounds. But it was an important victory to save us from snipers moving closer in."

"Are you alright?" she asked.

"Just a few scratches."

"Jefe?"

"He's okay. Torn up leg. Ripped up from a piece of metal from the barricade. Stitches."

She suddenly realized where she was, atop him, and she slowly crawled off him and into a kneeling position down at his feet. They stared at each other for another moment. She looked amazing to him, kneeling there. Then in a safe crouch she turned and disappeared down the hatch.

Filthy and exhausted, he rolled over to his red dragon silk pillow of dirt and looked for just a moment at the stars. He was fast asleep in less than 5 minutes.

Chapter 15
The King of China Walls

It had been another long day of dodging bullets and occasional cannon fire as Gunther made his rounds to visit Jefe at the hospital. He ate a gross dinner of "French Steak", horse meat and dirty rice, with Crippler, then he checked on the doctors and inspected various barricades. He roved until midnight, then he slept.

Or tried to! A lung-shaking, horrendous explosion. A startled awake Gunther sat up. He looked at his pocket watch. It was 3 a.m. What was that rumbling bang? He stood, shook off his tar-roof stiffness and saw, over by the French Legation, roaring flames but on the outside of the walls, not inside. Once at the roof's edge, he saw people below were clamoring to the back French building which made up much of the wall section. Men were yelling. He buckled his pistol belt on and threw his rifle over his shoulder and left for the French embassy.

It was a 4-minute jog to the French headquarters location, a section of random sized stone and cement buildings whose collective ragtag back stone walls were the main wall separating the compound from the rest of Peking and the enemy. He entered the building and followed hustling French soldiers to the rooftop.

Once atop he saw other soldiers and embassy workers looking over the edge but none shooting. Outside and down below, men were moaning and screaming. Arriving Boxers and soldiers were scampering among the dead and wounded. Chinese houses and buildings down near them, already blasted to bits, were again on fire where something existed still burnable.

"What happened?" he asked a woman. She shook her head, unable to speak English.

"A bomb," a nearby French officer said. "*De...de* Boxers try to dig under *de* walls at night, under *de* buildings...mines... and put bombs under us."

Gunther quick-counted some 25 Boxers lay dead on the ground, and many more wounded.

"It looks like *dey'* touch off their own bomb by accident. Thank goodness *dey'* did not set *de* bomb under us as planned."

Yorkie showed up on the roof, followed by Smithe.

"Buggers," Smithe said, peering over the wall at the human devastation. "We should shoot them all, but they looked hurt enough. It wouldn't be cricket to shoot now."

Cricket again, Gunther thought.

"Mining," Yorkie told Gunther. "They try it every few days. They've had some good results, collapsing some of the border buildings and blowing holes in the walls. This was a *helleva* explosion."

Swoop Swellen showed up to Gunther's left, leered over the wall, grunted, and pulled his slung rifle off his shoulder to start shooting. Gunther lunged out and grabbed the rifle's barrel, hauling it skyward.

Swoop looked at Gunther and Gunther shook his head, no.

"Something to do with cricket," Gunther explained. "I'm with you on this but let this one pass."

Swoop lowered his gun in impatient disgust.

Gunther turned and left. Another thing to worry about. Mining. Underground bombs.

******

At 10 a.m. sharp was now the new daily security committee meeting in Semitagold's office. Semitagold's adjunct read off some statistics and opened the floor to the military commanders and few civilians for questions.

"Mining," Gunther spoke up.

"Mining," Captain Smithe repeated.

"Mining in the U.S. means coal mining or gold mining, but here it must mean tunneling to plant bombs."

"Yes," Smithe said.

"It seems to be a real threat. What are we doing about mining?"

"We are hoping to respond…"

"Respond? Are there not lookouts working overnight, worried about this?"

"There are…there are in places. For example, there are no mining…tunneling, bomb attacks on the Tartar Wall. And inside our walls are stacked, or are being stacked with sandbags," Smithe said.

"I see," Gunther said, "what about the floors? Tunnels under us? Just a hodge-podge of walls? Of varying shapes and sizes on some sections, not like the Tartar Wall. These are invasion weaknesses. What if they tunnel past the sandbag walls?"

"Each commander here is given the responsibility to watch and cover their walls that border the outside world."

"Are they now?" Gunther said, standing, looking around the room. "Are they all? Last night the French weren't."

A French captain made a disgruntled face and shifted a bit in his chair.

"There needs to be a team whose duty it is to watch our outer walls 24 hours a day. Spy mining. Tunnels. It could be volunteer civilians, could be anyone..."

"Coolies," an Austrian said.

"Anyone. We can't have these people digging under our walls and blowing us up."

"*That* settles it then," Semitagold said. "Major Gunther, you are now the chairman of the new Wall Committee."

"Well..." Gunther said.

"Hear! Hear!" came the cries of the commanders.

Smithe smiled, at least Gunther had an official assignment.

"Post your committee in the park boards. Ask for volunteers, and by God get this going!" Semitagold said.

"I need soldiers," Gunther said, sweeping a hand across the room.

"My men," a Japanese commander said, "are very busy with security. If the wall is broken? I can send men, but I cannot have men watching the walls all day and night long."

The commander of each nation present declared a similar thing.

Once adjourned, Gunther left the meeting and Crippler was waiting outside for him.

"And how did that go today?" she asked.

"I am now the king of all walls," Gunther said in an air of frustration as they walked to the tea committee's tea bar in the park.

"One wall or..."

"All walls."

"All walls. It could be worse," she said. "You could also be the king of doors and gates too."

They walked on. She hooked his arm in hers.

"I have discovered there is a lot of...of interactions going on around here," she said.

"Interactions?"

"Many...affairs going on here. Men meeting women."

"Oh."

"Meetings in the parks. Meetings here and there...slipping around. There are numerous...things...going on! And some ministers are having a devil of a time keeping the German soldiers away from a bevy of very, shall we say, buxom Chinese girls next door."

"It's the war. The *battle*," Gunther said sarcastically.

"I see. The war...and battle."

"I mean, look at me? A poor, poor common soldier with no future, and yet, you seem to find me..."

"The king of doors and gates."

"Walls, my lady, the king of walls. Someday I will conquer the doors and gates, too."

By the afternoon, Gunther and Crippler found Helga Louvard, the head of the News Committee, in a large, multi-layered dress and top, hair in a well-kept bun, sitting in a courtyard of the German legation.

"Mrs. Louvard, I am Johann Gunther, the head of the Wall Committee. I understand you are the head of the News Committee," Gunther said in German.

"Yes, and you are from Germany?"

"Yes, from the Black Forest area, but I speak better English." They switched over.

"You," she pointed to Crippler, "are the sniper woman. The sharpshooter. We thank you oh so much for help."

"Suzannah Crippler," she said, extending a hand. They shook.

"I need to announce the new Wall Committee," Gunther said, "and we need volunteers to stand guard at night, to prevent the Boxers from sneaking along our walls and digging tunnels..."

"*Ja! Ja*. The mining."

"Yes, the mining. This is dangerous, and it can't go on."

"*JA!* I can make up the posters, and in all the languages here. We have a handbill printing machine and..."

She stood.

"...and we can call for a meeting. What is your plan?"

"Well...I think we need teams of two in every other building rooftop or something like that. Two people every 50 yards. Just the three walls, sides and back. The Germans and Americans are always on the Tartar Wall. Both keeping watch but one must be a runner..."

"Run...ner?"

"*Läufer* or a *Läuferin*," Gunther translated.

"*Ja*, A runner. Man or woman."

"Yes. One will run to tell the soldiers of an attack. The soldiers will make a plan for what to do."

"When?" she asked.

"When?" Gunther repeated.

"The meeting. When do you want the meeting?"

"Is…is tomorrow too soon?"

"NO!" she declared abruptly. "We work very fast here. With the news!"

"Can everyone meet at the park at…3 p.m.? Tomorrow?"

"*Ja*. It will go on the poster. The News Committee will start right away."

"*Danka*," Gunther said. "the entire Wall Committee…me…thanks you."

She turned and briskly entered the main German building.

Chapter 16
China Krupps, Doctors, Preachers and Soldiers

The morning of Gunther's 8th day started with cannon fire. As a graduate of West Point, schooled and experienced in various forms of artillery, these were "modern" sounding eruptions, not old China war cannon sounds. He walked to the wall of his rooftop and saw a round hit a building and demolish a corner of it, scattering people in fright.

He pulled a pair of binoculars off a sandbag and looked north. And there far away, too far for regular rifle fire, was a team of five Chinese army soldiers, not Boxers, on a rooftop, running a cannon-like gun.

"Damn," Gunther muttered. "Krupp. 50mm."

The German Krupp family were masters of armory and while these guns look like the common cannon with a cannon centerpiece and two large wheels, they were rapid fire, breach loaders. These guns were sold all over the world. Easy to disassemble and move even in the jungles of Siam and the Philippines. And rapid fire they were, as the rounds hit all over the compound and the Tartar Wall.

Gunther stepped over to the west wall that looked over the British courtyard. Down below, some people dashed about fearing more incoming, and Gunther called to them.

"Get Crippler! Get Crippler and her rifle up here!"

A group of women acknowledged him and ran into their building.

Gunther waited. Rounds poured in, one every few minutes, pacing out the fear nicely. Finally, Suzannah Crippler appeared in the hatch, with her gun case.

"How far?"

"Far," and he pointed north.

He opened her gun case as she looked at the horizon with the spyglasses.

"Can you do it?" he asked, screwing the barrel in.

"I can do it."

She finished up prepping her gun, pulled a chair to the sandbagged wall, laid the barrel on the wall, and fell into the trance of a professional shooter. Gunther took up the binoculars.

"Who first?" she said in a calm whisper.

"The man behind the gun, the one who looks like he is sighting the gun in. The shooter is to the left, pulling the draw string, anyone can do that. The man sighting the damn thing might be irreplaceable. But an idiot can eventually walk rounds in with a Krupp. If we can get them all, we…"

She shot.

And sure enough, the soldier working the sights toppled over, his head exploding like a smashed melon.

Bolt-action.

Bam!

Part of the drawstring operator's body disappeared.

The other two men spun around, shocked, their mouths appeared to be yelling. They ducked down flat.

"Can I shoot somewhere on the cannon?" she asked.

"Honey, that thing is solid steel. But...but there is a sighting device on the back, like a...like a pipe sticking up, it's metal, but..."

"I got it," she whispered.

Boom.

"I think you busted it apart," Gunther said putting the binoculars down, absolutely amazed.

The distant German and American Marines on the Tartar Wall turned to them and started jumping up and down, yelling and some waved their hats at them. They knew what had happened, what Crippler had done.

"You have an approving crowd. Many fans," Gunther told her, as she stared into the scope.

"Windage. Elevation. You see those Chinese pennants on the roof behind them? They tell me everything I need to know. Plum stupid of them to set up in front of those flags."

"Plum," Gunther repeated.

Bam!

The third of the gun team was knocked face down as he tried to run across the roof.

"Onnnnne more," Gunther said of the man hiding.

"I can wait," she said. "I waited about half a day to bag a beautiful, record breaking elk in Montana. Squirmy, smart thing in a valley of hills and ravines."

"You did?"

"I did. It was a hunting contest in 1895. I won. I waited and I won."

The fourth man got up and lit off for the rooftop door. She nailed him in the small of his back and he dropped like a stone.

"I will tell our little cannon crews," Gunther said, "there are three crews you know, to try and play with windage and elevation and blow that Krupp off the roof."

There was a barrage of rifle fire that unleashed upon the legation. Revenge fire. Gunther and Crippler hit the roof behind the sandbags.

They stared at each other, their faces inches apart.

"Johann Gunther," she said very seriously, lips pursed, "I am going to take you to my bed."

"You don't have a bed."

"I'll make a bed."

"Okay."

"I must tell you," she said. "I am engaged to be married. I am not now married. I am engaged."

"Okay. Engaged. Engaged is not married."

"You're not married. Are you engaged?"

"I am not engaged," Gunther said.

"I *am* engaged to a very nice man. He's from Omaha. And I feel…but I feel like we…we have been through a lot together and I cannot let…I just cannot let this chance for us pass…"

"I agree."

He kissed her. They embraced as a few of the rounds hit their rooftop walls.

"They know we are here," she whispered.

"I told you they eventually would."

"You did."

And they kissed again and again.

"Where is this bed that I now dream of?" Gunther asked.

"I don't know. I will see. I have to keep my lady-like reputation with all the women downstairs."

"You just saved about 2000 people from dooming, one-a-minute, Krupp gunfire. Your reputation is quite intact, ma'am."

She threw a leg over his legs. There was no more talk about engagements.

******

Six hours later, Crippler and Gunther, carrying a clipboard with blank paper in hand and a few pencils in his pocket, wandered to the park by the bulletin boards at 2:50 p.m. expecting no one "wall-watching" volunteers. As he got closer, he saw quite a large group of mostly women and some men, and he wondered what group they were there for. But as he closed in on them, they all turned to him and started clapping. His eyebrows shot up in surprise. He whisked off his hat.

"Major Gunther," a French woman said in English, "it is about time someone did something about this. We just can't all sit here and have the floor blow up from underneath us."

There were "hear-hears" and "yeahs" all around.

"There were some bastards creeping around out there last night," a man with an Irish accent said. "And some Frenchies ran them off."

"Well!" Gunther said, "I hate to disturb people's sleep, but there seems to be enough of you to spread the guard duty around. The way I see it, and I am open to suggestions, is that we need to man 10 pickets…posts…guard spots, each night. Two people at each one. If something is spotted out there, one of the two will alert the closest military for each legation, a runner so to speak, as well as alert me."

"Can we shoot '*em*?" a woman asked.

Everyone laughed.

"Yes! I certainly hope so. My answer would be yes but wait for the soldiers to help you. And…and …don't get yourself shot shooting at them!"

They laughed again.

"I am doing many chores through the day…" Gunther continued.

"We heard of your efforts, and we thank you," a lady said.

"And you too, Miss Crippler. Bless you," a man said.

"And I need a secretary to compose a list of people. We'll get a map, set up the guard posts and get things going."

"I will offer my services," an older man said in deep southern US accent. "Name's Willard Fit, one of the "*Fightin'* Parsons" they call us.

"I have heard of you. Six of you right?"

"Six parsons. Righty. And our flocks."

"Do you have a table and some kind of office? A parsonage?" Gunther asked him.

"Yes, we do and them Chinkos have tried to bust through our wall at night, too. But we parsons and our flock, we fought '*em* all backward."

"Good. A headquarters," Gunther said.

"We know Parson Fit!" a woman enthusiastically yelled out.

"I am sure most of you know that some of the embassies here have some ladders and ropes and they climb down over the walls sometimes and hunt around the outskirts. Looking for food and supplies. So, as we stand guard, we should not be surprised to see our allies do these things."

"Yes!"

"We will meet at the *Fightin'* Parsons headquarters, then," Gunther said. "Now can I get everyone to print their names and your legations on this list?" Gunther shook his clipboard in the air.

"I'll be handling that list, Major," Fit said, and Gunther passed off the clipboard, relieved.

******

At 5:30 p.m., Gunther climbed the stairs at the Tartar Wall and once atop took a long look around at the weary men in filthy unforms. Gunther spotted his goal. One Swoop Swellen. He was sitting on some wooden boxes, talking with some American Marines.

"Swoop."

"Gunther."

"Mind if I have a word with *ya*?" Gunther asked, nudging his head away from the others.

With a grunt, Swoop stood, adjusting the big Chinese sword on his belt to do so, and the two walked off.

"Hey!" shouted a U.S. Marine. "Are you that Major Gunny?"

"Gunther," Gunther said.

"Major Gunther! That there, woman rifleman…rifle-woman is a Godsend! She's got that rifle fine-tuned like a concert pie-any!"

"Yes!" Gunther said. "She does. Where you from, Marine?"

"Kentucky!"

"Never been. But I hope to. Hope to see that blue grass."

"It's a slice of heaven, sir."

"Stay well, Marine."

The two walked on.

"The other morning, I had the same feeling you did," Gunther told Swoop, "about seeing those Chinese outside the wall. Trying to blow us up. Trying to kill us. Smithe holding us back. Cricket they say. Cricket."

Swoop stopped and looked at him. "That's the truth."

"I have been assigned, and against my will, to be the head of a...one of these damn committees...a committee of the walls. The whole...thing," Gunther swirled his hand in the air, "the whole damn wall."

Swoop chuckled.

"We are going to have 12 two-man, well man and woman... and looks like a lot two-woman teams stationed all over watching for creepers at night. If they see any of these miners, they are to contact the local soldiers and me to...respond."

"Respond to do what?"

"Kill 'em."

"Kill 'em?"

"Kill 'em. No...cricket," Gunter said. "Kill 'em."

"Hummmm."

"What I was thinking was, when the watchers run for the soldiers, and for me...what I was thinking is, maybe they might run for you too."

"Me?"

"You."

"Humm."

"I think we need somebody like you on the wall. Not just up here on the Tartar, but the whole wall."

"Ain't you enough?" Swoop asked.

"You have more leadership experience on these things. I heard you ran whole forts in very, very hostile territories."

"That I did," he said, and they started walking again, slowly. Gunther kept up with him.

"What do you think...General?"

Swoop winced at the word 'general'. "This place reminds me of some forts. But are we stuck here until, until relief comes? Will it come?"

"Coming. Going. Stuck. All we hear are rumors we can't prove."

"Will our ship wait for us off the coast?" Swoop asked.

"I'm working on that."

They stopped at a wall lookout point and rested their elbows atop it.

"You can't live your life crawling on the ground. Afraid," Swoop said, glaring in at the rooftops across the canal and beyond.

"Nope," Gunther agreed.

"Like a lizard. Or a snake."

"Yup."

"Johann, I've not got much to go back to," Swoop said. "I am AWOL. I walked away from my last fort. I did. Didn't even steal my issued horse when I left. Just one morning I walked off. Changed clothes. Rode on a supply wagon train to St. Paul. Left. The wagon train soldiers all thought I was on some secret mission. HA! I was escaping and they escorted me! Just left because I knew that next treaty the government wanted was a worthless lie. Worthless promises. Horse manure. I knew, I could predict that in a year? Maybe two? I'd be *shootin'* those Indians over that impossible treaty. Gunther,

I am part-ways Indian. One fourth. A grandma."

"Oh?" Gunther let on he did not know that.

"Nobody in the Army command knew that. Secret. They all thought I hate Indians and wanted to kill all of them. But Indians are not all good, you know. Not all bad. Some need *killin'*. Some don't. The Army likes to tattle a tale about me *findin'* a dead family tortured by the Comanche, and since that day, I went Indian-killing crazy. I did see that dead family. One teenage girl captive was slowly burned and burned over 18 days of torture until her face was roasted away and her body was covered with bruises. She was still alive. They have a certain…expertise…in *killin'* people very slowly. Like these *fucken'* Boxers here do."

"I know. Seen things like that myself in Oklahoma."

"That made me a madman. Yeah. Sure. In a way. And I am a madman. When the fight starts. Any fight. When you see in their eyes that the enemy wants to kill you and yours. You just fight like a tornado from hell. It's a yes or no answer. A go or no go. A be there or not be there. Do or die."

"Yup."

"Where were you?" Swoop asked.

"Fort Sill, Oklahoma."

"Ooooh. The Indian territory."

"Yup. First at Sill. Cavalry. Mustered out, as I was through with soldering, I thought. Got in a jam with the KKK in Oklahoma as a lawman. Two governors sent me to West Point, more to hide-out from the KKK bounty on me. Then Cuba. Then the Philippines. Now?" he sighed, "now here."

"So, you just do what they tell you to do? Go where they tell you go. Shoot who they tell you to shoot."

"Pretty much."

"Hmmm. Nice not to think about it. West Point. All my promotions run in with blood. On the field. I probably couldn't last a minute at the Point."

"You *gettin'* along with Captain Yorkie?"

"I am. I am. He means business. He takes his responsibilities seriously."

"What will you do when we get back to the States?" Gunther asked. "You will get a considerable amount of money."

"I don't know. I don't know what I will do, even with a lot of money. I don't know how to spend money, Gunther. Considerable money. Damn sure don't want to pretend to be a preacher. I...like the ladies. But I don't know any considerable ladies that would consider me. Considerable money for an inconsiderable man. That! Is an odd combination. Anyway, I have to stay on the move."

"Well, maybe the Army will forget about you someday."

"*Shheeet*. The Army will never forget me! There's a $300 bounty on my head."

"That's considerable."

"There's a group of ex-Army NCOs, they hunt AWOLs for the bounty, and they never stop looking for me. They were all gravediggers. They are foot soldier, fucker-ups that were sent to gravedigging units for punishment. They call themselves the 'Gophers'. Yeah. They mustered out, and all they do is hunt AWOLs. They are always sniffing me out, at my heels because I was a general. Well, at least over here in China they'll never find me. For a while anyway. And what are you gonna do? Report me when you get back?"

"No."

"Nope?"

"No, Swoop, I am not. I am beginning to think about minding my own business for a while. And…you are not my business. And…you have a story."

"Excuses."

"No, sir, not excuses. It's a story not told."

Swoop grunted.

"And honestly," Gunther said, "I am beginning to think about what I want to do when I get back too. I still have 3 years left on this commitment. They'll probably ship me back to the Philippines right away when I get back."

"That's a hellhole mess. What did those people ever do to the United States of America?" Swoop asked.

They stared off at the short and tall, Oriental shaped houses and business, and their curved tiled roofs.

"SERGENT!" Swoop shouted out suddenly.

A Marine ran up to him. Swoop pointed to a distant rooftop. Gunther looked too. There were six Boxers with rifles on a roof, looking to organize some sniping. The Marine dashed back yelling orders to scrambling troops.

"That Crippler girl is a *helleva* shot," Swoop said.

"That she is."

"And a real looker too. She…is a considerable woman. Why in the Hell was her sister here?" Swoop asked.

"Just looking to spread her family business."

The Marines opened fire on the rooftop. The drilled tiles, stones, rooftops, and the Boxers split, shattered, splintered, bounced, and fell in a fusillade.

"Considerable people *gotta* eat things that taste special," Gunther said.

"We've killed for way less," Swoop said,

"That we have," Gunther said.

******

At 7 p.m. Gunther sat on a donated, ornate dining room chair beside the homemade cot Jefe was relegated too. The Filipino was not to walk for a few more days on the torn open leg, except for a quick hobble to and from the outhouse, using a splintered, 2x4 from a doorframe as a crutch. Jefe's bed was once a door in the Russian legation, elevated on rows of bricks. His bed was almost in the center of some 40 beds of the wounded and sick. In the far right and isolated, were some cases presumed to be smallpox.

"Here he comes," Gunther said, pointing to the hall's entrance. Jefe propped himself up on his pillow stuffed with cleaned, dead soldier uniforms, washed by the "Laundry Committee".

Gunther stood up and offered Mister Zin his chair. Zin sat. Gunther stepped around the bed and remained standing.

Dr. Bellmont saw the meeting and came over to listen in.

"Mister Zin, we need your help," Gunther said.

"What is it?"

"I am afraid that our ship out in the bay will give up on us and leave us, thinking we are dead."

Mister Zin listened quietly, staring at the marble floor.

"We need to get a message, a word to them that we are still alive and for them to wait."

"I can't go," Jefe added. "I would, but my leg is sewed up from above my knee to my foot. I can't bend it for a few days."

"Three days. At the very least," Dr. Bellmont said.

"And I would still need help getting to the spot on the beach," Jefe continued.

Mister Zin nodded.

"Do you think...do you think you can sneak out of here? Get to the Rio Lobos and tell them we are still alive?"

Mister Zin sat quiet.

"Back roads...ah...sneaking. We will pay you. A lot," Gunther added.

"I have to leave my family again," he mumbled.

"Yes, I know."

"Again."

"Yes. Again. We will pay you a lot."

"If the relief gets here," Mister Zin said, finally looking up at him, "if they relieve us and they rescue us, why can't you go home with your Army?"

"Who knows if they are coming? When can they fight their way up here? And, who knows when they will go home? This may be a long war. And I have a mission to finish. Without the Rio Lobos...well...I need the Rio Lobos."

"So how would I get to the boat? Signal the Lobos from the beach?"

"Each of us have a flare gun. We will give you one or two of them," Gunther said. "So, at night. Dark. You would shoot it in the air on the beach. The crew is supposed to be watching and waiting offshore every night for this signal."

"A flare...gun?"

"It's like Chinese fireworks."

"Oh, oh."

"We'll show you how they work. It's very simple. What

do you think?"

"I will have to ask my wife."

"I would go with you," Jefe said, but the doctor said I might split these stitches open."

"You would," Dr. Bellmont said.

"So, you will ask your wife?" Gunther said.

"Correct."

Mister Zin stood. A cannon shot landed somewhere outside. Mister Zin bowed slightly and walked off.

"What you think?" Jefe asked.

"I don't know," Gunther said.

"And I am, we are, really needed here," Bellmont added. He walked off to see other patients.

"*Very* tricky business," Jefe said.

"Yup."

"If we leave early? We are like *de*...escaping cowards. If we stay, maybe we all will die."

"Yuuup."

"It seems, he does not want to go, huh?" Jefe said about Bellmont.

"Doctors," Gunther said. "Doctors and preachers. They want to stay."

"They want to stay," Jefe repeated. "Soldiers? Soldiers always want to go."

Chapter 17
The Lesser Wall of China

"Major Gunther!"

"Wha…"

"Major Gunther. The Boxers are coming."

"Wha…where?"

"The Austrian legation. The Boxers are sneaking, single file along the wall. Maybe 200 of them."

He thought maybe it was a dream, but his sleepy, blurry vision focused in on the head of woman poking her head out of the roof hatch.

"Oh, oh, okay…okay. You tell the Austrian commander?"

"Yes."

"Is someone getting Swoop Swellen?"

"Yes."

"Okay, I am on my way."

She left, and Gunther stood and armed up.

He looked at his watch. It read 3:30 a.m.

"*Every* night, it's something," he grumbled.

The Austrian embassy grounds were major sections away

and Gunther was there in 10 minutes. Families, workers, and wounded soldiers cleared the way through the dimly lit Austrian lobby and stairs as Gunther dashed up and onto the roof. Dozens of soldiers and armed men and women were at the ready, waiting quietly for him.

"Look, Major," a woman whispered.

He peeked over the wall and saw the army of invaders. There were indeed in a single file and the line stretched way across the south wall.

"Tell the Italians to get up on their wall. Quietly. The line reaches all the way back by them," Gunther told the woman.

Swoop Swellen showed up, dragging large canvas sacks, his arms laden with coils of ropes from his shoulders to his hands. He dropped the sacks and let loose the ropes, the sections slipping off his limbs. He pulled his rifle off his shoulder.

The Boxers leading the way stopped below them. They produced tools that looked like shovels and picks from backpacks and started digging at the base of the wall.

"How many?" Swoop asked Gunther.

"Looks like 75? 100?"

They watched and waited as the Italian soldiers lined up on their rooftop wall some hundreds of feet to the west.

"Ready?" Swoop said in a loud whisper, looking at all the soldiers and volunteers near him. Gunther quickly shoved strips of cloth into his ears.

"NOW!" he yelled.

Everyone armed leaned over the wall and blasted away in an ear-splitting cacophony. The Italians caught on also and fired below them.

Gunther picked off two Boxers, who tumbled to the right

and left of other shot Boxers. It seemed like about 50 of them were killed in a few seconds! The last 50 or so on the far end took off.

"Cease firing!" Swoop yelled and waved his arm. "Cease!"

The gunfire from the two rooftops stopped other than the far Italian line shooting or chasing the Boxers off closest to them.

"Tell the Italians to stand guard," Swoop told some of the civilians. We are going over the side."

Gunther's eyebrows raised.

Swoop unraveled the sections of rope. There were large knots every two or three feet.

"Going…over?" an Austrian officer said in broken English.

"Hell, yes. There are guns and ammo and munitions down there."

Gunther helped him stretch out the knotted ropes.

"You've been busy," Gunther said, noting the many knots.

"Yeah. I sat around all evening tying knots. I figured we'd use these. Didn't figure it would be tonight! But we'd need 'em. I did this in two forts on the frontier. Sometimes we couldn't open the front gates, so we roped down the fort walls and picked up all the Indians' guns and ammo. Knives, jerky and such."

"Okay."

"You climb ropes back in West Point?" Swoop asked.

"Yes, sir. Everyday. I did and without knots."

"Then this will be a tea party. Hey, I am sorry about taking over like this."

"Hell, you're the general, Swoop. I am just the XO," Gunther said.

"Who here can rope climb?" Swoop shouted.

The officer translated.

To Swoop's surprise about 10 soldiers and three civilians shouted out and raised their hands. Swoop was a bit aghast, expecting almost no one to volunteer.

"They're fuckin' Austrians, Swoop!" Gunther said. "Mountains. Mountain climbers!"

Some of the civilians lit torches. They had six strands of knotted rope and they found ways to tie them off on rooftop structures. Swoop tossed the big empty canvas sacks off the roof, then Swoop, Gunther and four Austrian infantry went over the side and shimmied the 25 feet down to the ground.

It was a dark, dirt trail of suffering down there, the guts, the dead and the dying on the path.

"I would put these poor bastards out of their misery, but we need the ammo," Swoop said, picking up the rifles from the ground or yanking them from their hands or off their shoulders.

"Throw down one of those torches!" Swoop yelled.

One large torch flipped over the edge and landed nearby. Swoop yanked a body over close to another body and using the dead as a stand, he stuck the handle of the torch between them as a torch stand.

A rifle shot! From a wounded Boxer. An Austrian cried out and fell against the wall. Gunther pulled a pistol and shot the Boxer in the head.

Two soldiers hopscotched over the dead to their young comrade. The teenage soldier was shot in the chest.

"Tie him off and haul him up," Swoop ordered, while shoving more Chinese pistols, rifles, and ammo bags into the sacks.

This left Gunther, Swoop and one soldier to collect weapons. They tied the top-strings of the sacks, tied the sacks to two ropes and ordered the bags hauled up. The wounded Austrian and the two bags were lifted up the wall. The teenager was unconscious, the rope wrapped under his armpits. He bounced off the wall, awoke on the way up, and screamed with each bounce.

They stacked up weapons and even the shovels and pickaxes. The sacks were tossed back over. They filled them half-way when they heard an Italian woman screaming from down the wall.

"*Stanno Tornando! Stanno Tornando?*"

"What the hell's she *sayin*?" Swoop hollered up to the onlookers.

"They are coming back! They are coming back!" Another Austrian woman translated.

"*Sheeet*," Swoop growled.

Gunther stomped out the torch. They stuffed the bags even faster.

"Tell '*em* to shoot '*em*. Hold '*em* back!" Swoop yelled up.

The Austrian woman ran to the west of the roof and shouted to the Italians.

The Boxers were coming to the rescue, yelling, and shrieking like wild animals, no longer in a single file but what looked like in a mass of a hundred.

"You men! Up!" Swoop ordered to the Austrians. "Gunther! Up!" as Swoop loaded the bags.

"Nope," Gunther said. "Let's get these bags up first."

The duo tied the stock full bags to two ropes. Austrians pulled the booty up. Then they ran to the far two dangling ropes and started climbing. The Italians laid down a heavy field of fire on the mob. Some of the Austrians on the west side of their embassy roof had some access to shoot at some of the Boxers.

The Austrian soldiers made it over the top. Chinese bullets were now zipping by Gunther and Swoop as they climbed, knot by knot by knot. Some of enemy rounds were cracking into the wall and ricocheting off all around them, spitting brick dust in their eyes and mouth.

The rooftop rescuers now started pulling their ropes up, hoisting the climbing Swoop and Gunther higher and faster. At the top, many hands suddenly grabbed at their hands, arms, and head. A bit higher and bullets whipped through the air. Inches higher and arms scooped under their arms. Up. Up and half-over. Their stomachs were on the wall top as their legs dangled in the air. Hands on their legs! Their feet...they were over and dropped on the rooftop like sacks of potatoes.

The Boxers were now below their wall, howling and shooting upward.

"We may be using up all the ammo we just collected," Gunther said, rolling over to lay on his back. He wiped the brick dust from his eyes and lips.

Swoop, sitting up, smiled and his thick eyebrows rolled up. He untied a sack.

"Oh, I found something better than bullets!"

Swoop pulled out...dynamite. Sticks of dynamite, with fuses.

"Sergeant!" he shouted to the Austrians, "Get me your best sharpshooters ready and over here!"

"Ladders!" A woman with a pistol cried out, and she reloaded.

Gunther stood up and glimpsed over the wall. Sure enough, some of the Boxers were hauling long ladders with them and under the rain of fire, were struggling to set them up.

The sharpshooters knelt beside Swoop, surprised to see the sticks of explosives.

"I'm *gonna* toss these over the edge. I don't know how long these fuses burn. I want you to shoot anyone who tries to pick them up and throw them back at us. Ready?"

One translated and they all nodded. Still seated, Swoop lit a fuse, grinned, and tossed it over his shoulder, over the wall. The men stuck their rifles over the side and watched the stick sizzle, fly and land. Almost no one down below saw it in the darkness and within seconds, the blast obliterated the Boxers below, also wiping out the bottom of the ladder. Ten feet of the wooden ladder disappeared into red splinters. It slid sideways down the wall, toppling with desperate Boxers dangling and yelling.

Swoop stood, lit another and threw it further away. It blasted another 'hole' in the crazed forces. He lit another and threw it even further. Another explosion. And another further, and another further down the line.

Still, ladders abound, and they couldn't blow up all of them. Swoop saw one on his far left that had been spared the explosives. Men raced up the steps. Swoop ran over to it. Staying low. He had a second before the top man's head and shoulders appeared over the wall.

"Welcome to Fort Apache, *muther fucker!*" Swoop declared and inches apart, shot him in the throat with his pistol. The Boxer gurgled with the eruption, foolishly but impulsively clutched his throat and from that lost grip, dropped out of Swoop's sight. Swoop half howled and laughed. Gunther watched Swoop lean over the top and fire at any remining ladder climbers that weren't knocked off.

The bombing seemed to break the Boxers' spirits. They

backed away. They stumbled. They ran west into the city proper, from whence they came.

The Austrians cheered. The Italians cheered. The Boxers retreated.

Gunther and Swoop leaned on the wall, watching.

"I reckon you were at Fort Apache?" Gunther asked.

"Hell, yeah," Swoop said.

"Reload!" Swoop shouted. "Now we are going back down there to collect more ammo, guns and maybe even explosives."

Swoop waved the Austrian commander over.

"Nobody leaves," Swoop told him. "We need more knotted ropes and climbers. And we need rifleman on the wall as guards."

"I'll go tell the Italians to remain as guards. Check on them," Gunther said, shoving himself off the wall with his hands. "Good work, General."

Swoop wiped the sweat off his face with the sleeve of his shirt. He scanned the human debris below.

"I am going back down there too," Swoop said to himself, "I'm *gonna* see if I can find me a *helleva* sword."

******

At 1 p.m., the new Wall Committee met back at the *Fightin'* Parsons' headquarters. Parson Willard Fit held up an empty cooking pot and beat its base with ladle to get the congregation to order. When Gunther arrived, the some 50 men and women cheered and clapped.

"Thank you! Thank you!" Gunther said with a big smile.

Smithe emerged from the group and shook Gunther's hand.

"If not for you," Smithe proclaimed, "your ideas and your

quick organization, Major Gunther, there is no telling what would have become of us last night."

"We have Swoop Swellen to thank for most of it," Gunther said, looking the crowd over for Swoop. Everyone's head swiveled in a search. Swoop was there, leaning against a far back wall, behind the assemblage.

"There he is!" a man announced and pointed.

All turned and clapped. Swoop stuck his pointy finger in the air and shook it a bit in acknowledgment, his eyes cast upon the ground.

Gunther smiled broadly. He was beginning to "get a handle" on this mysterious Swoop Swellen.

A sudden cool breeze rushed through the grounds to the oohs and ahhs of all, breaking the thick heat. The skies grew a bit darker.

"Lord o' mighty," a man said, "might there be some rain?"

"We all know our guard duties for the next few nights," Parson Fits said. "We all have other committee chores. Let us all go about our businesses. May the God Lord bless and keep us."

Many said, "Amen."

As the group walked off, Smithe stepped into a clearance, raised his arms half up and let the cool breeze surround him. He smiled broadly.

"It's going to rain, Major," Smithe said with delight.

"Yeah."

"Are you still sleeping up on the roof, Yank?"

"Yes, sir. I reckon I am. And I am thinking I might be of need of a waterproof canvas."

"Follow me, my good man. We have a storeroom of tents."

Chapter 18
China Night of 200,000 Shots

The next night and day, the rain fell in torrents. And with it, a barrage of rifle fire began mid-afternoon. It never seemed to stop. Hundreds of Boxers surrounding the west side of the siege fired their weapons over the walls and oddly, far over the heads of the captured.

Inside and dry, Gunther, Crippler, Swoop, Erasimo, and the three doctors crammed around Jefe's bed in chairs, waiting for the inimitable Mister Zin to arrive with his decision. The sound was deafening outside but tampered down by the doors and walls inside the hospital. Dr. Bellmont, heavy scissors in hand, decided to make the best use of their time and crack open the makeshift cast on the Filipino's leg and take a look. Hedgecock helped him.

"If we only had an x-ray machine," Hedgecock said. "We could do so much more around here, see shrapnel and broken bones and help all these people."

The cast was removed, and Jefe smiled in relief.

"There," Belmont said, "there, and that looks pretty darn

good, Jefe." Hedgecock leaned in and Telemore stood to get a clear look.

"How's it feel?" Telemore asked.

Jefe bent the leg slowly and they all watched the stitches.

"Okay. Feels good."

"Looks good," Bellmont said, reaching out and squeezing the skin a bit outside of the stitches. "If you'll wrap that up with some bandages, you are released."

Mister Zin showed up with a grim face.

"Well, Zin," Gunther said, "whatever did the wife say?"

"She, of course, does not wish for me to go anywhere. But my wife knows that we all need to know if help is coming or not, and we need to have good information. She agrees that getting information for us here is vital."

"It is," Erasimo said.

"And you will get great information from the Rio Lobos," Gunther said. "They have radios and are listening to all the transmissions. You would see a lot and hear a lot."

"Correct," Mister Zin said.

"So, you'll go?"

"I will go. I...I don't want to go, but I will go." Mister Zin turned to the doctors. "I am sorry that my real reason is information, and not to rescue you."

"It will still help us greatly, Mister Zin," Hedgecock said.

Gunther scanned the doctors' faces. Hedgecock and Telemore were excited. Bellmont was sedate.

Jefe stood and walked around the bed and group, shifting his weight leg to leg. He put his hands on his hips and declared, "I'm going with you, Zin."

Mister Zin seemed relieved at this.

Gunther nodded.

"I think if you wrap this up tight, you can go," Bellmont said.

"And there are medical supplies and a doctor on the Rio Lobos," Gunther said. "Zin, what do you think about this non-stop rifle fire outside? The rounds are just flying high through the air."

"The Boxers, Mr. Gunther. They are very superstitious. They think that they are shooting the evil demons in the air protecting us."

"Evil demons," Swoop muttered.

"Correct. They believe it will take hundreds of thousands of bullets to run them off."

"All those bullets have to land somewhere, onto...into... houses and people in Peking, somewhere," Erasimo said.

"Correct, but Boxers? They do not care. And unlike us, they have endless bullets to shoot."

"When should you leave? How?" Gunther asked.

"I have successfully, in the past, gone down the Tartar Wall into the dry channel and through the sluice gate, but it is now flooded from this rain."

"And you can't get that leg underwater, and in the muck and mud," Hedgecock warned Jefe.

Jefe nodded.

"Well, if you don't mind a shimmy," Swoop said, "we can drop you over the wall of one of these embassies by rope on drier land, and you can run into all the burned buildings out there right away."

"Shimmy?" Mister Zin repeated, unsure what that meant.

"Yeah. Climb down."

"Climb...down?" Mister Zin looked at Gunther's and

Jefe's faces.

"We can lower you down, Zin. Don't worry about it," Gunther said.

"I must ask you, Mr. Gunther. How much?"

"We will send you an additional $100 US dollars."

"I must ask you, Mr. Gunther, as my wife…she asked me to ask you. Can we come to America too?"

They all stared at Mister Zin, taken by surprise with this question.

"Mister Zin," Swoop interrupted, "life is very, very tough for Chinese people in the United States right now."

"Everywhere there?"

"I think everywhere."

"But there are Christians there. Chinese there. And churches of our Savior…"

"I know, but I am trying to warn you…I mean, Americans will not treat you well," Swoop warned.

"Zin, if you really, really want to, I can arrange that," Gunther said. "I know someone very high up in government that will make you, your wife and your kids, American citizens with…" he snapped his fingers, "the snap of a finger."

"Snap of a finger. Like that," Mister Zin repeated, with a big smile. "When you leave for America, can we leave with you?"

Thunder rolled outside, beating out the gunfire.

"If we all have to escape from here? It will be very dangerous for us as it is, you know this, and…and very dangerous for you, your wife and your children," Gunther said.

"Correct. We are ready."

"Or…we can arrange this trip after China is settled," Gunther added.

"China will never be settled," Mister Zin said. "We want to go with you. Now. With you all," he said, waving his hands over everyone.

"I don't know if we should leave now. They need us here," Bellmont interrupted.

Everyone turned to Bellmont, the silence revealed again the heavy rain and steady roar of floating-devil-killing gunfire outside.

"So, when do *we* leave? For the coast?" Jefe asked.

"We wait for the rain to stop? I hope this rain stops," Mister Zin said.

"No. The rain is good cover to get out of here," Swoop said. "Soldiers...guards...don't like the rain. Don't like standing in the rain."

"Okay. Tomorrow night. At 2 a.m.?" Mister Zin suggested. "I am now very excited to go and to get back. I will tell my wife to pack, so that when I return with news, we will know the Rio Lobos is there to take us to America." He said A-M-E-R-I-C-A with great fervor.

Mister Zin stood, bowed, and left the hospital.

"Well, he's motivated now," Erasimo said.

Gunther rubbed his face with both hands.

"Help! Help!" a woman caretaker cried out from across the hospital. A wounded soldier sat up and started vomiting blood.

The three doctors dashed across the floor.

"This...this," Gunther whispered, "just burrows deeper and deeper."

Gunther and Crippler jogged briskly in the rain to the British Legation and once inside the embassy could speak.

"Bellmont does not want to leave," she said.

218

"No, he doesn't. I may have to knock him out, tie him up and cart him away."

"I have to run," she said. "I am the star of the Laundry Committee, and, by the way, your clothes smell like a cow pasture. You need them cleaned."

"I'll wait till the rain stops."

She kissed him anyway at the bottom of the stairs. They no longer cared who was around watching them.

He climbed the stairs but stopped at the top floor, no longer able to sleep on the roof, tent, or no tent. He took off all his guns and knives and laid on a dirty blanket, his head on another sandbag. He shoved his strips of cloth in his ears to hold off the thunderous, devil killing, gunfire.

******

In the morning, the intense shooting stopped, but the storm continued. Down in the lobby of the embassy, Gunther poured himself a cup of tea and ate a small meat pie, no doubt made of horse.

"Sleep well? Sleep at all, Major?" an Englishman beside him asked.

"I did. I covered my head and stuffed my ears," Gunther said. He noticed the Brit was one of the college professors on the embassy staff.

"200,000!" the man declared.

"200,000?" Gunther repeated.

"The night of 200,000 shots. My colleagues and I have deduced that those bastards fired about 200,000 rounds over our heads, yesterday and last night." He stirred his tea with an elegantly carved silver spoon. Pinky up.

"You can cipher that out?" Gunther asked.

"Yes, it's simple mathematics, dear boy."

"My Chinese friend tells me they were shooting at evil demons hovering over the legation," Gunther said.

"Well, the buggers must be shot full of holes," the man said with a laugh. But methinks they are still up there laughing."

Gunther stepped outside to the paved sidewalk before the open patio of the courtyard, but just in from the rainfall.

"Major Gunther! Major Gunther!" came a man's voice from a distance.

Gunther turned to spot what he would call a rickshaw, a two-wheeled seated cart, pulled by a stout Chinese woman.

It was Semitagold in the covered seat, waving his hand. Gunther set down the teacup, ran through the rain and slipped in under hood for a seat next to the English commander.

"The Japanese," Semitagold said. "They crept out last night on a hunt for food. Damned if they didn't bag a Chinese officer."

"They did?"

"That they did, sir. They jumped him, stuffed his mouth, tied him up and put him in a big bag and hauled him in."

"He's a prisoner."

"That he is, my boy. We have had a few but none of this ranking. We might call him a colonel."

"Boxer?"

"Regular Chinese Army."

The barefoot, solid woman grunted and coughed as she pulled the vehicle across the legation. She stopped at the front gate of Japanese section. Gunther noticed Semitagold did not pay her. Gunther reached into a pants pocket and gave her a British pound. Semitagold noticed this and said in a huff, "We feed her and her mother every day, and that's enough of payment."

They crossed the front grounds and Semitagold led them to a two-story cement and tile building. Gunther read the long list of multi-national words beside the front steel doors and stopped reading when he saw the words, "Bank of Japan," in English.

It was a bank, but an empty bank. Three Oriental female tellers were still on duty behind a long counter, dressed for work in tidy white uniforms, apparently doing nothing but smoking cigarettes. There was an inch of rainwater flooding the place. A soldier led the pair to a back door and down a mini-waterfall of stairs.

Down the stairs there was a stone basement in a half a foot of water. The back wall was full of brass safety deposit boxes. The area stunk of stale, moist air. Five officers circled a desk and a man in a chair in the middle of a poorly lit room. A sweating, naked man in his 50s sat in the wooden chair. A desk was beside him. A mallet laid atop it, its one wooden head corner painted in red. But the closer Gunther got, he could see that the red "paint" was blood from the man's bashed hand, for it too was atop the desk. Tied down. Crushed. Flat.

Gunther could see every bone in that hand was mashed and broken. The appendage barely resembled a hand. The prisoner was in a state of shock, so weak and confused that his jaw hung slack. He shook not from the cold water covering his bare feet, but from nerves. He babbled quietly and nonsensically.

"What has he said?" Semitagold asked a Japanese commander.

"He said that our forces have taken the Taku Forts and the city of Tientsin. He said that the Queen Dowager Empress does not know what to do. Does she support the Boxers, as they are popular, or...not," the Japanese man said in perfect English.

The men tied the prisoner's other hand to the desk. One soldier shrieked and barked at him, and Gunther couldn't tell if it was in Japanese or Chinese.

"Well, he's shat himself now," Semitagold whispered to Gunther.

"He says that there are many generals outside our walls, assigned to sections. They do not all agree with each other as to what to do with us."

The Japanese interrogator hit the man's other hand with the mallet. After crying out, he said even more.

"He said that some, not all of the generals think they need a truce here. That our armies are coming north to Peking and they need us as prisoners here to perhaps barter."

"Hostages," Semitagold said.

"Yes."

"YAAAAHHHHH!" The man screamed. He stuttered out more information.

"He said that some of the generals will not accept a truce and will still attack us. Others will use the truce as time to restore their ammunition and build better walls around us."

Now exhausted, the man's head dropped low. He could only moan.

The Japanese commander nodded to the others. An officer drew his Samurai sword, lifted the katana high and with a deliberate practiced blow, chopped the Chinese officer's head off. It hit his knee and then rolled on the floor, splashing into the flood water.

"Do you believe him?" Semitagold asked.

"We believe so. Yes."

"How did you capture him?" Gunther asked, worried he was set up to be captured.

"Our men caught him 10 city blocks out. He was walking his dog and smoking a cigar."

"In the rain?"

"Yes."

"Alone?"

"He had an aide with him. He was killed."

Gunther nodded. He didn't ask about the dog.

The headless body then gave out and tumbled forward until it hung from the lashed arms to the desk.

"Thank you, sir, for your good work, help and information," Semitagold said.

The two climbed back up the wet stairs, crossed the bank lobby and left the building, where they were so deep in thought, the steady rain did not affect them.

"A coming truce that is not a truce," the Brit muttered.

"Yes."

They saw the woman and her rickshaw outside the gate, waiting.

"I guess the information is good," Gunther said.

"The poor bugger. If he was caught to mislead us? He paid for it dearly. Dearly. No jail cell for him. Just...just chop-CHOP! These...these Chinese...Chineeesssse! And the Japanese. They are...are strange brew in their ways. I am afraid I will never understand them as long as I live."

They climbed into the tight fit of the cart, and the sopping wet woman began the pull them back to the British legation.

"I guess we will await the word of the false truce, but at least we have more information that our Tommies have won down south and are in route."

"That is good news," Gunther said.

"Yeeesss, dear boy."

Chapter 19
The China Lure, the China Beauty, and the China Pain

At 2 a.m., a quiet group of men and two women congregated in the rain on the Russian Legation rooftop wall that bordered the outside world of Peking. Gunther, Swoop, Erasimo, the three doctors, Semitagold, his aide, Captain Yorkie, and a few of his Marines. Jefe and Zin. The two women were Mister Zin's wife who came to say farewell, and Crippler.

Jefe dressed as a common Chinaman, and Mister Zin dressed in his normal Chinese clothes and carried a soft, travel bag. Jefe had a brown duffel bag slung over his shoulder that contained clothes, some jerky, flare guns and ammo. Inside his big duffle he also had a sawed-off, lever-action rifle, that he'd been customizing in the Rio Lobos workshop this last day aboard. The barrel and stock were shortened so it would fit inconspicuously in the duffel, alongside his set of Filipino Arnis fighting sticks. Under his bulky jacket were three pistols and several knives.

The Marines tied off the ropes on rooftop pillars, while some peered over the edge of the roof, looking for Chinese guards or patrols. One corporal signaled the all-clear. A harness was fitted around Mister Zin.

"Find out all you can," Semitagold told Jefe. "Tell them we need help up here."

"I will, sir," Jefe said.

Captain Yorkie handed Jefe an envelope, very quickly protecting it from the rain.

"Hide this on your body," Yorkie said. "It is an official letter from me, telling the reader who you are and what you are doing. It's in English and most of the Chinese can't read it. The Marines are here, on the coast and probably marching this way, to quell this mess, they have to take Peking. This may get you out of trouble."

Jefe nodded and shoved the envelope inside his shirt.

Mrs. Zin hugged Mister Zin after the harness was secured around his chest. She tearfully whispered to him in Chinese. Mister Zin remained stoic, nodding his head.

Jefe approached Gunther and it looked like they were about to shake hands, but their hands passed and instead they gripped each other's forearms.

"My friend," Gunther said.

"My friend," Jefe said.

Jefe turned, grabbed up the rope and went over the wall, rapelling like an expert mountaineer. The Marines lifted Mister Zin's shaky legs and whisked him to the edge. He looked at Gunther on the way with changing expressions of fear and courage and then fear again. They hauled him over the wall and four Marines slowly lowered him down the 40 or some feet to the ground.

Gunther took off his hat and peeked over the top, the rain

quickly seeping through his hair and down his face. Jefe was already kneeling on the ground, searching the area. Mister Zin spun in slow circles as he descended, his eyes closed.

Crippler, now hatless too, joined Gunther, her long brown hair quickly saturated from rain.

"Will they be okay?" she reflexively said.

"Jefe is an amazing scout and a Filipino warrior. I think they will be fine. Maybe better than us left here?" He turned to look at her. Their faces were inches apart.

They donned their hats and the brims of their hats touched. The others began to leave the roof, the last to leave was the sniffling Mrs. Zin.

"Tomorrow, Johann," Crippler said.

"Tomorrow?"

"Tomorrow, we will have a courting. There will be a small concert by the Bell Tower and then..."

"And then?"

"And then, we will have our...our special date."

"You have...found a real bed?"

"I have. Mrs. Engelston's room in the British Legation."

"Where will poor Mrs. Engelston sleep?"

"She has hall duty in the building and the grounds. All night."

"Mrs. Engelston's loss is our gain. Does she..."

"Know? She...suspects, but she...approves."

"You know I too must keep up my sterling reputation as a West Point officer and a gentleman," Gunther whispered and kissed her, then said, "The wonderful, obliging, concerned, approving Mrs. Engelston."

Gossip of a pending truce of some sort was welcome news to the weary, and it traveled like the several inches of flooding waters through most of the legations. The positivity swirled around the evening concert. Some volunteers from different nations erected various sections of canvas tents with no side coverings that backed up to a stone wall of the clock tower. The steady rain pelted the top in a hum of popping sounds as various people free of duty arrived, dressed up as well as they could be, shaking and spinning the water from their umbrellas. An array of different sized and colored drinking glasses filled with water mixed with cornstarch and sugar lined several tables. Early arrivals, such as Suzannah Crippler and Johann Gunther had chairs up front, the rest in the rear were content to remain standing to observe any scrap of entertainment and escapism.

America's *"Fighten'*Parsons" were first on the stage, armed with lyric cheat sheets and banjos. They sang the "Star Bangled Banner", "America the Beautiful", various religious hymns like "Buried with Him in Aversion", "Fully Saved Today", and a few more popular tunes like "Oh Suzannah", at which point Gunther squeezed Crippler's hand. Some Brits took the floor and sang "God Save the Queen" and other songs. The Germans were next with "Watch on the Rhine" and other local favorites. An Austrian solider in uniform was next with a violin who played several beautiful pieces unlikely recognized by the attendees. Not to be outdone, some Russians rendered "Madame Pokolitov", and a few other of their local songs. A resplendently dressed Chinese woman from the suffering, nearby Fu grounds stepped up with two men who carried in a harp. She played an amazing song which reminded almost all of the culture, the confusion, the lure, the beauty and the pain of the grand China experiment. Then at the end, a wounded American Marine limped up with a bugle. He blew a solemn "Taps", and from most in attendance, tears fell like the pattering raindrops on the canvas cover above.

The show was over, but people remained seated and standing for a moment. Clapping. Then they gathered themselves up and left the clock tower grounds. Crippler took Gunther's hand and led him to the British Legation and into the chipped and battered embassy building. They passed and nodded to Mrs. Engelston, climbed the stairs, and entered her room. It was small, dark, and musty, with the outer wall and window lined up with the sandbags of different materials and colors.

There was wine! As the elite members of each legation still had some bottles stored away. They drank, they undressed slowly, and Crippler descended upon Gunther on the bed, her long brown hair and body engulfing his world.

Later, Mrs. Engelston on her guard duty made the rounds of the outside perimeter and the insides, floor by floor. As she passed her room door, she heard Gunther whisper, "Oh Suzannah…oh, Suzannah…" She stopped for a few seconds and smiled.

******

Morning. Still raining. Random gunshots outside. Gunther and Crippler lay on their sides, facing each other.

"I am betrothed," she said.

"You told me."

"I will be marrying a man in Nebraska."

"As you said."

"Yes."

"Are you…feeling guilty?" Gunther asked.

"Yes and no."

"Are you officially engaged?"

"Not yet…officially. Expected."

"Okay. Well. you know…this is not a good conversation for a man to hear a morning after we did what we did. And so well."

"I know, but…"

"You must remind me," Gunther said.

"I must. He is a very good man."

"And I am not."

"You are too. You are, but you are different. You are…look at you. Look at what you do."

"I won't do this forever."

She dropped heavily on her back in the bed, in a frustration, with a sigh. She stared at the ceiling.

"You will probably do something the like this forever. Ernest…"

"His name is Ernest?" Gunther asked.

"Yes. Ernest. Is a very stable man. He is a farmer from a good, big family. He is an excellent business manager. Our families are long-time friends. He is someone…"

"Who is stable."

"Yes. He is like a very stout…like a stout, farm horse. You are like a wild horse or, or better a racehorse. The Army has barely tamed you."

Now Gunther laid on his back. She grabbed his hand.

"The importance of being Ernest," Gunther mumbled.

"The importance of…?"

"…being Ernest. It's a play by Oscar Wilde. English, but run in America, too."

"I'll have to see it someday," she said.

"And I will dream of taking you."

"Have you thought about having children, Johann Gunther?" she asked.

"Well, no, I haven't…"

"Do you believe in the fear of God, Johann Gunther?" she asked.

"This must be very serious questions, because you are using my full name."

"Do you?"

"Ahh, well…" he stuttered.

"You must have taken oaths. You were a deputy. You are a soldier. You have sworn in with the word of God."

"I have, I have, but…I haven't thought about it too much."

Silence.

"I gather your Ernest is religious?" he asked.

"He is. Quite. He is a Baptist. He is very busy with…"

"Suzannah?"

Knock, knock, knock.

"Suzannah?" It was Mrs. Engelston.

"Yes?" and Crippler, naked, ran to the door and opened it an inch.

"Suzannah, Semitagold is looking for Gunther and all the military leaders. It's an emergency. He…he is still here?"

"Um, yes. Thanks, I will tell him." She shut the door, turned to see Gunther already pulling his pants on. She rested against the door and watched.

In a moment, Gunther was full dressed and buckling his

gun belt. He walked up to the door and kissed her.

"Must go," he said. "Racehorse business."

She stepped back and he left. The door closed and she leaned her naked back against the door again and stood there for several minutes, thinking about Johann Gunther.

Chapter 20
The Maze of China Maize

When Jefe rappelled the last few feet from his rope the night before, he dropped to a knee and scoured the terrain. Silence. Nothing. The trampled road outside the wall was wide and flat, next to burned out and blown apart houses and businesses. Mister Zin touched down and unwrapped himself from his harness, mimicked Jefe and kneeled beside him. Then the two ran off into the destroyed landscape.

They ran when they could in alleys, peered around corners, raced in splashes across wet roads, all the time, seeing no one. Mister Zin kept up with Jefe well, though Jefe, ever the scout, stayed ahead of him some 6 or 8 feet.

At times, Mister Zin whispered to Jefe and motioned him back, warning him of the bigger buildings ahead and smart places for Boxer headquarters. Each time he was correct, and they avoided those areas.

On the outskirts of a city border they stayed within some rocks and under some trees, sheltered a bit from the rain.

"Which way?" Jefe asked.

"This is the first field of a park, and it runs south for a few miles. Then there are woods, then is a vast plain, you say in English. Flatland. Is 'plain' right?"

"Yes. Plain is de right word."

"No trees. Miles and miles. It is planted with maize. This maize grows 14 feet high. There are hundreds of trails between them. But you cannot see the trail next to you, as you go."

Jefe was listening but he pulled his compass out of his pocket, leveled it, thumped it with a finger and in the darkness tried to read it. He leaned in, his eyes inches away to see the needle. South was through the park and the maze of maize.

"Are de trails straight? North and south."

"Mostly. They are crooked because we Chinese believe that evil spirits fly in straight lines, and crooked rows and roads prevent the passage."

Jefe nodded. "In the Philippines, we have many such ideas. We have de past of Muslim, Hindu, and Buddhist beliefs. Then de Spanish brought many Catholics. But we still have much witchcraft and superstitions."

"Yes! What are you?"

"I am a Muslim," Jefe said.

"I am now a Catholic. My wife and I."

"Yes," Jefe said, "and may peace be with the both of us when this is over," Jefe smiled and patted a hand atop Zin's hand for a second.

"Correct!" Mister Zin said.

They stood and walked to the edge of the park and its vegetation and headed due south.

"This is a shorter way than the main road to Peking we took from the coast. But it will be rough."

"We cannot take de main roads, anyway."

******

Sunrise came, and with it, the end of the rain. The sky was clear and blue, and with it the promise of humid heat. The dawn brought tens of workers with plows, hoes, mules, wagons, and carts. They tended the maize fields.

"We will just keep walking, like we are Chinese visitors. Travelers."

Jefe noted that the maize was indeed *very* tall. Eight feet and maybe even 10 feet in height.

They passed the growing numbers of workers unnoticed. Mister Zin selected a row in the crops and marched in. The road was muddy and flooded in areas. Not the slightest of breeze existed and the wet heat intensified as the sun rose higher in the sky.

"Whew!" Jefe said, loosening his clothes and squirming under the duffle bag, backpack.

"Correct! It is very hot day."

There was some brief respite as they crossed an occasional intersection to catch a breeze. There were more farmers with ladders and wagons working. The crossroads still remained slightly curved to disturb the evil spirits.

The zipping sound of a bullet ripping through rows of maize was new to Jefe. He spun his head to the crackling. Then came the blast, muffled by the tall growth.

"Down!" Jefe yelled in English.

Mister Zin dropped but the nearby workers froze and looked astonished. Zin warned them in Chinese, but it was too late for some. Bullets pounded into some of them, knocking them off their feet.

Then the roaring gunfire of war erupted to their west. Even through the maize Jefe could discern the sounds of Chinese firearms versus Western weapons. Jefe waved his hand to Zin, encouraging him to crawl and follow him. Mister Zin, new to crawling had difficulty covering the muddy ground.

Forty feet. Fifty feet. One hundred feet. They passed cowering farmers. Some wounded, crying and howling. A few dead. All from random gunfire. Jefe grabbed a farmer's fallen, double ladder and dragged it with him.

Two hundred feet south. Bullets flying through maize remained north of them. Jefe stood, opened the ladder. It was a six-footer and ran up the steps, until…the mud gave way and the ladder tumbled over, pitching the Filipino in the air and into wet ground. He rolled with a grunt, got up and reset the ladder, testing its stability. Mister Zin remained flat in a puddle.

Jefe scaled the ladder. At the top he couldn't see much, but in the Northwest, he could spot tall, colorful, Chinese war pennants and a bit south, India and US flags. A small war was unleashing about half a mile away.

Back on the slippery ground, Jefe grabbed Mister Zin's arm and stood him up. Workers were now limping and running past them to escape.

"Let's go. Come on," Jefe said.

They got a few steps down the trail, rounded a corner to see the stalled farmers that had passed them, standing, some with their hands up.

Jefe and Mister Zin slowed, but it was too late. Ahead, about 20 Boxers stood, rifles aimed at all of them. And, to their left through the maize more Boxers appeared, rifles up and at the ready.

"We are fighting for China!" one Boxer proclaimed.

"We are fighting for our country," yelled another. If the devils win, they will kill you all slowly anyway."

"The enemy is killing us now, over there!" another said pointing to the west.

The other Boxers handed out some pistols and rifles to the workers. They came around giving Jefe and Mister Zin rifles. Jefe was covered in mud, and his Filipino features were somewhat masked. Mister Zin held the rifle in disgust, as though it was covered in poison.

"We are ordering you now to help us fight the foreign devils," a leader said, waving a curved sword. "You *will* help us!"

"Now!" said another.

"Now!" said yet another.

Jefe felt the tip of a sword on his back, shoving him into the maize. Others were poked and prodded inside the row of crops. It looked like Jefe was going to be forced into shooting his allies, or be killed?

Chapter 21
Ride a Wild China Monsoon

Emergency? Gunther trotted out of the building in time to spot Semitagold and some 12 military officers from various armies leaving the British compound and heading for the Legation Street barricade. He followed them, running up to the leader. Semitagold was adorned in his British uniform and sporting a cavalry sword on his belt, sans guns.

"Good, they found you," Semitagold said.

"Where we going?" Gunther asked.

"A grisly place I'm afraid. Into Peking."

Gunther made a perplexed face.

"We have been invited to a truce meeting. There." He pointed ahead to a large red and yellow, newly constructed tent on the far side of the barricade wall that they could see over the barricades.

Ahead, Erasimo and others were opening a final passage in the thick debris of the street barricade. Erasimo raised his eyebrows when spotting Gunther and Gunther could only reply with his own quizzical expression, as he did not know what would happen. With great effort the last walkway was cleared, as tangled wood and metal furniture, fencing and wagons were dismantled. They walked on around the makeshift, crisscross security walls to the outside avenue, to see several hulking Chinese soldiers with folded arms at each corner of the rectangular structure. Other soldiers armed with rifles stood nearby.

"Is this a good idea?" Gunther asked.

"I don't know, my dear boy, and I am glad you are here. I did not invite the top military leaders for this, just some underlings from each army, in case this all goes bad there will still be experienced leaders left."

"I see."

"Yes, dear boy. You are expendable! As am I. But I have been exchanging messages with a military diplomat Tsang Wee and there seems to be an opportunity for a truce. We are at wit's end here and I think we should forge on. See what they have to say."

Right behind Gunther and the group, the force protection men charged up to the barricade, ready to fight against a surprise invasion if need be.

Expressionless, two Chinese guards opened the golden-fringed tent entrance and Semitagold strutted in with a stern expression, followed by the others. The interior of the tent was musty and hotter than outside. It contained a large ornate table and 10 velvet chairs in the carpeted middle. The tent walls were bordered by long pieces of dark wooden, carved furniture resembling dressers. In the far corner of the tent, three women busily set out cups and checked on a stove and boiling water.

"Gentlemen!" an older Chinese man at the end of the table said. "My name is Tsang Wee." He stood, smiled, and waved them to the table. To his left on the table was a tall stack of what appeared to be newspapers. Near him stood a high-ranking

Chinese Army officer, about 50 years old with a long mustache hanging down off his chin, something Texan Gunther would call a "longhorn mustache". Unlike Wee, the man was not friendly. Not smiling. He wore a black short robe under his weapon's belt. On the robe was a red design drawn to look like artwork on a wax stamp.

Some of the officers took seats at the table, but Gunther and a few chose to remain standing by some of the dressers, facing Wee and this hulking bodyguard.

"Good day, good day," Wee said.

"Good day," Semitagold said.

"Thank you for coming. First, may I offer you any green tea?"

None of the men accepted, likely fearing poison.

Wee looked at their expressions as a woman handed him a cup of tea. He sipped it and smiled.

"Here. I would like to offer you these newspapers from your various countries, that our embassy has collected. United States. England. Italy. France. I am sad to report that your Italian political leader has died, ah, died. Ah, passed away, as you say?"

The Italian captain grimaced.

"It is all in the newspapers," Wee said, and he pointed to the stack on the table. I am prepared to offer you some food and other supplies."

"Thank you," Semitagold said. "Why now have you offered us this truce?"

"Ahhh well, we have been talking about your truce, off and on, and we have offered more than once, to escort you to safety on the coast."

"Given the stories of your butchery, Mr. Wee, your sniping

and bombardments, we are hesitant to take your offer."

"Yes…yes well, I will confess that I…we are not in total control of all the Boxers here. And the leaders of various Chinese army units…well…they seem to have their own minds. One general wants peace you know. Another general wants…ahhh… to kill you all," Wee said with a smile.

"You then see my problem," the Brit said.

"General Heeung here is one such general who is very mad? Mad is the word? Angry? And wishes you harm."

"YOU!" the general stepped up. "You are not welcome here. If it were up to me to do…I would slay you all like dogs!" He growled this out in broken English.

"Oh, oh, now, you see my problem, Mr. Semitagold."

"I quite see," Semitagold said calmly and quietly.

"I have already killed many of you," the general continued. "I have killed your missionaries, one by one. The fathers first. Then the mothers. Then the children. By sword! I will get 85,000 soldiers and attack this place of yours, and skin you all alive."

Gunther wanted to shoot the general right in the mouth with his .38. Instead, he leaned on a tall piece of furniture, pushing his left hip outward, throwing back his jacket and exposing one of his two guns on his gun belt. The general glared at him. Gunther didn't blink.

Semitagold saw this exchange and said, "I do think I will have some of that tea. Yeees."

"Please, yes," Wee said.

The women scurried to oblige.

"So, you see my problem, gentlemen. I am riding atop a monsoon. I wish no trouble. But I…I cannot control these natures. These forces of nature, as you say."

"And *our* armies?" Semitagold asked.

"Ahhh. I am told that they think you are all dead already," Wee said with a feigned sadness. "Your armies are here. They are fighting on the coast and in Tientsen. And I must report, not doing so well."

"I see," Semitagold said, sipping his tea.

"What I propose is a truce. I can supply you with some food. And I will, during the truce, try to control the good general here and these other angry generals and prepare for you the safest, best escort out of here."

"How will you deliver this food?"

"Oh, right at the barricade outside, of course."

"Well then, Sir..." Semitagold stood up, "...we thank you for your efforts in controlling the...the forces of nature. We also appreciate the food. We of course would like to leave your country if this can be arranged."

"Truce? Then?" Wee said.

"Truce," Semitagold said.

They shook hands and bowed.

The others stood.

"Good day to you. And," Semitagold turned to the ladies and bowed, "and thank you for the tea."

They almost giggled but restrained themselves and bowed back.

"The newspapers!" Wee reminded, and two soldiers split the stack and carried them out.

As all the men left the tent, Gunther waited until Semitagold passed and he left too.

"Were you going to shoot that chap?" the Brit said out of the corner of his mouth.

"Yes, but I didn't think we would get out of there alive."

"Indeed. He was there to scare us."

"Indeed," Gunther repeated. "What do you think?"

"I think…we are all hostages to be traded for."

"Yup."

Anxious legation faces awaited their return as the news had spread about the meeting. Gunther saw Crippler, arms folded, craning her neck, along with the others searching for him. He waved. She nodded and stepped off to the side. Once all were inside, Erasimo helped with rebuilding the barricade. Gunther stopped where Crippler waited beside a grove of trees and in the shade. Military, civilians, men, woman, and children followed Semitagold like he was the Pied Piper, hungry for any news.

"What was all that?" Crippler asked Gunther.

"A truce, Suze," he said, "but for how long and what kind? I don't know. I think…we think…we are now just hostages to be traded. Probably our troops are advancing, and the Chinese government needs a bartering ace up their sleeve."

Semitagold stopped in the mid-British courtyard, turned, and advised the crowd some of the developments, not his suspicions. The people were amazed at the sight of newspapers and the hope of some peace.

"We'll read these newspapers for any information we can glean, then post them on the belltower as soon as we can. Now if you will please excuse us, we have much to think about, much work to do, as do you all?"

"When will the food come?" a man yelled. "What kind of food?"

Semitagold turned back to say, "I am to presume… CHINESE food, dear boy!"

Chapter 22
Death on the China Road

The Boxers shoved Jefe, Zin, and the farmers northeast toward the gunfire. One shirtless farmer dropped his gun and tried to run off, but he was shot down by a Boxer. A rifle round hit the right side of his torso and tore him off his feet. He landed, first in shock, then in screaming agony.

"Come on! Come on," the Boxers insisted.

Jefe kept going with the group, but steered himself toward the lethally wounded farmer, slowing down near him. The man was squirming mostly on his back, yelling out inarticulately for help. Jefe saw his naked torso, the bullet hit him in the spine and exited like an explosion out his stomach. He was bleeding profusely. Legs still – disconnected. His guts were destroyed. He was doomed to die a dismal death in the stinking wet, mud. Jefe lifted his Boxer rifle and shot him in the head, ending his misery.

With the explosion, all the Boxers and farmers stopped and turned. Jefe remained expressionless and resumed his pace, in an effort to be ignored for what he'd done. He did not forget which Boxer murdered the farmer. Somehow, he would kill him too.

The small war was nearing ahead and to their left, through some rows of tall maize. Jefe saw no way out for the farmers, Mister Zin, and his mess. What could he do versus this group of spread out enemy soldiers?

But then, a lung shaking, horrible thrashing, roar sounded. Jefe grabbed Mister Zin's shoulder and tossed him face down as he dove down beside him. The thick maize rows to their left, were being splintered and cut in half from a machine gun. Jefe recognized the pounding kill sound of the Maxim machine gun.

It ripped through about six of the Boxers behind them, and several of the shocked farmers, virtually cutting two of them in half just as if they were maize. The belly high wave of high caliber rounds at some 450 per minutes zipped over Jefe and Mister Zin's head and tore north. Alerted, the remaining boxers and farmers dove ahead of the mayhem.

"Shoot back!" a Boxer ordered.

From a prone and then kneeling position once the machine gun scourge passed them, they shot west without visible targets, without aim into the maize, from whence they assumed the machine gun attack originated. The farmers did also. Mister Zin did not. Jefe rolled onto his back, pulled his two pistols from under his baggy shirt and got up on his feet. He ran up the line behind the men. He passed the farmers and picked off the heads of the prone and kneeling Boxers. The first three didn't see him, but the upcoming four Boxers began catching the motion and sounds behind and beside them and saw by their sides, their comrades' heads splinter and drop forward. The deafening Maxim in the distance had weakened their ears.

Each Boxer turned to see Jefe and they began a twist of their torsos to shoot him. Jefe swung out on the path even wider making them twist backward even more. And never missing, one by one, Jefe, from his right pistol then his left, then his right and left, blew holes in their faces and heads. One of them was the Boxer who killed the farmer.

Then Jefe kneeled and reloaded as he shouted to the farmers in Chinese, "Go! Run! Go. Go!"

The land men abandoned their guns on the ground, scrambled to their feet and ran off through the rows of maize behind them.

Mister Zin remained on the mud, watching as Jefe stood, holstered his gun, and buttoned his bulky shirt.

"You alright?" Jefe asked.

"Correct!" Mister Zin said.

But they weren't really "alright". Five rows of maize were shot down by the Maxim, leaving stalks about 4 feet tall. Jefe looked over the 40 feet to his left to see about 50 U.S. Marines in their tan uniforms, their unique Western-style tan hats, rifles, and gun belts, on that trail, glaring at him.

Jefe raised his hands in surrender.

"U.S. Army! Don't shoot!" Jefe shouted.

But several of the Marines raised their rifles shoulder high and leaned in to take their own kill shot...

Chapter 23
The Carrier China Dog Powwow

Several wagons of bread, meat and vegetables appeared at the barricade each day, along with the friendly faces of Chinese citizens and even official soldiers. It was not uncommon, while extremely odd before the truce, that even in this siege environment some of the Chinese soldiers or citizens would at times try to walk up to the walls, talk to the legation guards, even pass them some eggs or tobacco, then be shooting at them hours later or the next day from down the street.

Gunther and Erasimo watched the international "gate" guards haul back the right side of the street barricade, where they grabbed the neck yokes and pulled the big carts inside. Hand waves were exchanged. Thanks, said in several languages.

Gunther took note of the zigzag breastwork walls that were built on their side to slow any invasion down into tight, turning corners and furthermore create a quagmire trap for any intruders trying to dash their way in. The pathway was about 15 feet across. But since the truce, to facilitate these deliveries, a straight path all the way through was opened way on the right side, protected by only one wall.

"Any day, it could all be poisoned," Erasimo mentioned of the food.

"Any day. I reckon you all can extend these zigzag barricades back all the way to the right?"

"Yes, *sirree*, we can. Are they still shooting at us from the north side?" Erasimo asked.

"Yup. It's let up a bit," Gunther said. "But that general over there still wants a war going on, it seems. We're shooting back on occasion. And on the southwest side, too. Our lookouts report that the Chinese are busy re-fortifying their positions."

"You West Point fellers call it, 'a truce to reload', huh?"

"That we did. There's a rich history of it."

"We still get hit with the wide mix of ancient and modern weapons up here. Liable to have anything from arrows to Krupp shells slamming in. Some Boxers throw bricks and stones over the barricades. Others set off packs of firecrackers. You know… just to make us nervous.

Before the guards rebuilt the barricade, a Chinese man walked up with a German Shepard looking, "mixed" dog. The dog wore a red vest with large pockets on each side containing papers. The man stopped and the dog continued into the legation property, welcomed by some British aides of Semitagold. They kneeled and petted the happy, tail-wagging dog and it turned down the avenue, bound for Semitagold's headquarters. The dog followed.

"Comes every day or so, Wee and Semitagold trade messages with that dog," Erasimo said. "The dog seems to love it. I hear the Brits pet it and feed it, then another message gets packed in the vest and off the dog goes back to Peking."

"Not a carrier pigeon. A carrier dog," Gunther said.

"It's...China! Upside down!"

"Yup."

"How's Swoop doing?" Erasimo asked.

"He's on the Tartar Wall all day and night unless there's an alarm of night invaders."

"He's as tough as a woodpecker's lips. I haven't seen him since Jefe and Zin left. Need to go parley with the old bastard."

"I wonder," Gunther said, "I wonder if he might consider staying on here?"

"Huh? Hmm. Well, he has his real problems back home. *Whatcha thinkin'*, Major?"

"Nothing much, right now. Just *thinkin'*."

"What about the docs?" Erasimo asked.

"Okay. They're okay. I check in on them every day. Since the cannon fire and shootings have slowed, they are catching up on the patients."

"No medical supplies in these shipments?"

"None," Gunther said.

"Telling."

"I guess."

"Look at those newspapers any?"

"I did. There's no news about China in any of them, but there are pages missing in each paper. Cut out with scissors," Gunther said.

"Telling."

"How's that Crippler woman?"

"She fine. She's..." Gunther stepped back about seven steps and smiled, jerking his head toward the tallest British building.

Erasimo's eyes followed him and looked up. Off in the

distance, there was Suzannah Crippler on the roof, looking over the landscape with a pair of binoculars.

"I would not care to fall under her sights," Erasimo said.

Gunther smiled, knowing that Crippler had all kinds of different sights to fall under.

Erasimo walked through some guards over to stone shelves on a building wall and grabbed a *goat's bladder*, bota bag. He rested his rifle on the wall and screwed open the cap on the end, lifted it high and drank some. He offered Gunther some, but he shook his head, no.

"Wine!" Erasimo said.

"Too hot a day to drink hot wine."

"Hum! Short powwow," Erasimo said, looking past Gunther. He moved to open the passage, where two aides were walking back with a happy dog.

On the far side, the Chinese escort briskly approached the opening. No words were exchanged between the dog walkers. The dog passed through, and they left. The guards reconstructed the main barricade.

******

When the deluge of rain stopped, Gunther returned to sleeping on the roof, a few stories higher than most of the mosquitos, fleas and flies traveled, and cooler. Crippler also slept with him now, showing up that first return-to-rooftop, rain-free night. She built a net over them to help against the few higher-flying bugs.

If they weren't exhausted from chores and patrols, if they had baths in cool water from one of the five wells on the grounds and the one designated for bathing, they made love. The first time on the roof, Crippler seriously said, once again, it was the last time. Then the next time was also the *last* time. Then the times after that, she continued to say it, but it became a joke. They would stack a few colored sandbags on the roof hatch to prevent embarrassing interruptions.

She also built a sandbag wall in one corner to hide a small fire and they brewed some green tea each night.

"This is a lot like camping out on the range with my Daddy and the boys," she told him, sitting "Indian-style" on the rooftop, eating cookies, and holding a metal cup."

"Did you do much of that?"

"Yes. Until they laid tracks for the railroad, right up to our yards."

"And someday, you will run all of that, huh?"

"Yes. Now that my sister is gone, I will run it all. The food business. The restaurant businesses. Cattle business."

"Can you?"

"I can," she said positively.

"How will your father handle the death of your sister?"

"He will be...he'll be crumbled. His heart will be crumbled. I have to live through all of this, Johann, because if he lost the two of us...in China! Over vanilla and spice sales? He would crumble into bits of nothing. I hate the thought of telling him. Where are your parents, Johann?"

Gunther finished his tea and laid back on a sandbag. "Suze, I don't know."

"You don't know?"

"When we got to New York City from Germany, we were with a bunch of Germans kinfolk. We were all cramped up in tenement in the Bronx. My mother and father told me that I was to stay with these people, and they were continuing West… out West…for…to…build a future. Our future. They left one day, and I've never seen them again."

"When was this?"

"1883. The Spring of 1883."

"What did you do?"

"At 15, I joined the Army. The first time. Lied about my age. Stationed in Oklahoma. Just a… a cavalry man. *Fightin'* Indians and outlaws. Parading around. Mustered out in 88, became a deputy in Northeast Texas. Paris, Texas, for about 6 years. I…I then…it's a long story Suze…but I solved a whole bunch of murders in the region. The KKK came after me…"

"Oh my…"

"Yeah. They almost killed me in an ambush shoot-out in Oklahoma. They put a bounty on my head. KKK-wide. Two governors got me a spot in West Point to get me far away from them all. Four years away in New York State. That's the second time around for me and the Army. This time, Cuba. The Philippines and here I am now."

"And you never looked for your parents?"

"I've been kind of busy. And after a while, I quit thinking about it."

"My word," she said. "You have lived a strange man's life. Ever think about that?"

"No. No, I don't."

"It's not a happy life, Johann."

"I am happy right now. Right here with you."

She put the cup down and laid beside him. Without the net up they had a clear view of the moon and the star-enriched sky.

"Can you dance?" she asked.

"A little. There were balls at West Point, and we all had to attend."

"Where did the ladies come from?"

"New York. All over. Officers' families."

"I suppose you're a *helleva* dancer?"

"I am. Well, men are usually a few dance steps behind women in dancing…and in life. In general. But we had to ballroom dance at West Point. I can do that."

"I can imagine you in your West Point uniform, Major Gunther," she said.

"Cadet Gunther. At the time."

"I wouldn't know whether to slap you or kiss you."

He shook his head and smiled at that.

"Have you ever been happy?" she asked.

"I have been happy a few times, I reckon," he said. "Yes. I usually read a lot of books. I like music. I *kinda'* like the Army. I liked being at West Point. I didn't think I would, but I did. I like to study. Learn things. And for some reason, it interests me to work on how to shoot and fight. You know, it's all fun."

"Fun…"

"Yes, fun. I learned some French Savate from my old Texas police chief – he was from France."

"Savate?"

"Yes. A French fighting system. And Jefe is an expert in Filipino Kali, another fighting system, and we exercise it when we can."

"What about Germany?" she asked.

I was a very happy kid in Germany, growing up. I remember

that very well. Being a kid. Funny *lookin'* knickers. It was...is... very different from America. But my parents and their friends insisted we leave for America. The American dream. It's a tough dream in a tough land. I don't think I wound up living the American dream they had envisioned."

"You mean a life of...of adventure isn't the dream?"

"Killing people is no dream," he mumbled.

"I live the American dream," she said wistfully. "If I can get back to it."

"Back to the ranch," Gunther spoke for her, "the restaurants, back to the business. Back to...Ernest."

"Oh, shusssh-up."

"And Ernest, what would he think of all this? Us? Here?"

"I'll never tell him."

"Ernest...being so religious and all, has he ever fooled around with a woman?" he asked.

"You call this just *foolin'* around?"

"No. I don't," he answered quickly.

"I doubt that Ernest has ever...*been*...with a woman before."

"And then, does he expect you to be a virgin, too?"

"I expect he expects so."

"And he won't know?"

"I don't think he knows how to know," she said.

"And...your wedding night? You'll be like a master chef without any cooking lessons?"

She laughed a bit at that and said, "Am I a master chef?"

"Ma'am, you are master-sous chef."

Just a bit embarrassed, she smiled at that. "I will cross that bridge with him when we get there."

"You're a smart woman," Gunther said.

"You're no master chef," she said with a tease, "more like a chuck wagon cook in a cattle drive..."

"Oh well, thanks for the compliment, ma'am. Now, pass the beans."

"But you'll do. Don't you have any girlfriends? I'll bet you have lots of girlfriends."

"Nope. In the last 5 years I have been in West Point, Cuba, and the Philippines. Some girls...around, but no girl-*friends*. I had girlfriends in Texas. My last two years at West Point, we had a lot of weekends off. Some of us would take a train to New York City. I met a few girls. Saw plays, concerts."

"That when you saw this 'Important Ernest' play?"

"Yup. And Shakespeare..."

"Oh, very *flowerdy*' speech," she said. "So then, you had some Yankee girlfriends in New York?"

"Yes."

"What happened to them?"

"I don't know. They are probably all married by now. Kids. I am a *looonng* forgotten memory. Lest ways, I hope so."

"I'll bet they still daydream about you."

"Oh, I *highly* doubt it."

"What exactly did you do with these girls in New York City?"

"Well like I said, plays, walks in Central Park. Restaurants. Just about everything you do with a girl in New York City," he said.

"Oh, every...thing?"

"My secret plan in life is to find very smart, beautiful women, trick them into liking me, then making me smarter."

She slugged his arm. "Is *that* what's going on here?"

"Exactly."

"It is highly unlikely that I will ever forget you, Johann Gunther."

"It is highly, *highly* unlikely I will ever forget you, oh, Suzannah."

******

In the mornings they had more tea and posted themselves with binoculars at the walls to survey what might have changed through the night. Each day they saw more Chinese fortifications, barricades, machine gun and cannon nests.

One morning they awoke and scanned the horizon to see even more entrenchments.

"Look at the birds!" she said. "Flocks of birds. They are coming back."

They looked skyward to see hundreds of birds in various groups swarming here and there.

"We'd better hide our teabags," Gunther said.

They watched the flocks of bird, twist and turn in a freestyle unison way above them.

Then the two returned their watch to ground level.

"Those black flags and pennants," he said.

"I see them," she said. "They are everywhere. Overnight!"

"That red logo is the same one as the Chinese general wore in our first, so-called, truce meeting in the tent on Legation Avenue. He's hell bent on killing all of us."

"The one with the longhorn mustache?" she said.

"Yeah. All this, it's all a...truce to reload," Gunther said. "The birds will be leaving again. Very soon."

256

Chapter 24

Howling Jack McGovern on the Peking Trail

"Don't shoot! I'm with the U.S. Army!"

Some of the Marines ran through the chopped rows of Maize at them. Mister Zin stood up and ran beside Jefe.

"Get your hands up," Jefe ordered. Zin did.

The Marines got closer, but many found the rows of crops very difficult to cross. They stopped about 15 feet away.

"Get over here!" one ordered, and the two, hands held high, crossed the rows until they were standing before the wide trail of Marines.

Jefe looked north and south to see tens if not hundreds of Marines, horses, and wagons. He couldn't help but smile.

"Something funny to *ya*?" A stocky sergeant said.

"Good to see relief," Jefe said.

Three of the Marines that coaxed the two off the side road, threw Jefe and Mister Zin onto the mud, but Jefe stood right back up. Zin pushed himself up knee-high.

"I am Lt. Jefe Cocoy, 9th Filipino Scout, augmented to *de* United States Army. Major Johann Gunther and I were sent here to rescue three doctors shanghaied and kidnapped by *de* Boxers." Jefe tried to rub some of the mud off his face. The men squinted at the process.

"Filipino?" a Marine said.

"Yes! I am with the U.S. Army."

They didn't believe him.

"Then who's the Chink?" another said.

"Hi name is Zin. He works for *de* Legations, *de* embassies in Peking you are going to rescue. Your people. He is a messenger and now a spy for us. Helping us. A Chinese Christian. We were also sent from there to tell you they are alive and need great help. They are under siege now. Under gun and cannon fire very day. Running out of food. Running out of medical supplies."

"So, then you speak Spanish?" a Marine with a heavy Hispanic accent asked him.

"Si," Jefe said. "Tagalog. Spanish. Some Chinese. And English. I graduated *de* University of Madrid, Spain."

The Marine rattled off a question in Spanish. Jefe answered him back in Spanish and the Marine nodded to his team. "How many Chinese speak Spanish?" the Marine said.

"I don't believe him," the sergeant said, raising his rifle.

"Wait! Wait!" Jefe said. "I have a letter from a Marine captain. Captain Yorkie." He slowly reached inside his shirt and pulled out the envelope.

"Let me see that!" the sergeant growled and snatched it from Jefe's hand.

Others gathered around, and some more Marines walked over to them.

"What's going on here, Sergeant?" a captain asked.

"Sir, these two chinks claim they work for the U.S. Army,

258

and..."

"I do," Jefe interrupted.

"SHUT UP! They come *outta'* the crop lines over there where them Boxers were shooting at us, sir."

"And I killed seven of *de* Boxers," Jefe said.

Mister Zin nodded and said, "He did!"

"Seven? With what?" a Marine said.

Jefe slowly opened his bulky shirt to expose two US Army issued, Colt revolvers on a gun belt. The Marines started to mumble among themselves.

"And they say they have a letter from some Captain Yorkie *sayin'* so, sir," a Marine corporal offered.

The sergeant looked up from the letter and at them. He started to tear it into pieces. Jefe grimaced with each tear. "But I don't believe *'em*," he growled and lifted his rifle.

With this weapon lift, the group's aggressive positioning intensified. The sergeant aimed at the kneeling Mister Zin's chest. Jefe stepped right in front of Zin.

"He has done nothing but help *de* legations," Jefe said. "And the Americans. Risking his life. He does not deserve to die. He is a Christian with a wife and children, trying to help us."

The nearby Captain thought this sudden act of selfless protection odd. He leaned in and pushed the sergeant's rifle down.

"Now wait a minute," the captain said. "Did you say Captain Yorkie?"

"Yes, sir," Jefe said.

"Where do you know Yorkie?" he asked.

"First, from the Philippines, sir. I have fought *de* Insurrectionists beside him in Manila. Army and Marines together. I have been sent here with an Army Major Gunther to rescue three

American doctors from de Boxers who were shanghaied from California. We found them, but had to flee, sir, to Peking where we have been now for three weeks. Under siege. There, we met many soldiers and Marines from many armies. And our friend, Captain Yorkie was there with a contingent of Marines. He is six foot tall, blond, but losing his hair all around the top of his head."

"Where's he from in the States?" one asked.

"I don't know," Jefe said.

The Marines stood aghast at the story.

"We have a gunboat off *de* coast...to rescue *de* doctors... waiting for us and we thought de ship might leave us, so...so I am a trained scout and I volunteered to go to *de* boat, and Mister Zin...Mister Zin brought us first to rescue *de* doctors, then escape to Peking. And now he is helping me get back to *de* coast. To de boat. We hope it is still there! He knows *de* way back to *de* coast!"

Silence.

"It is...was...all in *dat* letter!" Jefe said angrily, looking at and pointing to the torn scraps melting into the wet ground.

"Private Willard!" the captain shouted over his shoulder.

A teenage Marine's head snapped up from several yards away. He ran up to them.

"Private Willard, this is Lieutenant..."

"Cocoy," Jefe said.

"Lt. Cocoy and..."

"Mister Zin, my volunteer ally and guide," Jefe said.

"And Mister Zin. You will escort them to the coast and ensure them safe passage and explain their presence to any of our allies you might incur. And you will kill any and all enemies you may incur along the way that interfere."

Willard looked them over, eyebrows raised.

"Get them some water and supplies," the captain continued.

"Yes, sir."

"When done? Attach yourself to any Marine unit we can rendezvous again in Peking. Now, go on, you have your orders."

Jefe offered a hand to Mister Zin and Zin stood. He was trembling.

The group began to disperse.

"Hold on," the captain said. "You men are in the presence of United States military officer. If you don't want to be digging deep shitholes in China, you best salute."

"Yes, sir!" they said in a staccato unison.

They saluted.

Jefe saluted back, with an extra glare at the trouble-making sergeant.

"Lt. Cocoy," the captain said, "if you live long enough to see Captain Yorkie again? Tell him you ran into *Howlin'* Jack McGovern on the Peking Trail."

"That I will, sir," Jefe said and saluted *Howlin'* Jack.

"This way, Lt. Cocoy," Private Willard said, pointing to a supply wagon, which for the moment was stuck in the mud. "This way for water and some chow. We have a long way to go."

He pushed his hat back on his head. They started walking to the wagon. Jefe was relieved, but Mister Zin was almost giddy, looking over his shoulder as though the quick redemption from Boxer to ally was too good to be true. Then came the next dampening news.

"The Boxers have been closing in behind us when we pass 'em, Lieutenant. *Pickin'* us off from rear," Private Willard said. "I hate to say it, but this sounds like a dang suicide mission to me."

******

Fed. Watered. With Private Willard in the lead, then Jefe and Zin the trio headed south, walking beside the multi-national troops heading north. The trail was littered with fainting and recovering men, mostly from the muggy heat. The roadway was covered with abandoned kit. Haversacks, left hats, helmets, blankets, and gear. Some of the men, ignored marching orders, stopped, and built shady shelters by the maize. Some of the colorful 8th Cavalry, Bengal Lancers trotted by with their long spears and high turbans, followed by Indian foot soldiers.

When not suffering from the heat, slogging through the mud, or distracted by their own thoughts, the troops acknowledged Willard but grimaced at Jefe and Mister Zin.

After four hours, they saw the last of this line of allied advancement. Willard agreed with Jefe and Mister Zin that they needed to cut way east of maize rows in fear of the Boxers closing in behind the allied militaries. This clearance took another hour of "arm swimming" through row after row. After row. Finally, they saw open land and trees.

"A breeze! Thank *ya'*, Jesus!" Willard said, once free of the maze of maize. It wasn't much of a breeze, but it was moving air.

They sat under some long sweeping branches of Chinese willow trees, for some jerky, bread, oranges, and more water.

"I think from now on, it might be wiser for you to be dressed like us?" Jefe said.

"Holy cow, sir. I think you're right, but I don't have a costume change."

"We'll see what we can find along the way. What were *de* coastal battles like?" Jefe asked Willard.

262

"Brutal. Just brutal. All the troops ran over the forts on the coast by the time we got there and landed. The generals decided that we need to take the city of Tientsin before we could move on to Peking. We had us a total of 6,000 men and they 30,000. Boxers and Imperials. The land around the city was terrible. Flat. Marshy. Irrigation channels. Lagoons.

"As soon as we came into sight we came under sharp fire. I was completely scared. Bullets kept a *fallin'* all around us. Then came the shells, as we tried to close in. We got nowhere, fast. But the Japanese? They never stopped. They turned failure to success. They blew open the city gates, they ran in and then we ran in behind them."

He reached into his side pouch and pulled out an orange. "Lieutenant, do you know how many times the word 'dreadful' appears in the Bible?"

"No," Jefe said.

"The word, 'dreadful' appears 25 times in the Bible. And in the city, it was dreadful. The Japanese cut and stabbed the Chinese. You know, when we got there we saw many Chinese hung and pinned to wooden walls by Japanese bayonets. Like... like they don't need their bayonets no more? Just leave *'em* there? Stuck in bodies? There was...was crushed skulls on the streets. Heads on sticks. Dead folk. I think many of the dead, were dead Christian Chinese families, killed by the Boxers before we got there. After a short bit of *fightin'* the Boxers all fled. They ain't like a real disciplined army."

He spit out a few pits.

"I...killed three men there. Shot *'em*," he said quietly. "*Ya'* know, *ya'* know first time...*fer* me."

"I am so sorry that I asked you," Jefe said.

"No. No. That's okay, sir. You know there are a lot of wars in the Bible. I ain't counted up all of 'em though. Just the word dreadful. I never knew what it would be like…to be inside a war. It was…dreadful."

They quietly ate and drank some more water. The sun was setting.

"Mister Zin, what is ahead of us?" Jefe asked.

"We have two more villages. The first one you have not seen. The second one by the coast you have, the one where we had our Boxer troubles at the pharmacy."

"It has been a *very* long day. I think we should stay here for the night," Jefe said, and the two companions agreed.

The next morning, they collected up their cold camp and with Mister Zin in the lead, working on his inner compass, they made their way through wooded and opened ground to that first village in their path.

Within eyesight, they stopped, kneeled and Jefe pulled out his binoculars and scanned the wooden and stone village of one- and two-story buildings. The outskirts were a blasted wreck.

"This village fell under cannon fire," Willard said.

Willard pulled open a small telescope. He and Jefe caught fleeting glimpses of figures darting through the rubble.

Within a few steps, and out from under trees, they saw the sky. It was full of tens, maybe a hundred big birds circling and diving into the village.

"Vultures?" Willard asked.

"Himalayan Buzzards," Mister Zin said.

"They eat up folks?" Willard said.

"They will eat anything," Mister Zin said.

"They are beautiful," Jefe said, admiring the many golden

264

and black colors of their wingspans.

"Should we go through this place? Or go around it?" Jefe asked Mister Zin.

"It would be faster to go through it."

"What do you think, Private?" Jefe said.

"Aw hell, let's go through. It looks whopped to me. And we need some more water and grub."

The three walked on, spread out, this time with Jefe in the lead. He pulled his sawed-off rifle from his backpack duffle bag and worked the lever action to ram a round in the chamber.

"What's the name of this village?" Willard asked.

"You couldn't pronounce it," Mister Zin answered.

They stepped through the rubble and once in the remaining village, took to walking single file beside the home and building fronts of a stone avenue. The intersecting side streets were packed down dirt, the few days of heat cooked off the mud to dry dirt. There were dead Chinese, mules, and horses in the street here and there in varying degrees of decomposition.

An elderly Chinese man opened a door, saw them, and quickly shut it. Jefe deduced it was probably the sight of a Marine in uniform that scared him. They carefully crossed one street and Jefe spotted something to his left and stopped.

"What?" Mister Zin nervously asked.

Just down the road, the men saw four thin people, presumably women with long black hair and bright, white clothes hanging from a two-story roof. Three upright and one... upside down? Two buzzards sat and squawked at the one hung from on the rooftop.

Jefe walked toward them with Mister Zin and Willard behind.

They were teenager girls. Near a second story balcony, the

upright three were hung by the neck, their necks unusually stretched, but the fourth was hanging by her foot, her white pants hooked by a red, wooden stud ornament protruding from the house front. She had a noose around her neck, but it was not taut, with a huge loop. There was no breeze and they all hung absolutely still.

Jefe stood right under her, their heads just five or so feet apart.

"*NI HAO!*" Jefe shouted up. Hello in Chinese.

The girl's body shifted slightly. Seeing this, Willard dashed right into the house. Jefe slung his rifle over his shoulder. Willard appeared on the balcony. He looked to see the four ropes were tied to the house eave above it.

"The girls were shoved or jumped from this balcony," he said.

Willard stood on a chair and with his bayonet, cut the hanging ropes. The three upright girls were indeed dead and dropped to the ground, stiff. He cut the upside-down girl's rope, which fell alone in a twirl to the dirt. She remained aloft from her caught clothing. Then he climbed on the wooden balcony fence.

"Oh, be careful," Mister Zin couldn't help but say.

Tottering, Willard reached out with the knife, holding on by the door frame with his free hand.

"Ready?" the Marine asked.

"Ready," Jefe said.

Willard started chopping on the pants leg material caught on the ornamental stud. With the fourth chop, she fell.

Jefe caught her, arms and legs in a tangled mess. The other girls had hit the dirt with stiff bodies, but this girl was supple...

and still alive.

Jefe set her on the wooden sidewalk in from of the house. Her back against the wall.

"Hey. Hey," Jefe said.

One eye barely opened.

Willard appeared from the door holding a clay pot of water. He handed it to Jefe. Jefe began trying to give her sips of water.

"The whole family is dead in there, Lieutenant. Looks like a grandma, grandpa, and mom and dad, and some kids. All dressed up. Cut wrists. Blood everywhere. Looks like suicide?"

The teen took some sips of water.

"*Zisha,*" Mister Zin uttered. "Suicide."

"Don't they cut open their stomachs with a curvy knife?"

"That's a Japanese way," Jefe said.

Willard turned back in the house.

"We don't have time for this," Jefe mumbled.

Willard came back out with some grapes and handed them to Jefe. Jefe tried to get her to eat.

"It's suicide," Mister Zin said, looking at the three girls. This can happen from fear of invading forces. They fear death by rape and slow torture. Cutting. Hanging. Throwing yourself down a well."

"Holy cow!" Willard said. "Down a well!"

"I will see if I can find someone still living around here," their Chinese guide said.

The girl spit out a grape with a cough, bouncing it off Jefe's face. But she did swallow some water and other grapes. Mister Zin returned with an old man and old woman. They took a close look at Willard's "American" uniform and froze.

"It's okay, he is with us. Helping us," Mister Zin assured them.

They talked in Chinese, the elderly couple quite animated, loud and tearful, while Jefe slowly fed the girl water and fruit. Then Mister Zin came closer to Willard and Jefe with what he found out.

"The Boxers were here, and they made the villagers fight the armed forces, like they tried to do with us. Some army came through...not yours," Mister Zin pointed to Willard's uniform, "another country these people did not recognize. And they fought the Boxers and their helpers. Big machine guns. Cannons. They said many people thought that the army would win and rape and kill them all slowly, so there was a lot of suicides here. Whole families. They knew this family and these girls. They are upset."

"Ask them if there are any Boxers left here?" Jefe asked.

Mister Zin asked them.

"Yes, maybe. Hiding."

"Will they take care of this girl?"

Mister Zin nodded and asked them.

"They said yes. They said she is a lovely child."

"Private," Jefe said standing up, "there's a well in there?"

"Yes, sir. A hand pump well."

"Fill our canteens. Take whatever food we can carry." Jefe handed him his canteen.

"Yes, sir."

"And see if you can find some clothes and hat to cover your uniform. And your face."

Mister Zin handed Willard his canteen, and Willard ran back inside. The couple crouched down around the girl. They removed the loose noose from around her neck. Jefe pulled the rifle off his shoulder and scanned the streets. Willard emerged in a dark blue, long gown like shirt stretching down to his shins. Atop his head was a conical hat that covered his light-colored hair.

"Water," he handed out the canteens. "Some bread and fruit." He shook the canvas sack strapped over his shoulder.

"Let's go," Jefe said. He tipped his hat to the elderly couple and the three left for the main avenue. Jefe and Willard had their rifles at the ready.

Hugging the wall, they passed several very still, stinking death scenes, interrupted by the buzzards. The birds made raspy, drawn-out hissing sounds, along with grunting noises that could sound like hungry pigs or dogs barking.

They proceeded past the horrors, but then stopped short. They heard men yelling and arguing in Chinese, their angry voices echoing off the buildings from just around the next corner, and then...a gunshot!

Chapter 25
The Alamo of China

July days past into August. The food deliveries and messages became scarce. Some small sections of the Legation seemed to be under almost constant fire, some not, some not at all, but a doom was pending.

Gunther checked on the main street barricade. Erasimo and the team decided to close off that temporary open passage and rebuild the complete zig zag composition of four "hallways". Gunther laid down his arms and chipped in on the construction. It took almost all day. Gunther sat on the cobblestone street beside Erasimo and a chalk of tired guards, all pouring sweat.

Semitagold saw them and walked up.

"Brilliant," the Brit said looking over the breastwork. "That should slow any bloody bastards down. Right, left, right, left."

Some of the men said thanks. "Any of you men familiar with General Charles Gordon?" He looked them over and it seemed no one was.

"Major?"

"Chinese Gordon," Gunther said.

"Yes, yes, that was his byname. And where would an American learn about Chinese Gordon?"

"West Point," Gunther offered.

"Yes, yes of course...yes." He put hand on his sheathed sword handle, cocked out a hip, propped a foot up on a block of wood, and struck a statuesque pose.

Two Chinese women came up with a big ornate pot and dipped metal cups into it, handing water to the sweating men.

"Gordon Pasha. Gordon of Khartoum. Put down the Taiping Rebellion in the 1860s. Sometimes I feel like Gordon, here. He was in the siege of Khartoum. A serious revolt broke out in the Sudan, in the 1880s. led by a Muslim religious leader and self-proclaimed Mahdi, Muhammad Ahmad. The Crown sent in Gordon. He held out in Khartoum for about one year."

"One year! What-some-ever became of him, sir?" an American soldier asked.

"He died! He was killed. The story goes stabbed on a stairway by a heathen's spear. In the chest. The moment has been captured in a heroic painting, actually. By George Joy. 'General Gordon's Last Stand'."

"Sounds horrible," another soldier said, wincing. "Right up in the gizzard."

"Yes...yes. By a ghastly large Middle Eastern spear head. Like a large knife on a stick. His reinforcements, his relief came but two days late. The poor chap."

"Any new hope, sir?" Erasimo asked.

"None, dear boy. None. Communication has ceased."

"Our general friend we met last week with the long mustache," Gunther said, standing and dusting off his pants, "his flags are now all over the city, all outside our little Khartoum here."

"Eighty-thousand men," the Brit added. "A bit, quite a bit like your Alamo, yes?"

"And we didn't do so good there either," Gunther said.

"Allmamio?" an Austrian soldier said.

"Al-a-mo," Gunther said.

"I hope ours ain't two days late *a comin',*" a Marine said.

Gunther slipped on his brown vest, his two-gun belt, rifle, and hat. He walked off and Semitagold walked with him.

"When they come," Gunther said, "I'll probably make a stand with these boys right here, but I will go anywhere else I might be needed."

"Your Thermopylae. Your Gates of Fire."

"Perhaps," Gunther said.

"Keep that girlfriend of yours on the roof with her spot-on rifles. I will ring the big bell tomorrow and announce our emergency plans. Every man and woman must take up a position. With a rifle. Count their ammo. Count their blessings."

They walked a bit in silence, the distant sounds of random, slow gunfire echoed down the avenue.

"There is an old pamphlet written by Gordan 'Pasha' at the behest of the Chinese government, then our ally in the 1860s. It advised the Chinese on how to wage war against foreigners. Gordon recommended that they should never show themselves in the open and should gradually wear out the enemy by constant firing, even by night. Oh, the irony, Pasha!" he said skyward.

They stopped at the British Legation gate.

"I suppose we should warn everyone," Semitagold said solemnly, "as you Yanks did versus your Comanches and so forth. Save a bullet for yourself sort of thing."

"That would be wise, sir."

"Yes."

Crippler moved about the roof, watching the Chinese army busy themselves with taking up positions around the compound. Then she spotted Gunther and Dr. Bellmont walking the grounds talking, but both had compelling argumentative arm movements. Then 10 minutes later she spotted Gunther on top of the Tartar Wall, in a deep discussion with Swoop Swellen, Swoop's arms were also waving about in some emotional discourse. She watched as Gunther pushed his hat way back on his head in an act of frustration.

Later that night, sitting by their small rooftop fire, Gunther broke the bad news.

"Suze, it looks like our days here are numbered."

"I know."

"The communication between the Chinese and Semitagold has ended. And we know they are building up out there like never before."

"I know."

"We have to think about, we have to discuss what to do at the very end."

"Yes."

"A plan."

"Yes."

"In the cavalry, out west, we had a rule. It's a rule of the outlands really. Save the last bullet for yourself. Save yourself from the...torture."

"You said so on our way here," she said.

"I will...probably die...down there, somewhere, and I will die if I must as I try to kill the enemy to the bitter end. You will be up here shooting. Shooting until you run out of ammunition."

"I will."

He reached over and held her hand that rested on her knee.

"Oh, my sweet Suze...oh..." he tried to be stoic, but his eyes welled up, "what...will you do?"

She reached over with her other hand and held his hand with her two.

"One of my favorite places to go," she said so solemnly, "as a little girl and a teenager...family trips to Three Rock Falls outside of Omaha. My sister and I would hold hands and jump from the highest rock, the third rock into the lake below. We would fly though the air. I suppose...when cornered. I will... jump right off this roof. I will fly off. I will fly and fly and dream of Nebraska. Until I hit the ground."

A single tear rolled down Gunther's cheek.

Chapter 26
China Train

His hat removed, Jefe peered around the corner of the building to spy on the source of the arguing voices and the gunshot origin. Thirty feet away, facing away from him, stood four Boxers and one Chinese Army soldier. Kneeling before them, almost naked, bloody, beaten and cut were American or maybe English or European soldiers. Two white. One black. The three looked exhausted with their heads bowed. One, a fourth prisoner was down and quaking, groaning, and gasping…the victim from that gunshot they just heard. Jefe jumped back out of sight.

"Five enemy. Three tied-up prisoners. Our armies. They just killed one of them."

Willard grimaced. Mister Zin's jaw dropped an inch.

Jefe tapped Willard's rifle and, said, "You take *de* two on the right. I will swing left, out of your way and get *de* three to *de* left. The prisoners are low, kneeling. Shoot chest high." He pulled his two pistols.

"Are we *shoutin'* out anything first?" Willard whispered.

"No. We are shooting them in *de* back, I hope," Jefe answered.

There was no time to think or say any more about it. They bolted around the corner. Rifle up, Willard began shooting. Jefe ran wide, both his guns blazing. Right to left, three were shot in the back, the next turned slightly and was shot in the side, the fifth turned around and tried to raise his rifle. He took pistol rounds to the face, arm, and chest. In the next two seconds, Jefe peppered all of them with support shots until he had two rounds left in his pistols, one in each gun.

"Cover! Cover me," Jefe half shouted.

Jefe holstered one gun and pulled his Filipino kris knife from his belt. He cut the prisoners' rope bonds.

"Come on!" he pulled one man with him to the side of the street and into the front hallway of a closed shop. The other two half-crawled with them.

Looking up and down the street, he reloaded his Colts.

"How many?" he asked.

"Just them," one said.

"Can you walk?"

"Yes."

"Our gear, our clothes *is* in them bags out there," said the black soldier.

Willard and Mister Zin ran up to them and kneeled.

"Everybody okay?" Willard asked.

"Get them some water," Jefe ordered, as he dashed out to the street. There were three satchels on the dirt road between the bodies.

"Zin!" he called out and pointed to the bags.

Mister Zin met him halfway and got the bags. Jefe began dragging the bodies across the street into the hallway of another closed shop. He took their Chinese rifles and ammo.

"Private Willard, United States Marines."

"Private Kane, Army."

"Corporal Wilder, Army."

"Corporal Spool, Army."

They men opened the bags and started sorting out their clothes and gear.

"This here's Mister Zin, our guide," Willard said, "one of the good guys. And that little firecracker of a wildcat over there, is Lt. Jefe Cocoy, U.S. Army Filipino Scout. We *is* on our way to the beach on a special mission."

"We were told to scout out this burg, but we got spun out and lost," Wilder said, "then these fuckers bounded in on us."

"Who's he?" Willard asked, pointing to the dead soldier.

"Jared Mullhaney. Hailed from Tupelo. A Mississippi boy," Kane said, watching Jefe drag his battered body across the street too.

"We can't burry him, *ya'*know. No time," Willard said.

The men understood. They painfully pulled their clothes on.

"One of them dead rat bastard has my boots on," Spool said.

"I reckon, best you go get them now," Willard said. "We've got a *fur* piece to walk yet, and you'll be *a needin'* 'em."

Spool stood up slowly and limped across the road, telling Jefe his plans on the way. "My boots!" he told him.

A minute later, Jefe and a shod Spool joined the rest with lots of firearms and ammo.

"I speak for all of us, Lieutenant, when I say God-almighty thanks. They'd a killed us for sure, like Jared."

Jefe nodded and said, "We are bound for de beach near de forts. You men can turn south to de Taku Forts. We own them now. There, you can get yourselves situated. Can you all walk?"

"We've been tied up tight for a day and half. They beat us pretty good. They questioned us, *yellin'* all mean in Chink. Nobody speaks any Chink to answer them! But we *gotta'*walk, no matter what," Kane said.

The six stood.

"Let's go," Jefe said.

More woods and farms. They passed rice patties with women knee deep, bent over at work, as though the world around them wasn't at war, but all about the rice.

"Huh. Life goes on *fer* some, huh?" Willard said to no one in particular.

They decided to walk around the outskirts of the village that Jefe had his first troubles in and in two days they trudged up on a breezy hill where they spotted the Pacific Ocean. A few more steps and visible to the south were the Taku Forts. With a squint or binoculars, they could see about 40 or 50 allied ships busy in the bay and ocean. The bay was at peace.

"Compadres," Jefe said, "we now go this way, and you go that way."

The men said their grateful goodbyes with hugs and handshakes and the three soldiers turned off for the Forts.

"I am an islander. It is very good to see *de* ocean," Jefe confessed, taking in a deep breath.

"I am not an inlander," Willard said, "and I am a damn sight happy to see it, too."

"Correct!" Mister Zin declared.

It took another five hours to get near the water's edge. Night fell and Jefe knelt out on the beach sand, opened his duffle bag and pulled out one of the flare guns. He looked at the starry sky, whispered a prayer to Allah, and shot the flare into the dark night. Then he doubled back to their rock cropping, pulled out his rifle and sat.

"We do not know who has seen *de* flare. Get ready," Jefe warned.

Willard took up a position to watch over the other side of the beach. Mister Zin sat in the middle of them, waiting.

"When your boats come," Willard asked, "should I leave you two and head south to the forts?"

"No," Jefe said. "I will not leave you here, alone. No! You must come with us to safety. It is, after all, your Navy. Marines are Navy. You are reporting to your Navy aboard this ship."

"I *foller' ya thinkin'*," he said, relieved. "I *foller' ya'*. At this point, Lieutenant, I'll honestly *foller' you* anywhere."

******

"Mister Zin! Mister Zin," Jefe said, shaking the Chinaman's shoulder.

Zin awoke and sat up. A red dawn was breaking over the seas. "*De* boats are here! Come on."

Two little black dots appeared on the waters. Then, the pair of common looking sampans grew closer. The first boat hit the beach and the U.S. sailors, dressed as Chinese coolies leapt overboard, splashed in and deployed knee-high on the beach in a triangle, rifles ready for an attack.

"Ahoy!" Jefe shouted from the rocks.

The three men ran to the water.

"Lt. Cocoy," one sailor said, "board the second boat."

When the second craft came close, the three climbed in,

with Willard giving a hand to Mister Zin.

"Welcome back," one sailor said.

"Muchas gracias," Jefe said with a smile, choosing Spanish over Chinese and Filipino Tagalog.

In moments, both sampans rowed out to sea, then switched over to small engines when out of hearing range of the land.

"Good to see you, sir," a sailor said in broken English. "We have been waiting a long time, but we have been following the military progress by radio and observation. We thought you might be…be stuck somewhere."

"Peking!" Jefe shouted over the engines. "We were stuck in Peking."

Shortly, the silhouette of the Rio Lobos gunship appeared on the horizon. It was dressed up as Chinese merchant ship at this moment.

"That's a warship?" a confused Willard asked, looking her over.

"Yes. Fearsome," Jefe said.

Showered and in the borrowed clean uniforms of Navy sailors, Jefe, Mister Zin and Private Willard sat at a long, Rio Lobos galley table with Captains Hoon and Delane. Cooks brought out four course meals and coffee to the delight of the weary travelers.

Between bites, it took Jefe a full 30 minutes to brief the two captains on the rescue mission progress.

"We have been monitoring all military action on our radios," Captain Hoon said, folding his big hands across his broad chest. "And we have been talking with them. The forces, as you have seen, have been advancing on Peking. Help is on the way."

"Then you must tell our allies about de Peking Legation,"

Jefe said.

"We will. Captain Hoon and I have been thinking," Captain Delane said, "that perhaps we should run up the Peiho River, to Tungchow east of Peking."

"Can you?" Jefe asked.

"We are a gunship. But still, a river boat. Big, mind you, but Captain Hoon knows the river. He said we can get quite a ways north."

"We can do this!" Hoon confirmed. "This boat only draws 30 inches of water when fully laden. When this mission is over? When we get you back to the States? We will be ordered right back here for river boat patrols."

"Hmm," Jefe hummed, thinking.

"We would be confronted by Boxers and inland pirates and thieves and perhaps even our own forces if we are dressed as Chinese," Delane said.

"We would have to change our disguises. Navy. Chinese. Navy. Chinese. It is not hard to switch," Hoon said. "Our militaries have been begging for supplies and men to be shipped up north and they may try to stop us and turn us into a military supply ship. Their ideas, their plan is not our rescue mission. Their plan is to take Peking."

"Take Peking? Take the country. Taking the capital, takes the whole country. But we have our rescue mission," Delane said, "and we cannot get bogged down in supply wars."

"In and out," Hoon said.

"In and out," Delane repeated.

"While we waited for you, we sent a few sampans in with our Chinese sailors, dressed as coolies to spy amongst the Chinese and Boxers. They blended very well. We learned that the Peiho River may now be mined by electric mines already, very near Peking."

"Electric mines. You could drop us off up *de* river *near* Peking," Jefe said. "Mister Zin could direct us back to the legations."

Mister Zin nodded.

"And we will get the major, the doctors and our people back to the Lobos. How far is Tungchow from Peking?"

"Twenty or so miles," Mister Zin said.

"As our armies go north, they are rebuilding the railroads and the telegraph lines. And from what we gather on the radio transmissions, Lieutenant, we will have to fight our way up the river, and once on land you'll have to fight your way to the legations, and…fight your way back to the river. Then we have to fight our way back down the river again."

Jefe nodded.

"Could you…" Willard interrupted, and they all turned to him, "Could you please pass them mashed *potators?*"

******

The next morning the Rio Lobos, in full American gunship regalia, minus any Chinese disguise turned up the Peiho River with the American flag up at full mast. Numerous allied ships were in the bay and smaller boats were running in and out of the mouth of the river around them.

With their travel clothes washed and pressed, rifles and pistols cleaned by the crew, Jefe, Willard, and Mister Zin stood on deck, fresh, rested and fed. Willard was in his tan Marine uniform, his China robes in a pack on his back. They watched the progress. The Rio Lobos was riverboat big and had to blast its horns several times to get smaller vessels out of the way. There was a flotilla of single mast, Chinese junks, some commandeered by Europeans, some shared by American, Europeans and Chinese, carrying provisions north. Both shores were full of activity as various armies worked with wagons and construction. Indian Lancers were loading train cars with gear and horses to railroad the troops as far north as was repaired.

"It would be nice to have some horses," Jefe said. "Mister Zin, de way to Peking from Tungchow, how hard would it be on horseback?"

"I think it would be very fast. There are trails, not important ones, we could take them to sneak in."

"Two horses in..." Jefe began thinking aloud.

"Wait just a darn minute, I'm *goin'* in with *ya*!" Willard said.

Jefe smiled at him. "Three horses in. We get in. What about getting out though? On foot? Because on horseback, we would need at least 12 horses to get everyone out."

"Correct," Mister Zin said. "At very least 12. My wife and children included."

"Three of us would have to lead 12 horses, so four horses each. Feed. Gear," Jefe said.

"Might be difficult, Lieutenant," Delane said, stepping up to them. "We understand that in the last delivery and trip north, only 60 of the 400 horses survived the long sea trip. And now this infernal heat. The troops are short hundreds of horses. They'll never give us any."

"Trains, Mister Zin?" Jefe quickly asked. "Surely, there are trains running from Peking to Tungchow?"

"Correct! But the Boxers have destroyed many train lines."
Then Delane added, "But all we know about are the destroyed tracks between Taku and Peking. Maybe..."

"Maybe they are not running, but *de* tracks are okay from Tungchow to Peking," Jefe said. He turned back to Mister Zin. "Coal?"

"Coal."

"Is there anyone here that can run a coal train?" Jefe asked Delane.

"Captain Hoon! Captain Hoon!" Delane shouted to Hoon, who was within earshot at the bow.

Hoon heard him and approached them.

"Captain," Delane asked, smiling as if he knew the answer. "Is there anyone in the crew that can operate a coal driven train?"

"HA! Chinamen *built* the trains from Sacramento to Vancouver," Hoon said. "Of course. Many of our crew worked on the trains. And anyway, it is not complicated. We have two men in our engineering crew that repaired coal trains."

"Can they also shoot?" Jefe asked.

"Yes, they can. They are sailors of mine. The Navy. They can shoot."

"I would like to take them inland at Tungchow, and see if we can commandeer a...train," Jefe said.

Hoon leaned into Jefe, put up a pointy finger inches from the Filipino's nose and said, *"That...is a very good idea!"*

Gunshots erupted ahead and on the shore to the right. The team of men grimaced at the sound.

"Captains!" a sailor shouted.

Hoon and Delane ran to the request, followed by Jefe and Willard. Mister Zin lagged.

"Captain, that rail line of Indian troops has fallen under fire from Boxers on that ridge," a sailor said, handing Hoon a telescope.

"Ready the starboard bow guns," Hoon said, spying through the looking glass, his hand waving to the machine gunners on the front right.

The long train was slowly moving north and catching a lot of rifle fire from that ridge. Maybe from as many as 40 or 50 snipers. Horses were dropping and some Lancers on the passenger and freight car roofs were hit, falling down and even falling off the train.

"Des...*TROY!*" Hoon ordered.

Three heavy machine guns were able to aim over the train and into the higher ridge of rocks and foliage. From three angles, framed by occasional tracers, these heavy rounds did indeed destroy that ridge. Rocks, plants, small trees, and Boxers seemed to melt into small fragments and crumble together down into a small landslide.

Rio Lobos was keeping pace with the train and the Indian troops on the car tops and from inside the car windows waved at them, cheered and war-whooped. Someone on the bridge blew the big ship horn to the delight of all.

The train stopped to collect those who fell off, and as the Rio Lobos sailed on north, the grateful cheers ran the length to the engine. Hoon went to the rail, took off his captain's hat and bowed. Those rescued could not determine in the distance that her captain and crew were in fact...Chinese.

******

285

The next morning, Hoon on deck and drinking a cup of green tea, ordered the gunship into its Chinese disguise. They had outraced the allied troops and were nearing Tungchow. Much of the crew were on deck observing the shoreline and the waters ahead for the rumored "electric mines", triggered to go off on contact by a plunger-sparking device. They passed some Chinese boats without much notice, though a few stared at them with curiosity.

Jefe and Willard were also on deck in their Chinese clothes, guns hidden underneath and in their satchels. Members of the crew used shoe polish to blacken Willard's hair, hidden further under a big hat. Mister Zin was…Mister Zin. Four crewmen in coolie clothes, two of which were their possible future train engineers, the other two there for security, stood with them.

"Mister Zin," Hoon said, "do you know where we are?"

"Yes, I do, Captain. I can see the towers of the local palaces. That is all I need to know."

"We cannot go much further," Hoon said, we will let you off over there. We will wait here, or just south of here a little bit, and…and…fish or something. Come back here. If we are not here walk south. If you see us, use your flare guns. If we are not here? The allies are coming and try to connect with them. I will stay as long as I can. Like last time. If the allies come, I will switch over to the American gunship. I can foresee however, some general trying to take command of my ship."

Jefe nodded.

A sampan was readied.

"And what are your names?" Jefe asked the four sailors.

They answered with very long, unpronounceable names.

"Oh, Allah be praised," Jefe muttered, shaking his head. "I

cannot remember those names. I am very sorry. In English they would say, 'my goodness', I must give you fast and easy names for me and them to remember. Since you two are de train engineers. You are 'Casey' and you are 'Jones'. Casey Jones is famous in America for a terrible train crash. You are 'Wyatt', and you are 'Earp'. Wyatt Earp is a famous cowboy. Casey (he pointed). Jones, (he pointed). Wyatt (he pointed). Earp (he pointed).

The four sailors nodded. Jefe eyed the four up. Young and strong-enough looking. Clean-shaven and short-haired under a variety of Chinese hats.

"We're ready!" a sampan sailor shouted.

"Let's go," Jefe said.

The boat ride. Disembarked on a rocky, brown dirt coastline.

"How far to the train station?" Jefe asked.

"Two, three hours," Mister Zin said.

Out of the woods by 11 a.m., they walked onto the packed dirt, cement, brick, and cobblestone streets of Tungchow. Men and women urgently hustled about with goods on foot, bicycles, and wagons.

"They are fleeing," Mister Zin said. "They know the allies are coming up the river."

They saw Chinese soldiers heading to the east.

"They are going to the main bay, to defend it," Mister Zin said.

In 30 minutes, Mister Zin had them turn left and soon they stood before an ancient red arch in front, and brick and tile building.

"Gentlemen," Mister Zin said, "I give for you...the train station."

They entered the large, covered, empty hallway. A booth for tickets was empty. Mister Zin read a poster that was glued over the glass.

"What's it say, Zin?" Willard asked.

"The station is closed. This station is used only for trips back and forth to Peking. Now for military use only."

Casey and Jones walked further in. They stood on the platform and looked around the trainyard.

Jefe jogged down the hall beside them.

"What do you see?"

"There are three sets of railroad tracks," Casey said.

"There are two engines over there. Cars attached to each one."

Jefe studied them. The front end of the engines looked universal. The engineer portion was an Oriental design, orange-colored compartment. Behind each engine was a coal car, then several passenger cars.

Casey and Jones jumped off the platform and ran to the first train. They climbed aboard. Wyatt, Earp, Jefe, Willard, and Mister Zin remained.

"Who are you!" A voice demanded from the street side of the hallway.

Three Chinese Army soldiers marched up to them, their rifles at the ready.

"We are trying to get home to Peking!" Wyatt said.

"This train station is closed."

"Can you help us? How can we get home?" Earp said.

"We cannot help you."

They lowered their rifles. But one soldier studied Willard. Willard looked at his own feet, hoping his big hat would cover his face.

"You!" the soldier said to him. He stepped up to Willard and near Jefe.

"Look at me!" he demanded in Chinese, but the Marine got the message.

Willard had no choice as he slowly lifted his face revealing his Anglo features.

The three soldiers looked at him rather shocked.

"He is the Chinese bastard son of a bastard son from the English army," Wyatt said, thinking quickly.

"What is your name?" one said, but of course, Willard did not understand this.

Jefe said in English to Willard, "He wants to know your name."

Willard looked at each one, one at a time, and he said, "Uncle Sam, motherfucker."

And he kicked the closest one right in the balls. Wyatt and Earp grabbed the one close to them.

Jefe lunged out and hammer-fisted the third in the nose with his right hand. His left fist followed and hit the lower face. He kicked the kneecap, he drew his kris knife as fast as a cat and shoved the edged weapon into the soldier's throat. Face broke, knee broke, windpipe ruptured in but three seconds, the guard tumbled down into a gurgling death.

Willard did not fare so well. His soldier bent over from the groin hit, but he charged into the Marine in a half-tackle. The two stumbled back across the platform, with Jefe in a dashing pursuit. In the chase, the Filipino flashed his knife side-to-side in two seconds, cutting the left Achilles tendon and the left lower hamstrings. The attacker's left leg "disconnected" like snapped guitar strings, and the soldier fell to the left and rolled over on his back. Jefe was still coming at him, but the man put his right foot of his still connected leg to kick at him and keep him away. One kick. Two...then Willard stomped the soldier's face repeatedly.

Jefe turned to the third soldier. Wyatt had one arm from behind, Earp the other arm in a wrestling match. Jefe charged. He cut an X pattern on the man's throat and then uppercut stabbed him just under the sternum, hitting the heart and lungs as he churned the handle of the knife in a circle.

The sailors hauled their gasping, dead or soon dead men out of sight from the big entrance hallway. Willard pulled his attacker out of sight, then grabbed Jefe's first kill over there too.

Jefe whipped the kris through the air to shed any loose blood or guts, then sheathed the knife under his decorative jacket, all the while staring down the hall. No one witnessed their actions. Willard caught his breath and smiled at Jefe. Wyatt and Earp, also out of breath, were somewhat shocked. Jefe was calm and not out of breath.

"Uncle Sam, motherfucker?" Jefe said to Willard with a smile.

"He's my uncle."

"We got a train," Casey said, running up to platform. "We have coal."

Jefe walked to the edge.

"Can you disconnect most of *de* cars? I think we need *de* engine and coal car, of course, and only two passenger cars at *de* most."

"Already have disconnected, sir."

"Good work," Jefe said. He turned to Willard. "Get these dead men in *de* last passenger car. We will kick their bodies out along the way. We cannot leave them here. They must disappear and not found dead. We have to return here or near here when we come back."

"Only one concern," Casey said, "as we go on this track to Peking? We don't know if there is a train coming back on the same track?"

Jefe was silent, pondering that.

"Have you ever seen a train collision?" Casey asked. He lifted his hands and jammed his fingertips together, then opened his fingers and rammed them palm to palm. "We must be ready to jump!"

Chapter 27
China Charge

Sunrise. The dreaded time had come. The dreaded gunfire increased. The dreaded cannon fire increased. Buildings' sections disappeared or splintered into pieces. Gunther was already down walking on the grounds, and he ran to the Legation Avenue barricades. Many of the men assigned there were also sleeping there too, night after night, some with cots, some without. Erasimo, ever the smooth con man, had a cot. He sat up among the explosions. Many of the guards moved down the zig zag pattern of wall till they saw the 30-odd, on duty, soldiers standing guard at the very front wall. Gunther and Erasimo followed the reserves. The men up front looked concerned.

"They have been building up over there," one said. "Noisy. Chanting."

Then suddenly, horribly, came the charge. The human wave. The yell. The bombs. Firebombs were tossed at the front barricade wall, and over the wall, exploding and landing on some of the soldiers, turning them totally aflame. The front thick wall of furniture and wagons, scorched from the summer heat, ripped into a roaring flame. All the defenders could hear was their war cries from the other side along with the pathetic, inhuman screams, howls, and yelps of the burning comrades.

Downward hacking swords and axes appeared above the barricade as the enemy began hacking at the wall. It was also apparent that bullets were being fired into the mishmash structure, the rounds stumped, thwarted, and deflected, but still splatted, tattled, and pinged. Bits of rounds and splinters were sparingly getting through.

As the guards had long feared, fire would burn their carefully structured frontlines. One of the soldiers shot to death a friend engulfed yet still alive. Rifle rounds began from behind, above and behind them from their compatriots, to include from Crippler's lofty nest pelted into the Chinese over the wall. Two men threw overhand bombs back at the Chinese which blew off with success, resulting in more bands of screaming wounded.

The guards retreated to the first zig zag turn. Once there, Gunther scaled the jagged construction, yanked off his hat to peek down the avenue. To his dismay, it seemed like 1,000 Chinese packed the avenue, waiting to burst in.

"We need the Maxim machine gun right there!" Gunther jumped down and advised an Austrian captain, pointing to a roof. "Up there. There are about 1,000 of them out."

The captain dashed off.

Several soldiers threw bombs and sticks of dynamite over the front wall at the attacking force. In turn Chinese firebombs flew over the first and second wall as Gunther and others dodged and dove out of the way.

How much longer the first breastwork would hold was... then the closing roar of wild men filled the air and the first sharp turn of the barricade filled with charging Chinese Boxers, shoulder-to-shoulder across the 15-foot-wide passageway. Some had spears, some swords, some rifles. Gunther and those with him were shocked at the sight, like red lava with spears, swords, and guns in the lead. The front wall must have collapsed from the flames and bombs, and some of the Chinese clothing was even on fire from their fast and climbing entry.

The Boxers with guns shot at the guards. Under the zipping fire Gunther raised his rifle and poured lead into every rifleman he could spot. Overhead the booming sound of the Maxim machine gun began its roar but not at the nearby charging crowd but rather out at the hundreds on the avenue. These invaders before Gunther and the Austrians were too close.

And they were closing fast. He dropped his empty rifle and pulled his two pistols. He picked the path in front of him and shot. Twelve times, with a steady system of fire, wounding and or killing. Some fell, some stumbled. The head and neck shots killed.

Closer! Closer!

They were on him as well as those beside him. Gunther dropped the empty pistols and pulled his Bowie knife as a Boxer swung a sword at his left side. Gunther stepped in and slammed the blade into the man's forearm of the attack. The sword went flying into the wall. The Boxer grabbed Gunther's shoulder, as Gunther pulled the knife back and sunk it into the right side of the Boxer's neck. Other Boxers dashed by them, screaming. He shoved the enemy aside into the wooden furniture of the wall.

Right behind that man was another with a spear and an angry face. Gunther hit the spear aside with the Bowie, then grabbed the spear with his free hand and drove the knife upward into the man's stomach, lungs, and lower heart.

Just over the spear man's shoulder, Gunther saw a rifleman aim at him and with a push and sidestep the round hit the back of the spear man, who was already gasping in the throes of dying.

Then they all were hit by what seemed like a stampede of buffalo, as all the Boxers and some Chinese soldiers rammed in. Gunther fell with the dying spear man atop him. Then another runner fell on them. Then another tripped and fell and 10 or more climbed over the pile, stumbling, crawling...

Gunther suddenly couldn't breathe as tens of men scaled the piles of bodies in the passage. A sandaled foot crushed his face. Then a boot, he tried to push these dead and alive people off him...but...

Blackness strangled at him.

Numbness.

Sounds muffled.

No breath.

No...air!

Blackness.

******

Voices, as if from afar on a snowy mountain. Or underwater? Gunther couldn't tell.

"Here!" he heard a bit closer.

"Here!" Better yet.

"Johann!" a man's voice?

"He's here."

Was he buried alive in the German Alps? An avalanche? Where...?

The weight decreased.

He saw Erasimo.

"Wha...?" Gunther tried to speak.

Erasimo hauled bodies off Gunther.

"Where are..."

The last body was overturned.

"Look," another man said, "look, this bastard's stabbed to the hilt."

"Me?" Gunther asked. Gunther's head tiled up and saw it was Swoop Swellen talking.

"No, the other bastard," Swoop said. He was smiling.

He watched Swoop slowly pull the knife out the Boxer's chest and wipe the blade. Both sides, off on the man's shirt. He stuck the knife back into Gunther's sheath.

"Ah, ah...the spear..." Gunther mumbled.

"*Killen'* to the very end," Swoop said. He spread his legs over Gunther and looked him over.

"Shot?" Swoop asked.

"I...don't think so," Gunther felt of his chest and face and had a flashback of a rifle barrel aimed at his head. "Somebody... somebody tried to..."

"I'll say they tried to," Swoop said with a chuckle.

"I...ah...I..."

Swoop leaned in and looked at his head. Gunther's face and hair were a bloody mess.

"Let's get him *outta* here," Erasimo said.

"My pistols!" Gunther shouted.

Swoop huffed, then started heaving carcasses like they

were sacks of wheat. Gunther tried to sit up with a little help from Erasimo. He looked around at the carnage. From ground level it looked like the whole length of the passage was three-deep in dead bodies.

"Here!" Swoop said. "And here!" He opened the cylinders and laughed.

"Both run empty, Trooper," Swoop said. He handed Gunther the pistols and Gunther tried to holster them but couldn't. Erasimo helped position the barrels.

"Yeah, ahhh, rifle? Rifle?"

"Jesus!" Swoop growled.

As Swoop searched, Erasimo helped Gunther to his feet. Gunther saw soldiers jump and step back and forth by him, some carrying dead men.

"Who's all dead?" Gunther asked.

"We don't know yet," Erasimo said.

"Here it is!" Swoop said, lifting the rifle in the air. "She's empty too. You must have run it dry, run *yer'* pistols dry and pulled *yer'* pig sticker. The Austrians said…as they were backing away, that you stood fast here on this turnpike like a goddamn fool, killing any and everything that came your way."

"I…I…a path…I, a path," Gunther babbled.

They each grabbed an upper arm and the three threaded their way hopping and dancing over the bodies.

"Is Crippler okay?" he asked.

"She's *gotta'* be fine," Erasimo said. "They really didn't get in deep."

"They came at me like a herd of buffalo! We stopped *'em?*" Gunther asked.

"We all did, Major," Swoop said.

"Gunth," Erasimo said, "in the middle of it all, we heard a lot of cannon fire, and heavy guns."

"Oh no."

"Oh yes, good, yes," Erasimo said.

"Our big American guns!" Swoop said, smiling.

"Then, then, in the middle of us almost losing, who come a *runnin'* through the legation but a got-damn Indian?" Erasimo said.

"Ahhh…what the hell kinda…Indian? Commanch? Apache?"

"Shit-fire boy, you really don't know where you are yet, do ya?" Swoop said.

"A Hindu Indian! An Indian-Indian. From India. A Lancer!" Erasimo said, beaming.

"A Lancer?"

"Come all up a *runnin'* through here with a big ass turban twice the size of his head, and a mustache waxed out three inches from his face. Screaming 'we're here, we're here'."

"They're there?"

"They are here!" he weaved his way in and climbed a wall. "They are here, Gunth. The relief. The reinforcements. One of the British wives went right up to him and kissed him on the lips with an open mouth," Erasimo reported.

"The Chinese had to flee us and fight them. The relief is attacking Peking now," Swoop said. "He told us the Brits and American are right behind. Japanese, Russians."

"But I still hear shooting," Gunther said.

"Yes, sir," Erasimo said. "They are still shooting in here and there, like always."

They laid Gunther into a cart, and a Chinese woman grabbed the handles.

"To the hospital," Swoop told her, motioning with his hand. He put the rifle in the cart beside Gunther. She nodded, and barefoot and at a speedy pace, off they went.

Gunther saw great damage on the way. Wounded citizens and soldiers. And many more happy survivors. He saw Lancers walking around inspecting, and talking with the population, in some spots, like a Sunday afternoon in Central Park.

"JOOOHANN!"

It was Crippler. She ran up to and then alongside the moving cart.

"Are you alright? You aren't shot anywhere?" She asked, looking him over.

"I think not, Suzzzze."

"Your head is covered with dried blood!"

"I've been stomped on. Feels like a mask. What's for dinner tonight? I think it's *gonna* be curry, huh?" and then... he passed out.

He awoke in a bed in the Legation hospital to the sound of random gunfire and a cannon blast. He saw Crippler sitting beside him reading a book. His body was aching and numb. Then he fell asleep again.

******

"Major Gunther. Major Gunther."

He awoke in the same bed from a tapping on his shoulder. He looked up to see Semitagold.

"Major Gunther, this is General Carr, British Military."

Gunther nodded.

299

An explosion roared outside.

"He is here on an inspection of the wounded, and several of his doctors will be assigned here for the duration."

"What happened to you son?" another's face leaned in and asked.

"Ahhh," his throat was desperately dry. Suddenly, Dr. Bellmont appeared and handed him a cup.

Gunther sat up and drank the whole cup of water.

"Kicked in the head, sir," Gunther mumbled.

He laid back down. He felt of his head and face, half expecting to touch the caked blood. He also felt of his teeth, rubbing them to see if they were all there. They were.

"The British are here now, Johann. The Japanese and the Americans," Semitagold said. "They are taking on Peking. It's a full on, bloody war."

"Take care of yourself, Major," General Carr said, and the group moved on.

Bellmont sat on the bed.

"Remember much?" he asked Gunther.

"Not much."

"You were on the front line of the street barricade. They say you fought like a demon."

A wounded Marine with a crutch was standing nearby. He said, "He did. Like Daniel Boone at the Alamo."

"That's Davey (cough) (cough) Davey Crock...Davey Crockett," Gunther mumbled, "anything broken?"

"No, sir. You've had a bad concussion. And your chest was horribly compressed by...by dead bodies, and other Boxers running over you and dead bodies, which could have killed you."

"That I remember...crushed..."

"Your head and face are bruised. You have been kicked in the head, head stepped on. But your head will clear up. You should be getting up soon. Walking around."

"Okay," Gunther said, and laid back down. "I'd like a barbecue sandwich and a beer."

"We have plenty of food now."

And in a moment, he was asleep again.

******

"Johann! Gunth!"

He opened his eyes.

It was Jefe.

"Jefe!" Gunther said. "I must be dreaming."

"I leave you and you almost die."

"It's all your fault."

Jefe handed him water and a sandwich. Gunther sat up a bit, drank and took a bite.

"I asked for barbecue and beer."

"We have to go," Jefe said.

"We...how...what?"

"We've got a train," Jefe said. "We came up the river east of here in *de* Rio Lobos, got into an abandoned train station and stole a train."

"A...train..."

"We have stopped the train a ways from here. In a roundhouse. And we have to get back to *de* train. We have four sailors guarding it. It is hidden in a stable in the roundhouse. Good spot. We must get to it, then get back to Tungchow and get to de Rio Lobos."

301

Gunther coughed. He slowly sat up and put his bare feet on the stone floor.

"Where are my clothes?" he asked with a mouthful of sandwich.

"Dr. Bellmont!" Jefe shouted.

Bellmont arrived bedside them, lifted Gunther's head up by the jaw and looked deep into his eyes.

"Follow my finger," the doc said, moving it back, forth, side to side.

Gunther tried.

"I don't know," Bellmont whispered.

"Tell the others, it's time to go," Gunther said. "I can't hold people up. We've got to move."

Bellmont sighed. "Your clothes are under your bed."

Jefe knelt down and pulled the pile of clothes and boots out.

"Crippler had them all cleaned," Bellmont said.

And at the moment, Crippler, book in hand walked in, shocked to see Gunther up and Jefe beside him. She hugged Jefe.

"We're going, Suze, get ready."

"Can you..." she asked.

"Got to," Gunther said.

Jefe explained the situation to her, as they both helped Gunther stand up.

"The Austrian doctor I told you about two weeks ago, Hans Gruber?" Bellmont said, "the one with the wife and kids..." Bellmont waved the doctor over. "Can they go too?"

The doctor ran up.

"Dr. Hans Gruber. Can you shoot?" Gunther asked reflexively.

The man's jaw dropped a bit and it shifted to the left and he said, "Ahhh...skeet."

"Skeet," Gunther repeated with a sigh, buttoning his shirt.

"We have two passenger cars on *de* train," Jefe said.

"Okay. Okay. Pack. Pack light. We meet at the British Legation courtyard in 30 minutes."

Gunther saw a white man in Chinese clothes standing a few feet back.

"Who's he?"

"That is 'Uncle Sam' Willard. United States Marines," Jefe said with half a smile. "He was ordered to help us and that he has."

Willard stepped in and saluted Gunther, waiting for a return salute. Gunther grabbed his wrist and pulled the hand down into a handshake.

"Uncle Sam, just call me Gunth. Let's got tell Semitagold what we are doing. Relief is here. They won't need us now..." Gunther stumbled a bit and Jefe caught his arm.

On the way, Gunther finished the sandwich and water, dangling the metal cup on a finger when empty. Despite the occasional bullet zipping through the air, and the distant sounds of battle, the legation people, Christian Chinese, and a plethora of relief soldiers were milling around. U.S. Army and Marines, Lancers, British soldiers were walking, talking, setting up tents and delivering wagons of supplies.

Gunther, Jefe and Uncle Sam Willard rudely marched into Semitagold's office. He was speaking with some soldiers, and Gunther recognized General Carr and recognized the ranks and uniforms of the men with him. He nodded to a U.S. Army Colonel.

"Major Gunther, you are up!" Semitagold said, not insulted with the sudden appearance. "And Lt. Cocoy! I think your success may have hastened our rescue! Thank you! Is our Mister Zin okay?"

"Yes, sir," Jefe said.

"Yes, sir," Gunther continued. "As you know of my mission, sir, Jefe has just commandeered a train. The Rio Lobos awaits us in...in..."

"Tungchow," Jefe finished for him.

"With our rescue, with the arrival of new medical crews, I think it's time we leave and complete our mission. We have no idea how long this war on China will last and we can't wait."

"Major Gunther has been sent here by Vice President Roosevelt to rescue several Americans," Semitagold informed the audience.

"Commandeered a train? Going east to Tungchow?" a man said in an army uniform. He stepped up. "Major Stanley." He shook Gunther's hand. "We are barraging and invading Peking now, but we need intelligence on the east side." He sat on a corner of Semitagold's desk. "Hmmm, well. What if...what if I sent a detail with you...small intelligence group. Help you get out there, and they can get back and report."

"How many, sir?" Jefe asked.

"Five or six men."

Jefe looked at Gunther with raised eyebrows and a slight nod of approval.

"Let's do it. But we have to leave in 30 minutes," Gunther said.

"We worry for *de* train waiting for us, Major. And *de* riverboat gunship waiting for us," Jefe said.

"Of course," Major Stanley said and turned to a lieutenant with instructions.

Gunther and Jefe shook Semitagold's hand.

"I can't say it has been a complete pleasure, dear boys, but it's been close. It's been more than a spot of bother. Godspeed."

"Allah be with you," Jefe said.

In 30-some-odd minutes, the ragtag group appeared in the courtyard. Soldiers, the Zin family, doctors, and families. Gunther looked over their duffle bags and luggage and counted the children. Five kids cowering with their parents. Crippler was wearing her rifle case on her back via a strap, and atop that a backpack with a Chinese rifle slung around her neck, hanging from the front, gun belt on her hips.

"That's a lot, Suze," Gunther said eyeing her up.

"The Russians recovered this rifle for me. It's a beauty. I'd like to try and take it back. I'll drop it if I have to."

"Okay."

Erasimo and Swoop Swellen showed up, tugging a two-wheel cart behind them, carrying rifles, pistols, and some small soft bags.

"Sgt. Lingstrum, sir," a soldier approached and saluted.

Gunther saluted back and then shook his hand. He acknowledged the five troops with him, looking each man in the eyes with a nod, an important quick connection, and a leadership tip he learned from West Point. He owed every man such a quick, personal connection.

Jefe, Erasimo, and Swoop handed all the doctors the rifles, pistols, and ammo. The medical men understood what this meant again, that certain switch of professions. They gave the two wives, Mrs. Zin and Mrs. Gruber, pistols. There were looping lanyards run through a rounded hook at the end of handles. Swoop helped them with the shoulder loops.

"Men," Gunther said to Lingstrum's soldiers, "show them how they work."

The instructions to the doctors and wives were brief, and Gunther waited.

"Gentlemen and ladies," Gunther spoke up. "Lt. Cocoy here and our guide Mister Zin will take us, hopefully, to a small train, awaiting us, for our trip east. From there, we hike to a riverboat, gunship for a run down the river and for the most of us, out into the China Sea for a Pacific Crossing. Whereupon we will refuel at various island stops on our way to America. You troops spread out among the civilians. Their safety is our priority. Our mission."

"We will leave out the main street barricade," Erasimo said, "and circle the south half of the legation walls, as all the main action has moved off the avenue."

"Ladies and gentlemen," Gunther shouted, "we are going into a war zone, as you can hear out there. Stay in a line, about two people abreast, or in the case of families, three people deep. You may have to pick up your children and run as fast as you can. Should you get lost from us? Should we fall? Hide and try to find the nearest ally army and explain your predicament."

Gunther then informed the civilians of common hand signals for stop, go, run, get down knee-high, lay down and the importance of silence when needed.

The group either acknowledged him, or some just stared at him aghast at what was ahead.

"Uncle Sam Willard," Gunther said. "You and Mister Zin take the point."

Chapter 28
Tied in China Silk

The group made its way through the zigzag barricades where Gunther almost lost his life a few days earlier. Many of the allied bodies had been cleared, but many not, along with the Chinese, who were frequently left to rot on the landscapes anyway. The rotting had well begun, and the stench was thick. Starving dogs and birds picked at the flesh and bones. Some of the group gagged, some covered their noses and mouths.

Out on the open avenue was the same look and smell. Death upon mangled abandoned death. Mister Zin told Willard to turn left, and the troupe followed. To the far south wall, a place of such prior fires, battles, and destruction, they trotted. Hyper-alert they scanned ahead and to their left, searching among the rubble of those once-established homes and businesses. The stretch ran along the entire side of all the legations.

At the northeast corner they waited and kneeled, with Mister Zin, Jefe and Willard peeking outward.

Gunther approached and asked, "What?"

"Over there," Jefe said, "Boxers and Chinese Army."

About 100 yards away, 50 men were moving east also at a run. They were being fired upon by allied soldiers out of Gunther's sight.

"I think…" Mister Zin said, "we can move into the ruins a bit and…"

Suddenly, a cavalry of horseback Japanese soldiers galloped into view, their Samurai swords held high. The men and steeds in colorful regalia, crashed into the rear of the formation of fleeing Chinese, slinging, and chopping the razor-sharp swords into their enemy. Heads, arms then bodies dropped.

Mister Zin collected himself from the vision, gulped and continued, "We can get into the ruins and still head east."

Jefe agreed.

"Let's go," Gunther said.

The group picked their way through the ruins and crept through the outskirt dirt and paved streets surrounding Peking. They were seen at times by otherwise preoccupied, frightened residents, busy with their own hoarding or escape plans. Cannon fire and explosions rattled the unbroken windows and at times, shook their lungs. They only caught glimpses of fleeing or repositioning Chinese soldiers and Boxers. Most of the streets were empty and many houses had long poles of abandoned laundry left hanging. Broken and abandoned carts and wheelbarrows, some with the ingenious wind sails posted atop them to help push the heavier loads along, cluttered the avenues and alleys.

Two hours later, Jefe stopped the group near an industrial area, pristine from the war damage, but devoid of people. The group kneeled between two towering racks of wood and metal bars. Two of Lingstrum's men moved to the rear to cover.

"I will go ahead;" Jefe said, "de train engine is in a round-house in a stable of engine stables. It is a good hiding place. I will tell the sailors to bring it out, connect to de two passenger cars and get it ready to go. Mister Zin will show you the way. Come in one hour. If it is not safe? I will return."

Jefe took off in a dash, darting between the piles of raw materials.

Then there was an odd bark in the distance. A single bark from a dog.

"Major! Sergeant!" One of the rear guards said.

Gunther and Lingstrum went to the rear of the supply row.

"We are being followed," a soldier said. He pointed.

Gunther pulled his telescope from his jacket, breast pocket, and waited.

"Yeees," Gunther whispered. Chinese Army. The colored brand uniform of the angry general I met. They have tracking dogs."

He handed the scope to Lingstrum. Lingstrum's four other soldiers gathered around by them.

"There's a platoon of Chinese soldiers about 250 yards behind us. They have tracking dogs. Bloodhounds." Lingstrum told his men. "They are hunkering down right now wondering if and where we are in this supply yard."

Gunther, in a crouch, ran back to the rest of their troop.

"We are being followed by soldiers with dogs. We've been moving fast but they will catch up with the help of tracking dogs."

The civilians fretted and the men cussed.

"We are going to have to move on to the roundhouse and not wait. Get ready. You know the way, right, Mister Zin?"

"Oh, yes. Correct."

"Pick a path that will catch Jefe in case he has to come back to us. Suze, come on back with me," Gunther said. "Mister Zin, come on too."

They hustled and kneeled at the rear. He handed her his telescope and pointed to some piles of factory parts about 250 yards away.

"I see *'em*," she said.

"You see the two big dogs?"

"Yes."

"They are tracking us and closing in. They will catch up. Here's the plan, Suze, we need to move on, but they will catch up with us following our scent."

"We leave a parcel of smells for sure," Lingstrum said.

"We left no tracks in the city and the dogs tracked us by smell. Can you shoot the dogs? The handlers?"

"She can...?" Sgt. Lingstrum said.

"She can," Gunther confirmed.

"I can," she said. "I'll shoot the handlers, the loose dogs will run after us, faster than the men. They will just try to corner us. And I'll shoot some of the other men too."

"You have to catch as many of the men out in the open. You will give away your position. They will return fire."

She nodded.

"I will stay with..." Gunther said.

"No, you are certainly not!" Crippler demanded. "All these people up there need you."

"Two of my men will remain with her," the sergeant said. "Major, you take the group off for a head start. Two men and the missus here..."

"Suzannah Crippler," she said.

310

"Miss Crippler," he said, "will stay here, take the shots and then run off. A bit back a ways my two other men will set up and lay down cover fire for you, until you three catch up with them. Then all five of you run off. Myself and my last trooper will be a *waitin'* even further back. We'll set up for even more cover fire, then the seven of us will run off and catch up with you all."

Gunther thought about it for a few seconds and said, "That sounds like a good orderly retreat, Sergeant." He looked at Crippler. "We will follow the path we saw Jefe take.

"It's smart, Johann. I'll be alright," Crippler said.

He squeezed her hand.

"We have to run through the silk factory," Mister Zin suddenly added.

They all turned to Mister Zin.

"There are big fences on the front sides of the factory. We jumped the fences. We did, coming back to save time…but…I had much trouble with the fences. The factory is empty as everyone has fled. These fences are very tall…the children… my wife…will have trouble…"

"Okay," Gunther said. "Okay. Through the factory."

"We better get going," Lingstrum said.

"Yup," Gunther said.

Crippler opened her gun case and constructed her rifle. Lingstrum and Gunther dashed back to the group. Lingstrum gave the spread-out, cover, set-up orders to his men.

Gunther said, "Let's go. Now!"

Within minutes, Crippler and the two soldiers were spread apart and prone. She looked at the Chinese group through her rifle scope as they knelt making plans. The two soldiers with her just had iron sights on their rifles.

"You boys can shoot?" she asked.

"Yes, ma'am," one said.

"We'll just aim a little higher," the other said.

They waited about 5 more minutes until all the Chinese came into sight from their covered pow-wow. There were at least 30 of them. Two of them up front worked the charging, excited dogs, and tried to slow them down.

Crippler shot the first handler. Bolt action. Shot the second. The dogs ran free toward them. Several surprised soldiers tried to chase them, grab their leashes but...

The two beside Crippler, aiming a bit high, opened fire into the group. Crippler fired with precision, dropping three. The Chinese soldiers dashed back to their original cover behind rows of raw materials.

Crippler and the two shooters got up with a slight crawl-back and ran full out for the silk factory. Crippler abandoned her rifle case. Some Chinese rounds clanged off the rows of metal bars and boxed machinery nearby them. They hustled toward the factory, and they spotted their next two soldiers in the retreat path, waiting for them. One had binoculars.

"They haven't followed you yet," a private declared, "but them dogs are a *comin.*"

Then those five took off for the factory. They could only hear some random gunshots behind them.

Finally, they spotted the last two soldiers kneeling behind some rusty, heavy duty factory equipment. Sgt. Lingstrum was one of the two, also with binoculars.

"The Chinese hadn't left their cover yet across the yard," he told them. The seven took off for the factory some 25 yards away.

The double back doors of the filthy, tall building of metal and stone were wide open. The seven slowed and stepped inside to the thick smell of chemicals and machine oil. They immediately heard distant yelling in Chinese from the far side.

Lingstrum made hand movements for the group to spread out and advance. They passed rows and rows of sewing tables and seats that processed cloth from bins and spools above. At the end of a row of some 50 such workstations, they walked quickly forward through a second long row of labor desks. The yelling got louder.

"That's Mister Zin," Crippler whispered.

The closer they got, the worse it appeared. They crouched as they moved in. Then stopped. Their whole troupe was stopped near the doors to the front lobby. A large Chinese man in work clothes held the female child of the Austrian family with one hand, and the other held a long knife at her throat. A second worker stood nearby with a wide, long sword! Mister Zin stood in view, no doubt begging for the girl's life and for their passage.

Crippler, now about 50 feet away and a bit to the right of the scene, laid her rifle barrel on a wooden podium and got behind the gun. With a round already chambered, she held her breath and squeezed a shot off, hitting the worker in his weapon-bearing shoulder, ripping most of it off his body in a popping mist. It looked like the shoulder was hit with a sledgehammer. The knife went flying and the man fell backward.

From her limited vantage point, the second man with the sword was then hit with rounds in the chest, one ricocheting off the broad sword with a spark. He dropped the same time the sword did. As she expected, Gunther, pistols drawn, walked up to study the downed men. The newly-freed Gruber's daughter ran crying to her parents.

Crippler and the soldiers made it to the front.

"They musta seen us coming, hid, and jumped out and grabbed the girl," Erasimo explained.

"I tried to reason with them," Mister Zin said, "they are just floor supervisors here, workers, not soldiers. Not Boxers, but they would not listen. I do not understand."

The wounded man, now missing his right shoulder cursed in pain and crawled away. Gunther kicked him hard in the head twice to knock him out.

"The dogs?" Gunther asked.

"They are free from the handlers," Crippler said. "They'll run up to the back doors. We closed them."

"A good tracker could still follow us in here, with the dirt in the yard. And these floors are dusty. And...them!" Gunther pointed to the workers. "Let's go!" he ordered. He shoved Mister Zin up to the front.

They climbed a flight of stairs and entered the front office and the grand lobby, exquisitely appointed with marble floors and Oriental adornments. They dashed across the lobby and out onto the avenue. It was an industrial area. Few locals could be seen here and there, but they were preoccupied with chores.

"This way!" Mister Zin said. "Not far!"

Fueled by adrenaline, being chased, they ran. The Austrian doctor Gruber picked up his two children one in each arm. Uncle Sam Willard grabbed up the youngest Zin child, Erasimo grabbed the middle child and one of Lingstrum's men got the third. Gunther slipped back to the rear, waving his arm to be passed. He would keep up but keep an eagle-eye out for the pursuers.

Up a grassy unkempt hill of wild trees and bushes and then bounding down, they all saw the train roundhouse. Lingstrum put an open hand up for them to stop. They knelt or sat, all of them sweating profusely.

"Drink!" Gunther ordered as he approached Lingstrum and Mister Zin.

"There it is, Johann," Mister Zin said.

The structure was large and indeed round, wooden, with the center unroofed and open. They examined a myriad of train tracks into the many stables of the building, built to turn engines around for return trips, repairs or storage. The half they could see from the hill was empty and no workers or soldiers could be seen.

"There! Look!" Mister Zin said, as he pointed to the east of the roundhouse. "That is them. They are ready."

An engine, with smoke streaming from the chimney, a coal car and two passenger cars sat idling just 50 yards away. A man jumped up atop the first car and waved at them.

"It's Jefe," Gunther said. "Let's go!"

Lingstrum guided the relieved passengers aboard the first car. Gunther ran to and climbed into the engine compartment.

"Gentlemen," he said to the four grimy sailors.

"This is Wyatt and Earp. This is Casey and Jones," Jefe introduced the engine crew.

Gunther laughed out loud. The first laugh in several days and it felt good, despite his prior crushed chest problems. The laugh was met with big grins all around.

Lingstrum appeared on the side of the train.

"We're loaded!" he yelled, then ran back to get aboard.

"Chug *'er* up!" Gunther told the crew.

They did.

"We were followed by soldiers with bloodhounds from that crazy general I met," Gunther told Jefe.

"OH! Allah be praised, what happened?"

And Gunther told him of the events, as the train headed off east. The sun would soon set.

"Come on," Jefe said, "there is a wooden walkway beside *de* coal bin."

The two walked back to the front doors of the first passenger car.

When they entered, and when all the doctors, wives and children saw Jefe they all cheered and applauded.

Jefe smiled, took off his tan jungle hat and bowed like a British stage star.

Erasimo walked up. "We got two men in the caboose watching out behind us."

"Yeeees," Jefe said, "this of course is not over yet. We hope not to hit an incoming train head-on! Or, or be passed by a train of soldiers going to Peking. They could see us, stop and back up. Or...*de* tracks might be damaged ahead, and..."

"Okay! Enough!" Gunther said.

"I am just saying. Then we have to march to *de* river. I am just..."

"I know, I know."

"How long is this ride going to take?" Telemore asked.

"Could beeee...three hours," Jefe said.

Gunther saw that the windows had shades.

"Let's pull down those shades," he said.

Gunther saw Crippler sitting alone in the back, hat back

on a string around her neck. Navigating the train wobble, he shuffled his way to her and sat beside her.

"This seat taken, my lady?"

"I was saving it for a tall, blond, handsome stranger," she said, not looking at him.

"I am, at least, a bit strange," Gunther said. He could tell she was very nervous.

"You must be exhausted?" she said, looking at his bruised face.

"I could use a nice nap."

"I'm exhausted," she confessed.

"Just a few more hurtles to go," Gunther whispered.

Chapter 29
The Big China Derail

A rear guard soldier burst into the back door of their passenger car.

"Major! Sergeant! They're behind us!" he yelled.

All the passengers turned to him.

"They are in a train coming up behind us."

Gunfire.

"I'll tell the engine crew to pour it on," Jefe said and ran out the front.

Gunther, Erasimo, the soldier and Lingstrum took off for the rear car. When they entered, they ducked as a bullet bashed into the car.

"They're *shootin'* at us, Sarge!" the soldier posed at the back door shouted.

The men almost crawled to the rear and Gunther peered through the back window. There was a charging engine behind them, gaining ground, and several soldiers hung off the sides of the engine and one outside it crawled atop the engine itself and shot at them.

A large man leaned out of the engine car to look. It was that General Longhorn Mustache!

"It's him," Gunther said, "that *son* of a bitch. You'd think he'd have something better to do."

"What?" Lingstrum said.

"It's a Chinese general I almost shot in a 'diplomatic' meeting back at Peking. He swore he'd kill every foreign dog."

The train closed in even more and was but a few feet behind them now. That Chinese soldier atop the front engine crawled out further, with his eyes on the back of their passenger car.

Gunther growled.

He pulled a pistol and crawled to the back door, as the enemy bullets shot up the back of their car, breaking glass, splintering wood, and banging metal foundations. He shoved open the door and stayed low.

The roar of the trains was deafening. The wind blasted him. The Chinese soldier was at the front tip of his engine, propping himself to leap onto their caboose. He looked up to see Gunther's face. Gunther, flat on the platform, raised his pistol and aimed at the face, but with the wild waddle of the trains, he shot the man in the shoulder. The bullet and the rush of air took over his body and it bounced off the pursuing engine. The gunfire from the soldiers further back intensified. Gunther was suddenly hauled back into the train car. Lingstrum grabbed hold of his ankles and yanked him back inside. Erasimo slammed what was left of the back door shut.

"Should we shoot back?" a soldier asked.

The pursuing engine actually bumped their car!

Just then their train surged forward, as Jefe must have ordered more speed, rocking them back. Their train picked up the pace and gained a slight lead.

"Hold on!" Erasimo said. "Hold on there…I got something." He was laying on his back. He reached into a knapsack and pulled out a stick of dynamite. He grinned.

Gunther, Erasimo, Lingstrum and the two soldiers got up on their knees. Gunther leaned over and opened the back door. Erasimo lit the fuse and they all watched it burn down half-way and he flipped the stick out the back, careful to aim for the center of the tracks, which were in a slight curve at the moment. The group peered out the shattered back windows and watched.

BOOM!

The rail section and ground exploded. General "Longhorn Mustache" leaned out of the engine side to look ahead. Gunther waved goodbye to him. The engine did not, could not handle the erupted curve. It shot straight forward, the front end bucked up and then went deep down, as the cattle-guard rail sweeper entrenched into the rocks and dirt around the line. The sheer force of the train dug a rugged path for some 30 feet as the train lost its way. The pursuing train engine tottered to the side… tottered…tottered…

"Whoaaa…" Gunther and the watchers groaned. "Whaaaa…"

Then the engine twisted and fell onto its right side, bringing with it the coal car pitching coal, and then, like a writhing snake, multiple passenger and freight cars with it.

"WOWWW!" the watchers declared with grins. "YEAHHH!"

"*That*…was amazing. I wish Jefe was here to see that," Gunther said.

"See what?" Jefe said, entering the car.

"That!" Gunther said pointing out the back and to their left.

Jefe charged up the aisle to see the last bits of the chasing train bash and crash. The engine hit a small hill. The cars smashed, some bent up like bucking horses into each other, or splintered into bits. Jefe's jaw dropped.

"Dynamite. Tracks," Erasimo said with a giant smile, mimicking a toss out the back door.

"Well," Lingstrum said, "I guess I won't be returning by this train to Peking."

"Sometimes, Sergeant," Gunther said, "to save a train, you have to destroy the tracks."

"That sounds like another one of those riddles of war, Major."

"Yes. Yes, I guess it does," Gunther said.

"As a trained scout," Jefe said, "I say, you can always walk back near *de* tracks, when you are done spying."

"Yup," Lingstrum said, disenchanted with the suggestion.

Their speed picked up and a slight turn rocked them all sideways.

"I'll tell them to slow down," Jefe said.

"Okay, wait!" Gunther said. He was looking out the windows and the car's shades were all up. "The telegraph wires. Look."

They all did.

"They are all tight and up," Lingstrum said. "They know we are coming."

"Yes," Gunther said.

"We can't ride into the station. It'll be a trap," Erasimo said.

"How much of that dynamite you have left?" Gunther asked.

Erasimo lifted one of his shoulder satchels.

"Twenty-seven," he said, "thanks to a search of the dead Boxers outside the legation."

"Each one has a fuse?"

"Yes," Erasimo said.

"How long?"

About 12 or so seconds."

"I think I have a plan," Gunther said.

"Oh, no," Jefe said.

******

The train rounded a bend and into the sight of the Tungchow train station. It was moving slow. At about 15 or 20 miles per hour, as one might expect in a station approach.

The Boxers and Chinese Army, alerted by telegraph that the enemy was arriving by train, were hidden throughout the trainyard. Troops were behind parked engines, freight, and passenger cars. Troops were inside rooms of the big empty station, platform hallway.

When the train entered the official grounds of the station a Chinese commander watched intently, waiting for the proper moment. He waited. He waited...

"NOW!" he cried out in Chinese.

Some 50 men opened up on the train with rifle fire. The barrage was thorough and intent, blasting, blasting, blasting every inch of the vehicle, until pieces of it flew off in an apparent disintegration, all except for the solid metal engine which deflected the bullets with sparks and metallic clicks and clangs, and the coal car of thicker wood.

The train maintained its same speed. The commander thought that perhaps they had killed the engineers? He hadn't thought of that event, only planned a gauntlet of death. He ran out from the main office and stood, sword in hand on the platform, watching, inching off to the right side of the platform as the train continued in. Would the train stop without the engineers if they were dead? He looked at the tracks. There was a small rubber and metal barrier ahead, would it stop the train at this speed. He moved more to the right. The train continued at 15 to 20 miles per hour.

It broke the barrier. It traveled across 15 feet through the dirt, it crashed into the platform, crushing it, bending it, and breaking it to pieces. It dug into the station hallway. The men nearby scrambled away. The steamy, broken engine hissed off into silence. Many sighed in relief. Some shouted success, coming forward, rifles up and ready.

They couldn't hear the more subtle sound. The sound of 27 sizzling fuses, moments earlier pulled out and tied off in one long strand, a giant fuse lasting several minutes. The commander pulled his pistol and slowly approached the hulk. He heard something funny. Something odd. Even smelled something other than the crashed train engine.

"Wha...?"

The coal car erupted into a gigantic red-and-white flashing, ear-splitting ball explosion. The force threw rocky pieces of coal, almost bullet speed through the air throughout the station grounds. Like a meteor shower, they tore into and through everything for several hundreds of feet.

All the men behind solid objects were down and stunned. The others exposed and approaching the train, were down and dead. The commander was riddled so his corpse was unrecognizable.

******

323

Scurrying down the sloping hill, Gunther and his rag tag parade of men, women and children all heard the detonation. He and Jefe exchanged glances. No time to gloat. Gunther's plan of plucking the fuses from each and tying them together in a long strand worked. They all kept looking over their shoulders to spot the Chinese sailor nicknamed "Casey", to appear, for he alone remained on the train, in the engine, to ensure its slow passage into the station. He lit the fuse! Did he jump out in time? Did he time his escape well? Did he...?

He suddenly appeared behind them, bounding down the hill between trees and scattered houses.

On a rise they glimpsed the river. But Dr. Telemore saw something else off to their left.

"Look! Other there!"

They all turned to see soldiers, about 100 yards away in the denser parts of the city, also heading toward the river, appearing, and disappearing behind house and buildings, parallel to their descent.

"They see us!" Dr. Gruber shouted.

"This way!" Gunther said and cut their direction off more to the south.

Mrs. Gruber fell, a child in her arms and they rolled downward until one of the soldiers helped them back up.

They heard a gunshot, but from where? The city bay was to their north. Then it was apparent that gunfire and now even cannon fire discharged from the bay. The allied invasion had begun.

The fleetest of foot, Jefe, took the time to stop, knelt and pulled out his telescope, searching the northwest to northeast. He collapsed the device, jumped up and dashed through the group up to Gunther.

"They are following us," he said, jogging beside Gunther.

"Men from the station?"

"I can't tell."

"How many?"

"I can't tell. Looks like at least 20."

"I may have to stop and give cover fire," Gunther said. "Get everyone down to the river. Make Crippler go with you if you have to drag her. She'll want to stay with me."

Erasimo yelled out, "There she is!" He reached into a pocket and pulled out his flare gun. "The Rio Lobos!" He yelled again and at a dead run, fired a red flare toward the river.

"He's right!" Gunther said.

Crippler fired her flare gun too, also while running.

A small ditch-like valley eliminated their view for a few seconds. One of Lingstrum's squad raced ahead waving his arms at the ship. He crested the next hill. He was shot dead.

"Damn!" Gunther said, turning around. The Boxers and soldiers were charged after them, emerging from the outskirts. It looked like 30 of them, now!

"Go Jefe!" Gunther ordered. He took the rifle off his shoulder and laid prone. He started firing at the charge.

"Get him aboard," Sgt. Lingstrum ordered. He dropped down 10 feet away from Gunther, rifle at the ready, then began firing up the hill, at the attackers. His men grabbed up the shot soldier. Jefe grabbed Crippler's elbow, Mister Zin, and the doctors grabbed up the kids, and off they stampeded to the river. Erasimo fired another flare on the way down.

Lingstrum and Gunther exchanged serious looks. For them, this was…it. The last stand. The final end. Their real "Alamo".

Two versus 30. Thin them out, slow them down. Make time for the recue. Make each bullet count, and save one last bullet for...

BOOM! BOOM! BOOM!

The attackers were rocked by cannon fire. Lifted. Thrown. Tossed. Then came intense machine-gun fire chewing up the slope north of them. Gunther looked to the river. Captain Hoon! Captain Delane! It was the Rio Lobos. That beautiful *gotdamn* ship! Those beautiful, *gotdamn* Chinese sailors, blasting the hillside from what seemed like a mile away!

Lingstrum and Gunther now grinned at each other in amazement. They half-stood and took off for the river, the hillside behind them a churning graveyard of death and craters, as only the Rio Lobos could produce.

As they ran close to the riverside, they saw the sampans rowing toward the shoreline and the group waiting with mixed emotions, glaring over the dead Army soldier, yet the thrill of their rescue imminent.

"Who was he?" an out-of-breath Gunther asked Lingstrum.

"Corporal Haliburton Reedem. Port Aransas, Texas," the sergeant said.

They ran the rest of the way. Silent. As they descended, they saw the gunship's crew at their posts, watching for any enemies.

Once at the water's edge, Crippler hugged Gunther and held on to his arm. Mister Zin hugged him. Jefe nodded at him. At river level, they heard more of the battle rage north at Tungchow's Bay. Gunther walked out knee deep and looked north. He still couldn't see much, but he pictured the devastation in his mind. Minds. Bodies. Souls. Buildings. Landscapes. Cultures. Crippler followed him into the water, still clutching his arm. He sighed and shook his head.

Boats ashore, the men, women and children from the Peking siege boarded them, bound for the mothership. Gunther told all the soldiers and the Marine to board the last boat with him.

Sgt. Lingstrum pondered this. As the commanding Army officer, Gunther ordered Lingstrum and his men to accompany them back to the U.S. as it would be a deadly mistake for them to remain so alone and isolated. And with a casualty. And they needed protection from pirates to escape China waters.

"And I'll think up some more reasons as we go. We'll radio and wire the intelligence back to Peking that your colonel wanted."

He also ordered Marine "Uncle Sam" Willard to return with them stateside.

"I am not sure Captain Howlin' Jack would approve, Major, he told me that…"

"Uncle Sam," Gunther interrupted. "I know people in very, very high places."

Jefe raised his eyebrows and nodded.

"Yes, sir," Willard said.

"You all have been invaluable to me and Lt. Cocoy. This will be noted all the way to the White House."

Then their eyebrows raised.

They boarded the last sampan. They circled the Rio Lobos over to the far side away from the battlegrounds. The crane hooked the boats and hoisted them aboard one by one.

The last sampan swung up over and settled down on the deck. Hoon and Delane stood there, beaming.

Gunther stood up and still for a few seconds and then said,

"Permission to come aboard, Captains."

"Permission granted," they both said.

******

Over the next 2 weeks, the Rio Lobos island-hopped for fuel and supplies across the Pacific Ocean on their return run to San Francisco, California. It took days for the group to rest up and even more days for the doctors, wives, and children to calm down. But the seas were calm, the sunsets and breezes amazing. Hoon reported good weather all along the way.

Gunther and Crippler were barely seen, and with the advice and "protection" of Jefe, they were mostly left alone. They ate alone, sat on the topside observation deck for hours alone and otherwise spent most of the time in Gunther's stateroom.

Then finally, San Francisco Bay…

Chapter 30
The Sad Pocket

The Bellmont, Hedgecock and Telemore families received somewhat generic telegraphs, as the mission was still to be kept top secret, from the vice president's office, announcing that Gunther's team had returned from China. The instructions in the messages were to contact Colonel Westways for a meeting place as soon as possible. Westways decided they all should meet at the officer's quarters, third floor conference room at the Presidio for a catered event.

Gunther, Jefe, in their class A dress uniforms, the Zin family, Erasimo, and the doctors, even Dr. Gruber and wife, burst into the big room to the delight of the families. Telemore's wife, Anna, and son, Timothy crashed into him with joy, almost knocking him over. Cheers and yelps abounded.

But Mr. and Mrs. Bellmont stood up from the sofa and saw no Dr. Bellmont. Their son was…missing.

Bellmont's face was puzzled, his hands opened, palms out in a questioning manner toward Gunther. Mrs. Bellmont's eyes were wide and stared at the room's double doors, awaiting her son, until one of the aides reached in and closed the doors.

Gunther suggested they walk off to the side as he removed his round, wide-brimmed Army hat, and from the right side, pocket of his jacket produced an envelope.

"What..." Mr. Bellmont said, leaving the revelry of the families and children around them.

Mr. Bellmont took the envelope. Mrs. Bellmont leaned in. The envelope was addressed, "Dear Mom. Dear Dad." Astonished. Concerned. He opened the letter.

Dear Mom and Dad,

I hope you will forgive me and understand why I am doing this. I am not returning with Major Gunther and my friends. I will remain in China. The situation is somewhat stabilized now. The allied armies have invaded and control Peking. The Boxers have surrendered. The Chinese government have accepted the terms. Things are quiet and safe.

The people of China, the people themselves are good people. And they need modern medical help. I have chosen to remain here and help them. In case you are worried, Major Gunther has arranged for my safety with an excellent bodyguard, a man named Collin Small. He has received some money from the Major to protect me. Major Gunther will vouch for him.

I will come home someday, of course. I do not know when. We can now telegraph and write each other as the systems are being rebuilt.

I am sorry, but I feel I must do this. It is like the calling of our church. I love you both. We will write each other very soon.

With love and hope,
Your son

330

Bellmont handed the letter to his wife.

"You have failed me," he told Gunther. "I told you to bring him back."

"Doing so, sir," Gunther said, "would at this time, be like shanghaiing him...twice. He told me he absolutely wished to remain."

"China shanghai, twice," he sneered and said, "you will not be rewarded by me, or ever work for me."

"As you can plainly see, sir, I work for the United States Army."

Bellmont grunted. Mrs. Bellmont finished the letter and her hand with the message dropped lifelessly to her side.

"He is in very competent hands. Safe. This...Collin Small... is no ordinary person. He will protect your son against any and all troubles if need be. Things have already calmed down and they will live safely within the new American Legation."

Silence.

Telemore saw this conversation ongoing and stepped over to them.

"He'll be alright," Telemore said. "He is with a great man for protection, and he just wanted to stay and help the people."

Gunther bowed his head slightly to Mr. and Mrs. Bellmont. "Ma'am," he said, "your son is an excellent doctor and a very good man." He turned to join the others. "Perhaps soon, when things calm down, you can visit him."

Jefe had been explaining to the rest about all the brave work that Mister Zin had done to make the rescue mission a success. He finished with, "...and our Mister Zin needs a job."

"Oh my, we can arrange that," Mr. Hedgecock blurted out.

Mister Zin was beaming.

"Vice President Roosevelt has promised me he will see to it that Mister and Mrs. Zin and their children will quickly become citizens of the United States," Gunther advised.

The room filled with cheers.

The Bellmonts gathered a few things up and walked out of the room, not saying goodbye to anyone.

"The Bellmont...boy?" Mrs. Telemore asked looking around, suddenly realizing that, *that* doctor was not there, and the Bellmonts were leaving.

"He decided to stay," Dr. Telemore said.

"Stay?"

They all looked at Gunther and Hedgecock and they nodded their heads.

"He decided to stay there. Practice medicine there," Telemore said.

The families were astonished.

"It's like a mission, Mother, A church mission."

"What will happen to you next? Where will you two go?" Mrs. Hedgecock asked Gunther and Jefe.

"I don't know, ma'am," Gunther said calmly. "We'll just go where we are told." Gunther put on his big hat. It was time to go and leave the reunion to the families.

All of them surrounded Gunther and Jefe, reaching for arm or a shoulder to hug them. They shook everyone's hands, with a long clasp with the two shanghaied doctors themselves. Mister Zin remained to speak with the Hedgecocks about a job.

Gunther and Jefe opened the doors to find Colonel Westways in the hall.

"A fine reunion I would say," Westways remarked as the three walked down the hallway.

"Come on down to my office. Oh, Major, I have something for you."

"Yes?"

They stopped and Westways reached into a breast pocket and handed Gunther a letter. The handwriting on the envelope was artistically beautiful. It was addressed.

"Dear Johann."

"This came for you, here to me, about an hour ago by messenger. I found it moments ago in my office," Westways said.

Gunther opened the envelope.

Dear Johann,

By the time you read this I will be gone, returning to my life in Omaha, and to my future that we have discussed so many times before. I thought it best that we should not say goodbye in person, because in your arms once again, we might not say goodbye after all. And, as you know, I simply cannot do that. I have many responsibilities, especially now, after the death of my poor sister and her husband.

I cannot write in words what you mean to me, and what we have gone through together. You will always be my beautiful racehorse.

With unforgettable love,

Suzannah Crippler

Gunther folded the letter back up into the envelope. He shoved it into his right-side pocket, the same pocket he'd just produced the Bellmont letter from, given to his parents. Gunther thought, in that second, it was a very sad pocket, indeed.

"Everything okay?" Jefe asked.

"Yes and no," Gunther mumbled.

He continued down the hall, followed by Westways and

Jefe. They went downstairs to Westway's office and sat in the leather chairs, Westways at his desk. Atop his desk was a folded *San Francisco Chronicle* newspaper. He passed it to Gunther. Gunther saw the front-page article on the "China's Boxer Rebellion", a summary after four weeks of battles and the surrender of Chinese forces.

"...The Boxers began their assaults in 1898. By May 1900, Boxer bands were roaming the countryside and around the capital at Peking threatening death and destruction to all 'foreign devils'. Acts of extreme torture and violence followed. Finally, in early June an international relief force of some 2,100 men was dispatched for protection.

On June 13, the empress dowager ordered imperial forces to block the advance of the foreign troops. The small relief column was turned back. Meanwhile, in Peking the Boxers burned churches and foreign residences and killed more Chinese Christians on sight.

On June 17, the foreign powers seized the Taku Forts on the China coast.

On June 18, the next day the empress dowager ordered that all foreigners be killed. Foreign ministers and their families and staff, together with hundreds of Chinese Christians, were besieged in their legation, embassy quarters. There, until 15 August, the international sieged group lasted 55 days battling daily attacks of raids, mines, gun, and cannon fire, surviving on rice, wheat, and horse meat.

Initial military sources suggest a total of up to 100,000 or more people died in the Boxer Rebellion conflict. The great majority of those killed were civilians, including thousands of Chinese Christians and approximately 200 to 250 foreign nationals (mostly Christian missionaries). Some estimates cite about 3,000 military personnel were killed in combat, the great bulk of them being Boxers, some Chinese Imperial Army, and other Chinese fighters.

"A China Alamo," Gunther said and handed the newspaper to Jefe.

Jefe intently read the news report. While in transit across the Pacific, island hopping for food and supplies, they had been out-of-touch with the latest news. All they really knew upon arrival in California was that the international forces had more or less "won" and order in the legations had been restored.

"And we received some bad news from Peking. Your man, the appointed commander Semitagold?" Westways added.

"What?"

"He was killed."

"Oh. Hell, no," Gunther said.

"How?" Jefe asked.

"The Legation still had some periodic invaders. He was stabbed inside a building, by a Chinese sword on a long stick, the *London Times* reported."

"A qiang..." Gunther said solemnly, "...which is the most common, long-handled weapon. Like a spear with a...a... machete on the end." He shook his head and whispered, "And so he dies, like Gordon on Khartoum."

"Hmmm?" Westways said. "Like Gordon?"

"A British hero of his. What's next, West?" Gunther asked.

"Vice President Roosevelt wired me to tell you to take a week off. He will contact me, or someone will from Washington about your next assignment."

"Probably back to the Philippines," Gunther said.

"Could be," Westways said. "I don't know though. I have heard some talk about Africa."

"Africa?" Gunther said dimly.

"This is my first trip to America!" Jefe declared. "I would like to see San Francisco and…and the museums, and…and…"

"I will arrange an escort to take you all over."

"I tell you what, we are going to get citizenship for the Zin family, Get Roosevelt to grant citizenship for Jefe too. He loves America."

Jefe's eyebrows raised. He beamed.

"I will ask Marie to marry me, Gunth," Jefe blurted out.

"There ya' go," Gunther said.

"What about you, Gunth?"

"I just might join him for that museum tour, but first, I might go see someone for breakfast tomorrow."

Westways knew exactly who that was.

Epilogue

The Carlton Hotel

Gunther, in a new civilian dark suit, white shirt, string tie and black boots, walked into the prestigious Carlton Hotel lobby the next morning, pulling off his black bowler hat. He stopped and took a good look around. A very old Chinese man with a long grey-haired, braided ponytail, in a white hotel uniform approached him.

"Hello, sir," he said with a smile. "Can I help you?"

"Yes. Yes, I am looking for a Clayton Alexander."

"Oh, oh, yes. But I must tell you, he has not done any work for anyone, for a very long time."

"I am not here to ask him to do any work," Gunther said with a smile.

"Okay. Okay. Good. For many, many years, many people come here still, in this lobby, looking for Mr. Alexander, to ask his help, just like this, you know. I thought you might be one of them."

"No. About three, four months ago, he invited me here for breakfast, and I thought I would take him up on the offer."

"Oh. Oh. Good. Well, he is in the restaurant. Breakfast now. Please to follow me."

The man led the way in. As they approached, the elderly gentlemen, dressed as if attending a grand ball, was starting his breakfast, sipping his coffee, and turned to see them approach. His grey, thick left eyebrow lifted, and he half smiled.

"This man…"

"Yes, Hey Boy, I know him. Have a seat, young man," he said.

"Johann Gunther," Gunther said with a smile, sat, handed the Chinaman his bowler and said, "I'll just have some coffee. I just ate at the Army mess hall."

"Any good?" the man asked.

"No."

And Clay laughed in a grunting style. "Not much has changed then. I noticed that a night or two after we last spoke on the docks…there was quite a fire. Quite an explosion."

"Is that so?"

"Yes. And the boat I pointed out…*and*…the man we discussed, were blown into very small pieces that night."

"I see."

"Where have you been these last few months? Anywhere interesting?" he asked.

"China."

He grunted again and grinned. He sipped his coffee.

"China! And into what the newspapers call the Boxer Rebellion? Ohhhh…an eight-nation fistula."

Gunther smiled, not knowing what "fistula" meant exactly, but he had a good guess. Hey Boy brought him a cup of coffee.

Gunther took a drink.

"This is excellent coffee," he said.

"From a particular mountain in Brazil. Not like the Army's. I see you are wearing a West Point graduation ring," the man said.

"Yes."

"I too have one of those, but I don't wear it. Rings and things hurt my fingers and hands these days, but I didn't wear the ring much when I was younger either. Oftentimes, it was not wise to draw undue attention to oneself. On one's business travels."

"I agree. So, I gather that you have parleyed your military time into a…" Gunther waved his hand in the air, "a lucrative business."

"That I have," he said between bites. "Are you a bit tired of the Army? Tired of being told where and when to go, here and there, and…who to kill?"

Gunther rested back in the chair and crossed his legs.

"Yes."

"Yes," the man repeated. "You know, I started a business years ago that allows one to pick and choose what one does. Where one goes. And who one…kills or doesn't kill." He wiped his hands with his napkin, then dabbed his mouth.

"A detective agency?" Gunther asked.

"Of sorts," he said.

"Sort of a lawman? I was one once back…"

"No," the man said.

"A…gunfighting…"

"No!" the man barked! "Certainly *not* a gunfighter. A problem solver, Johann. And sometimes, yes, that does involve guns. As a very last resort. Think of it as a much higher calling than simple gunfighting or killing. I have killed. Too much. Had to.

With regret. A person of a higher intellect and training must maintain a regret about such things, and seriously ponder such actions as gunfighting...or killing."

"Okay," Gunther said. "You sound a bit like my old police chief, who was first a Paris, France police detective. And then a warden at Devil's Island."

"Interesting fellow. Still alive?"

"I think so, yes. I have become so busy, I have lost touch," Gunther said.

"I had become someone who offers remedies to people's problems. How much time do you have left in the Army?"

"Two years, 10 months, 16 days."

The man smiled at that classic Army count down, then said, "Here's how you set up such a business." He took another bite before explaining.

"Remedies..." Gunther repeated in a whisper, then leaned in for the lesson.

"First, you have to..."

If You Like This, Take A Look At:
Be Bad Now by Hock Hochheim

HOW BAD IS BAD ENOUGH WHEN YOU MUST...BE BAD NOW?

In the 1980's a recession stampedes Texas. The oil industry dries up, laying high rollers low and sending the entire state of Texas into a tornado-like downspin. Northern mobsters invade these cracks in the Lone Star State. Their schemes: corruption, loan sharking, gambling, extortion, drug and human trafficking, and murder for hire -- all backed with strong arms swinging bats, psychos pointing guns, torture, violence and death.

The city of West Forge, a stone's throw from Houston, is Sgt. "Jumpin" Jack Kellog's town. When organized crime seeps in, Kellog's brand of justice knows no bounds. He tracks, fights, kicks and shoots his way through conspiracies, threats, ambushes and showdowns. Pushed to near-madness by angst with informants inside his agency and lurking everywhere, Jack tackles the thugs, bosses, lawyers, politicians and businessmen on the mob payroll, in a battle that takes him from the swamps of Louisiana, to the ghettos of Houston, to casinos in Vegas and even through the Halls of Congress in Washington D.C..

"If you like hard-core fast-moving police stories with a sense of justice, Be Bad Now is a definite read."

AVAILABLE NOW

About the Author

Hock Hochheim is a former U.S. Army investigator and 22 year veteran Texas police investigator, patrol officer, former private investigator and award winning author.

He currently owns and operates Force Necessary, an international combatives training company and teaches combat techniques and strategies in 11 allied countries around the world annually. He is the author of 10 non-fiction books and four fiction, and countless articles on policing, the military, street survival, close quarter combat and conflict psychology. He lives in Texas.

In 2013 Hock's book My Gun is My Passport won the Beverly Hills Book Award for Best Military Fiction. You may read more about him at http://www.forcenecessary.com or email him at hock@hockscqc.com